STALKING SEASON

A SEASONS SERIES MYSTERY

STALKING SEASON

MARYANN MILLER

FIVE STAR
A part of Gale, Cengage Learning

GALE
CENGAGE Learning

Detroit • New York • San Francisco • New Haven, Conn • Waterville, Maine • London

GALE
CENGAGE Learning

LIBRARY OF CONGRESS CATALOGING-IN-PUBLICATION DATA

Miller, Maryann, 1943–
   Stalking season : a seasons series mystery / Maryann Miller. — 1st ed.
    p. cm.
   ISBN 978-1-4328-2598-0 (hardcover) — ISBN 1-4328-2598-4 (hardcover)
    1. Policewomen—Fiction. 2. Police—Texas—Dallas—Fiction. 3. Murder—Investigation—Fiction. I. Title.
PS3613.I545S73 2012
813'.6—dc23   2012019916

First Edition. First Printing: November 2012.
Published in conjunction with Tekno Books and Ed Gorman.
Find us on Facebook– https://www.facebook.com/FiveStarCengage
Visit our website– http://www.gale.cengage.com/fivestar/
Contact Five Star™ Publishing at FiveStar@cengage.com

Printed in Mexico
1 2 3 4 5 6 7 16 15 14 13 12

Dedicated to Dany and Paul for never flinching when I called with another computer problem.

ACKNOWLEDGEMENTS

It is with much gratitude that I acknowledge the officers at the Dallas Police Department who shared their experiences and expertise with me when this series was first developed. I owe special thanks to the late Tim Huskey, a former police officer and a wonderful writer. For years he was the one who kept me on the right course about how police officers work and behave. I also want to thank Doug Grantham, a retired Dallas police officer who more recently has become an expert source on police procedures and policies. Thanks also go to my son, David, who assisted with much of the research, and particularly enjoyed visiting the gentleman's club. And finally, thanks to my husband, Carl, for supporting this writing addiction through the years.

PROLOGUE

The minute she stepped into the brisk January wind, Tracy regretted wearing the skimpy black dress she'd danced in. The beaded shawl offered little protection against the waves of chilled air, and the cold skittered up her bare legs like drunken spiders.

Pale halos of light illuminated the border of hedges flanking the cement steps at the entrance to The Club. Beyond the artificial light an impenetrable darkness shrouded the area, and Tracy felt her resolve slip. She must be nuts going out to meet some man in the dead of night. Amber had reasoned her past the initial fears, building on the sense of adventure that had led them here initially, but now she wasn't so sure.

Tracy angled to the right, away from the front portico where valets hustled to relieve guests of their cars. Once clear and facing a sea of parked cars, she wondered how on earth she'd find the man who had requested her company. Or was he going to find her?

She turned to see a big dark luxury car pull through the sweeping driveway and crawl to a stop beside her. The tinted window inched down, sliding with a soft whir into the well of the passenger door. Tracy leaned into the opening and a rich, pungent odor of leather tickled her nose. It reminded her of the smell inside her father's Jaguar, and the familiarity eased her remaining fears.

Tracy tried her best smile. "You want me to get in?"

The click disengaging the automatic lock answered her.

As her hand touched the cold metal of the door handle, caution made her hesitate. Once she got in, there would be no turning back. Did she really want to do this?

"I'm not waiting forever." The voice registered barely above a whisper, but it nudged Tracy to open the door. If she didn't, Amber would rag on her forever.

Settling into the soft embrace of the leather seat, Tracy welcomed the reprieve from the cold night air and gave the man a furtive glance. A gray Fedora shadowed part of his face, and long, thin fingers gripped the wheel as he maneuvered the car out of the parking lot.

"Where are we going?" Tracy asked.

He didn't answer, and panic fluttered in her stomach. What if she was supposed to have a place? Amber hadn't told her how that part of it worked.

Tracy fidgeted with the clasp of her purse, pushing it open, then closing it with a series of soft clicks. She waited for the question she wouldn't be able to answer, but the man remained silent. He held the car in the flow of traffic on Loop 12, then took a right on Harry Hines. Passing flashes of neon advertising GIRLS and GOOD TIMES, Tracy realized they were not in an area where they would find a Raddison on the next corner.

She swallowed a protest when he pulled into the parking lot of what Amber must have been referring to as a "no-tell motel." It wasn't the worst place Tracy had ever seen, but it was close, not a hint of an amenity in the pale, stucco buildings that formed an L on the debris-strewn asphalt.

Wondering if she could suggest an alternative, she turned to the man. Her inclination was cut short by his curt command. "Sign us in. Make up a plate number and don't use your real name."

He reached into the breast pocket of his dark suit and pulled out a slim wallet. Separating one crisp bill from others, he handed it to her. "This will cover it."

The thin, pale man at the desk in the tiny office kept most of his attention on a Mavericks basketball game blaring from the TV. Tracy was glad he didn't notice her shaking fingers as she signed the card he slid across the counter. He took the fifty she held out and handed back ten in change along with the key.

"Number fifty-two in the back," Tracy said, sliding into the passenger seat.

Tires making only a whisper of sound on the asphalt, the car rolled into the shadows surrounding the back rectangle of units. The man stilled the engine, then motioned for her to get out. She offered the key to him, but he waved her toward the entrance.

Tracy fumbled the key in the lock, then finally got the door open and stepped inside. A stuffy aroma of long-neglected dirt assailed her as she looked around. The room was a study in beige with a cheap copy of a landscape on the wall making a feeble attempt to break the monotony. She glanced at the bed, taking note of the obscure loops and swirls of a faded floral design on the spread. Trying to mask her dismay, she looked back at the man.

He closed the door, engaging the lock with a loud click, and Tracy wondered if she had made a huge mistake. *Don't be silly.* She stilled the yammering of her panic. *People do this all the time. He's probably waiting for you to make the first move.*

The man sat down on a chair by the long, dark drape covering the sliding glass door. It wasn't what Tracy expected, and she wondered what to do next. Disconcerted, she moved closer to the standard-issue low dresser. It hosted a television, a cheap plastic bucket wrapped in cellophane, and a dog-eared directory of local amusements. A chill tickled the back of her neck, and she pulled her shawl over her bare shoulders.

"Don't do that."

The command froze her in place. She was going to blow this whole thing. Think. What had Amber said?

Right. Take care of the money part first.

"Uh." Tracy cleared her throat. "The pay?"

He raised a questioning eyebrow.

"My . . . the usual's two hundred."

He pulled the leather wallet out again, removed two hundred-dollar bills and held them aloft.

Tracy quickly crossed the room and snatched them.

"You don't talk much, do you?" she asked.

He gazed at her with bottomless brown eyes and shook his head. The intense scrutiny sent her back to the middle of the room.

Now what?

"Would you like me to dance?"

A quick nod answered the question.

Okay. Play it like a game. One move will lead to another.

After putting the money in her purse, Tracy stood in the middle of the room wondering how to get past the awkwardness, finally closing her eyes against her inhibitions. *There, that's better.* She let her body sway to a melody playing in her mind. The moves felt stilted at first, like the music was out of sync and she couldn't find the rhythm, but she forced herself to keep moving.

Slowly, a memory of having done this before surfaced. Remembering brought back the delicious feeling of sensuality that had so excited her last year when she'd danced for Brad. She'd felt an incredible sense of power at that moment and now she drew on that power.

Confidence synchronized her movements and she let the inner heat build. In a crackling slither of beads she drew the shawl across her shoulder, then down over her breasts, feeling a surge of warm excitement as her nipples peaked. A quick tug on the back zipper released the fabric of her black crepe dress.

Drawing the moment out, she slipped one cap sleeve down her arm then the other. Free from restraint, the dress slid like a caress across her body, releasing a subtle scent of sweet perfume before settling in a soft puddle at her feet.

More daring now, Tracy opened her eyes and watched the man watching her. He lit a cigarette, the blue haze of smoke rising slowly to the ceiling.

She waited a moment for some word of direction, but he just smoked quietly. Did he just want her to keep on dancing?

Sliding her fingers across the tops of her breasts, she touched her nipples lightly then smoothed her palms across her stomach, rolling her hips in slow, flowing circles. She let the moves carry her closer to the man, searching those fathomless eyes for response.

Nothing.

"You should at least loosen your tie." Tracy tugged playfully at the knot, but the man pushed her hand away.

Uncertainty caused her to falter. Amber had said the only difference between sex with the frat boys at SMU and this was that they'd get paid for it. But the college guys had been direct in letting her know what they wanted. What was the deal with this guy? If he didn't like her, he certainly wouldn't have shelled out all that money.

Uncomfortable with her questions and his proximity, Tracy spun back toward the center of the room. Okay. She'd give him five more minutes. Then if he didn't do anything, she'd tell him to forget it. Give him his money back . . . God, she hated to think of having to do that.

She closed her eyes again, retreating into the insulation of darkness. Then she heard snatches of music from outside her mental soundtrack. It was him. He was singing. A familiar song.

What was it? A hymn?

Tracy stopped and stared at the man.

"Keep dancing."

She willed her body to move, to ignore the breath of unease that blew over her, and for a few moments it worked. Ignorance came easy in self-imposed darkness. Then his music again intruded on hers and she realized she'd changed her rhythm to match his song. What was he singing . . . ? "Amazing Grace" . . . ? What a ridiculous—

A rustle of movement startled her and she opened her eyes. He was standing now. Jacket off. Getting ready? It was about time.

Her soft sigh of relief constricted in her throat when she saw the glint of metal in his right hand. What the . . . ? There was no way her frantic mind could convince her it was something harmless.

". . . was lost and now am found . . ."

The voice was still a harsh whisper, but it hurled the words against Tracy like waves pounding a shore. A cold shudder of fear buckled her knees and she fell against the bed for support. She tried to voice the scream that built inside, but no sound squeezed past the tightness in her throat. Terror clamped an iron hand on her body. Her mind screamed, "Run!" But her muscles froze.

"Not a breath of noise and you won't get hurt." The man moved toward her. "Understand?"

Tracy nodded, even though the deep ache in her gut told her he was lying.

"Please don't kill me." The plea finally squeaked its way out.

"Quiet." The calculated menace in his voice invaded her body and rendered her helpless.

Helpless as he shoved her back on the bed, pinning her with his length.

Helpless as he murmured words next to her ear.

Helpless as he laid the cold edge of steel against her neck.

He was right.

It didn't hurt.

Rolling away from the spurt of blood, the killer ran smooth hands over the contours of Tracy's body, still warm and inviting. But it wouldn't be desecrated anymore. She was redeemed now. She had paid for her sins and no one would touch her body again.

A thumb, dipped in the river of blood, traced a crude cross on the dead girl's forehead. There, my sweet. Sleep now. And do not think too badly of what I had to do. You left me no alternative. You were the only one who had a choice. The Father wanted only goodness for you. Instead you took the path of evil, offering your body on the sacrificial altar of man's depravity. But it is over now. Your own blood has joined the Blood of the Lamb. You have been saved and are now His.

". . . was blind, but now I see . . ."

Loving hands arranged the body in an acceptable pose for the Lord. Covered modestly.

"There now. Isn't that better?"

CHAPTER ONE

Angling to the far-left lane of the I-75 overpass, Detective Angel Johnson admired the dramatic skyline of Dallas. Sleek lines of brick and glass cut deeply into the brilliant azure sky, slicing the lavender clouds in half. She loved this spot. Up here, away from the endless parade of dead bodies and remorseless killers, it was possible to believe that the city lived up to the perfection presented in a view that could be a postcard.

She took a deep breath to stifle the morning's frustration. She had gone with her partner to interview a woman who had witnessed a drive-by shooting, but the woman had nothing helpful to tell them. No description. No nothing. Angel wasn't sure if it was because the woman didn't want to help or if she honestly had not seen enough to help. It was always hard to tell in those neighborhoods terrorized by gangs.

"Stop!"

The sharp command jerked Angel's attention to Sarah Kingsly who was looking out the passenger window.

"Now? Right in the middle of the freeway?" Angel asked.

"We've got a jumper!"

Glancing to her right, Angel saw a young man with one foot over the railing. It didn't look like he was there to share her delight in the view. She edged the car off the lane until the faint scrape of metal on concrete told her she had gone as far as she could. Before the car came to a complete halt, Sarah pushed the door open and stepped out.

Screaming tires marked her passage across four lanes of traffic. Thankful that it wasn't rush hour, Angel hastily punched numbers on her cell phone. With any amount of luck, her partner might actually be able to dodge the cars and arrive at the other side intact.

Physically, that is.

Mentally, Angel wasn't sure how intact the other woman was. Six months of partnership-on-paper hadn't moved them more than an inch toward partnership-in-reality. And these stunts. *Shit! She's going to get us both killed.*

Angel quickly briefed the dispatcher, slammed the phone closed, then scrabbled across the seat to exit through the passenger side. When she stepped out, the stench of exhaust gagged her, but at least she didn't have to worry about being hit. The traffic crawled across the overpass as gawkers leaned out of car windows to catch a glimpse of the drama unfolding at the side of the road.

Cautious, so she wouldn't alarm the young man perched precariously on the guard rail, Angel sidled up to her partner. Sarah seemed oblivious to everything but the pathetic guy who didn't seem to have anything to live for, if appearances were any indication. A tattered sweatshirt offered his only protection against a cutting January wind, and jeans that weren't distressed for style encased legs no thicker than the rail they straddled. Wild, frantic eyes were buried in a mane of hair that flowed into a scraggly beard.

The eyes could see, but they didn't communicate.

Angel was mesmerized by the soft, soothing voice of her partner gentling the man the way she'd once heard her brother do a horse. "It's okay . . . I'm not going to hurt you . . ."

As Sarah spoke, she moved slowly toward the man, gliding as if the concrete had turned to ice. Angel held her breath while the moment stretched to eternity.

"Stay away!" The man's harsh shout jangled the airwaves like a stone disturbs a still pond.

Angel watched Sarah freeze for one moment, then move forward again, letting her voice ease the coming. "Shhh . . . Take it easy . . . We can just talk a . . ."

As Sarah moved closer to the man, Angel could no longer distinguish words in the soothing wash of sound. Could she rush him while Sarah had him distracted?

No. She was still too far away.

Turning her head slightly, Angel caught the faint wail of a siren growing stronger. The man gave no sign of hearing it, but he would soon. Would it provide the impetus to push him into the flow of traffic on the concrete river a hundred feet below?

A sudden rush of adrenaline sent her heart on an erratic trip through her chest as Angel watched the next few seconds play out in excruciating slow motion . . .

The man turned his head toward the scream of the sirens.

Sarah lunged forward.

The two of them tangled in a macabre embrace, teetering on the edge.

The man fought to pull away.

Sarah clung to his ragged shirt.

"If you go, I go, too." Sarah's words were oddly calm in the frenzy of emotion. "And killing a cop is a death-penalty of-fense."

Angel found the pronouncement absurd. What was that honky bitch thinking? If this guy even cared about the future they wouldn't all be here.

Willing her feet to cross the distance in time, Angel broke the slow-motion lock.

She grabbed Sarah's bright red jacket, and a sudden weight threatened to pull her arms out of their sockets as first the man, then Sarah, went over the side. Angel could feel the momentum pulling her toward the edge. Her Reeboks slid across the loose dirt and gravel like skis, slamming Angel against the rail with a bone-crushing thud. "Sarah! Let him go. I can't hold you both."

"He doesn't really want to do this."

Angel risked a glance over the edge. Her partner was stretched between a grasp on a steel support beam and a fistful of fabric. It was the only thing holding the man from certain death.

"Could have fooled me." Angel flexed her knees to lower her center of gravity and tried to ignore the sear of pain in her arms. She couldn't hear the sirens anymore. Did that mean some Uniforms would rescue her at any moment? She fervently hoped so. She didn't know how much longer she could hang on. And she didn't know if she was willing to go over the edge with her partner.

The alternative wasn't even worth consideration.

A momentary flare of anger distracted her. Why didn't one of the bloody gawkers stop and help? This wasn't some reality TV show.

The burning pain in her muscles gave way to numbness, and Angel felt the fabric of Sarah's jacket start to slip through her fingers. She willed her grip to hold. "I'm losing you!"

"You're not dying today. You got that!" As Sarah's words drifted up to Angel, it took a moment to realize they were directed at the man.

"Let him go, Sarah! You're not going to talk him out of this."

"The hell I'm not! The deal hasn't changed. You go, we all go."

Sarah's comments didn't make sense, even when Angel realized the last two were spoken to the man again. She fought an urge to let go, to punish Sarah for being so obtuse as to think some sappy appeal might work.

Suddenly, the balance of weight shifted, easing the burden on

Angel's trembling muscles. Had her partner lost her grip on the man? Angel took another look over the railing. Sarah's face bore a triumphant grin. Then Angel saw the man clinging to the support beam next to her partner.

A car braked to a sharp stop behind her, and Angel turned to see two patrol officers throw the doors open and run toward her. They reached over and helped haul Sarah and the man back to the roadway. Her partner didn't let go of the guy until he was handcuffed and in the grasp of the officers who walked him in an ungainly puppet-dance to the car.

Now that the man was safe in the back seat of the cruiser, the sharp edge of tension eased, but anger smothered Angel's relief. Sarah's face still wore that goofy grin, and she shrugged before starting across the street. Angel reached out and pulled the other woman around.

"Don't you ever do anything like that again."

"Hey. We saved a life. You should feel good."

"Pardon me if I don't cheer. I came too close to dying to be happy."

"You need to lighten up, girl." Sarah pushed at straggles of blond hair the wind kept tossing in her face. "It's all part of the job."

"No." Angel poked a finger at the other woman's chest. "What you do can no way be considered normal."

"If we were normal, we wouldn't be cops."

"Forget it." Angel threw up her hands, checked for a break in traffic and stomped back to the car.

"You want me to drive?" Sarah called, her footsteps padding softly behind Angel.

"I don't think I trust you right now."

Back at the Municipal Building, they rode in a stony silence as the elevator hummed toward the third floor. Trying to formulate an icebreaker, Sarah watched Angel pick at a nonexistent piece of lint on her blue linen jacket, refusing to make eye contact. A muscle worked in the woman's jaw, rippling skin the color of coffee with light cream. The tension was so thick, it was suffocating.

Any opportunity to speak was lost when the doors whooshed open.

In the hallway, Sarah stepped around Chief Dorsett who was talking to Lieutenant Scrubbs from Vice. Then she followed Angel and the silence through the security door leading to the Crimes Against Persons section of the Dallas Police Department. Gladys pressed a button on her side of the door so the detectives could enter. Sarah gave the woman the briefest of nods then broke eye contact. Known affectionately as "the keeper of the gate," Gladys had an uncanny ability to read the people who sought access to the department. Sarah didn't want to reveal too many pages of her private book just now.

A bustle of activity operated independently of them as Angel and Sarah passed through a maze of desks where detectives responded to the shrill ring of the telephone, traded information on cases, or pecked out reports on computer keyboards. The cacophony of noise bounced off cinder-block walls, drab in their blanket of gray. The place always reminded Sarah of the cellar of her early childhood in the hills of Tennessee, but instead of housing snap beans and peach preserves, this room was home to cases of burglary, assault, and a host of other crimes.

News of the rescue had obviously beaten them to the station, and their descent down the four steps to the Homicide section was greeted by a few cheers that were quickly quelled when Lieutenant McGregor rounded the corner from his office. "Knock it off. You sound like a bunch of kids at a rock concert."

Then he turned his hard, dark eyes to Sarah. "Superwoman's a myth, you know."

Sarah bit back the smart remark that came to mind and nodded. McGregor looked like a pressure cooker ready to blow—a giant pressure cooker—and she didn't want to be the one to open the valve.

McGregor reached under the bottom of his navy suit coat and pulled a rumpled handkerchief out of his back pocket to attack the perpetual film of sweat on his face. "What the hell were you doing?" He paused to stuff the handkerchief back. "Risking your life for some asshole who's probably madder than I am about it."

Sarah did her best imitation of contrite, fighting back the smile that threatened while McGregor sputtered. He turned his full force on Angel. "And you couldn't do a damn thing to stop her?"

Risking a glance at her partner, Sarah waited for the answer. Would Angel let her anger erupt in an indictment? Watching the woman, whose face remained impassive as the six-foot-plus man towered over her, Sarah let air out in a soft sigh when Angel merely shrugged.

The drop in the temperature of the tension signaled the other detectives that the diversion was over, and they shuffled back to their desks. Chad Smith gave Sarah an encouraging smile, teeth brilliantly white against his mahogany skin. She savored his silent encouragement as she waited for McGregor's next move.

"Okay," he finally said. "You two want to be heroes. Go make a case on that Pilcher woman. Some Uniforms found her holed up at her sister's place. Still had the gun stashed at her house and Ballistics matched it with the slugs taken out of the late Mr. Pilcher. But she swears she didn't do it. A confession would be a nice thing to take to court."

For a moment Sarah wondered if it didn't matter to him whether the woman was guilty or not, then she chased the thought away. McGregor had his faults, but trying to make a case that wasn't there didn't appear on the list. They had some pretty strong circumstantial stuff on the unhappy wife. Coupled with lab reports, it would probably be enough to indict. But McGregor was right. A confession could seal the case.

Nudging Angel's arm, Sarah flashed a quick smile. "Ready to roll, Robin?"

"That's not funny," McGregor called out, but the laughter that followed them down the hall belied his pronouncement.

Sarah paused at her desk and made a call to have the Pilcher woman brought up from Holding. When the suspect arrived, Sarah took note of the woman's faded camp shirt that was tucked into seasoned polyester pants stretched over ample thighs. Lank hair surrounded an unadorned face where striking blue eyes gazed out of the beginnings of what would become a maze of wrinkles in a few years. The overall effect stirred a sympathetic response. It looked like Mr. Pilcher had fallen short in his role as provider.

But divorce would have been a smarter option, Sarah reminded herself. Then the woman wouldn't be facing the prospect of trading one life sentence for another.

Angel hung back by the door while Sarah got Mrs. Pilcher settled in one of the chrome and vinyl chairs bracketing the wooden table that had seen plenty of distress over the years. Each cigarette burn, each water stain, had a story to tell, and Sarah thought perhaps it had been sentiment that had kept the table here when the interrogation rooms were modernized a few years ago. The institutional walls were now covered in a fabric that looked like indoor-outdoor carpeting—and probably was. It didn't create ambiance, but then, photographers from *Better Homes & Gardens* seldom showed up.

After a nod from Angel, which Sarah interpreted as a go-ahead to take the lead, she sat down opposite the woman. "Mrs. Pilcher, do you know why you're here?"

"Please call me Adelle. I told you there was no need for formality."

Now Sarah remembered something else about her first interview with the woman. Under that frumpy exterior lived a lady of some intelligence and refinement. Sarah could only imagine what it must have been like to disintegrate over time until nothing remained of the person you used to be. The woman might have kept a lid on her emotions for a long time, but everyone has a breaking point.

Pushing those thoughts aside, Sarah leveled gray eyes on the woman. "You understand that you have been charged with first-degree murder."

It was half-question and half-statement, but Adelle didn't respond to either. "What we need to do now is get your statement," Sarah continued. "So I am going to advise you of your rights."

"I'm well aware of them."

"It's procedure. And we will be taping this interview."

Adelle nodded impassively, remaining so as Sarah recited the *Miranda* wordage. The woman seemed equally unconcerned when Angel opened the door and Eric slipped in with his video camera mounted on his shoulder. Wearing his trademark jeans and leather vest over a denim shirt, Eric took a position in the corner, then gave the high sign when the tape was rolling.

Sarah dictated the relevant information that established the who, what, where, and when, then asked Adelle if she wanted her attorney present.

"That is not necessary."

"Let the record indicate that the suspect has waived right to counsel."

Sarah paused a moment to let those words have their impact, then systematically took Adelle through her previous story of not being home when her husband was shot. "We now know that wasn't true," Sarah concluded.

Only the slightest interest flickered in clear blue eyes.

"There's no doubt you will be standing trial for murder. Now it's only a question of whether there are mitigating circumstances that will keep this from being a capital case.

"That means the death penalty." The words echoed hollowly in the room as Sarah waited for some reaction from the woman.

Was she made of stone?

Then, very slowly, the expression on Adelle's face was transformed. A flush crawled up her cheeks, igniting a fire that smoldered in her eyes and turned them into granite hardness. She hissed her words. "There is no way. No way in hell I will die for that bastard."

The force of emotion pushed Sarah back in her chair, and she reeled from the impact. Then she glanced at Angel, who shrugged as if to say, "Let her go on and see where she takes us."

So Sarah did.

Adelle darted a quick look at the camera, and Sarah had to wonder. Was the woman's apparent concern for incriminating herself? Or for having her lapse of refinement caught forever on tape? But Sarah stopped speculating when Adelle's voice cut into the silence.

"Roy was every woman's fantasy at first. Kind. Attentive. Supportive. I tried to remember that when things started to go bad. I wanted to believe they could be good again. That he would somehow revert back and be the man I fell in love with . . ." She let the words trail off and appeared to go deep inside to recapture the memory.

"Did he abuse you?" Sarah asked, her voice soft and encouraging.

Adelle gave a short, hard laugh. "He didn't think so. I tried to talk to him. Tell him I wasn't something he could just keep locked up when he wasn't interested in playing with me. He didn't get it. If I didn't have any bruises, it couldn't be abuse."

Sarah wrapped herself in a professional cloak to keep a new wave of sympathy at bay. "Did you plan to kill him?"

"Oh, heavens, no." Adelle laughed again, softer this time. "Always considered myself above such things. It was just that moment. The opportunity. And I took it."

"Okay. You need to tell me everything that happened that night."

Adelle nodded.

Sarah gestured for her to begin, then sat unmoving as the woman detailed the fateful evening, beginning with Roy Pilcher's arrival home from work and ending with his demise.

It was the in-between that tore at Sarah's gut, the belittling, the goading, the whole sorry mess of emotional bludgeoning that left a person cowering. A long time ago she'd seen the same thing happen to her aunt, Dorothy. Sarah had been too young to know exactly what was going on, but she could still remember the tension tinged with fear that pervaded her aunt's house. At first she used to wonder why her mother always kept their visits so short, but eventually some instinct told her Dorothy's house was a terrible place to be.

The first time Sarah had questioned Adelle, she had seen the same fright reflected in large doe eyes staring back from the past into the present.

"After I called my sister to have an alibi, I hid the gun and called the police. The rest you know." Adelle finished.

Sarah gave a slight shake of her head and leaned forward. "We'll type up your statement, then you'll have to sign it."

Adelle nodded.

"You want anything? A glass of water?"

Adelle nodded again.

Outside the interrogation room, Sarah paused to rub the

tightness out of her neck. "I almost wish we didn't already have her in lock-up."

Angel turned to give her a puzzled look, and Sarah shrugged. "It sounds like she was punished enough before the fact."

Angel stopped and faced her partner squarely. "You'd let a murderer go?"

"Of course not. I'm just saying justice is skewed." Sarah thrust her hands deep in the pockets of her jeans. "You know what I mean."

"So we just skip the judicial system? Try the cases in the interrogation room?"

"That's not what I said."

"Sure as hell sounded like it to me."

Not giving her partner a chance to respond, Angel whirled and stomped off. Sarah released her frustration in a long breath, thankful for the reprieve. She didn't want to talk anymore. She didn't want to fight anymore. She just wanted her life to be normal again.

Fat chance of that.

CHAPTER TWO

Driving to the address McGregor had given her, Sarah nursed her Honda Civic along, and tried to figure out when she might have time to look for a new car. This one had served her well, exceedingly well if truth be told, and some loyal part of her cringed at the mental picture of the venerable old thing being turned into somebody's lunch box. She knew the idea was absurd. People didn't even use lunch boxes anymore. And the car was just a thing, an inanimate object that had run well past its warranty but now sputtered and choked in protest of cold mornings. But she'd formed an odd attachment that was hard to break, even though she knew she had to.

Okay. Next week she'd go to some dealerships. With any amount of luck, this current case would wrap as quickly as the Pilcher one.

McGregor had called Sarah this morning before she left her apartment to tell her they had a body. Young girl at a crummy motel. She should go there and meet Angel. So now she turned into the lot of the Anchor Inn Motel and nosed into a parking space next to a patrol car. Then she stepped out into a morning so glorious it should have been October. The sun rendered the clear blue sky iridescent and warmed the breeze that tugged lightly on her scarf, tossing it over one shoulder of her tan jacket.

Sarah inhaled the fresh air, thinking that nobody should have had to die on such a perfect day.

Noting the two patrol officers who were keeping gawkers well away, Sarah took a moment to survey the area close to room fifty-two. Scraps of litter rode gusts of wind until they were trapped in a hollow where the sidewalk didn't quite meet the wall. Down the uneven walkway, dark brown doors contrasted sharply with the pink stucco, but there was nothing to indicate that one of life's cruelest acts had occurred just beyond the doorway in front of her.

Steeling herself for what was inside, Sarah showed her shield to the patrol officer standing next to the open door, then stepped over the threshold. Her eyes couldn't adjust to the abrupt switch from the brightness outside, and she was cast into a world of dim shadows. Then one of the shadows moved into a shaft of sunlight that had pierced a hole in the cheap drapery.

"Detective Kingsly?" A young patrolman with a liberal sprinkling of freckles and close-cropped red hair stepped forward.

"Yes." She looked at him closely. "Rusty, isn't it?"

"Yes, ma'am."

"Sarah will do."

"Yes, ma'am."

Sarah decided against correcting him again. "What do we have?"

"Female victim." He gestured toward the bed, all business now. "It appears that her throat was cut."

"Who called it in?"

"Manager."

Sarah stepped closer and tried to look dispassionately at the body of a young woman that was covered to her chin with a faded bedspread. It could have been a child lovingly tucked in by a parent, except for the russet stain of dried blood on her forehead.

"What do you make of that?" Sarah pointed to the odd marking.

"Some kind of symbol?" Rusty shrugged. "Pretty weird."

"I'll say."

The girl might have been attractive once, but death's pallor was too stark against the dark puddle circling her neck and cradling her head. A sour odor of long-dead blood mingled with the distinct stench of feces and urine. Pressing a finger against her nose, Sarah fought the wrench of her stomach as she turned back to the officer. "Any ID?"

"Nothing in her purse. She was registered as Tracy Smith. But the manager said he doesn't know her."

"I bet half the guests here are named Smith." Sarah forced her gaze back to the victim. She was young. Maybe eighteen, tops. And so innocent looking, with slim, smooth hands folded over her chest.

Sarah pulled latex gloves on and bent closer to the dead girl's hands, lifting one finger. "She definitely wasn't a two-bit whore. Not if she could afford to have her nails done like this."

Rusty leaned closer.

"And look at this ring." Sarah turned the stone toward the officer. "I'd bet my next paycheck that's a genuine sapphire."

"What do you think?"

"I don't know." Sarah straightened. "She could've had some rich patron. But then why was she in a dump like this?"

"Maybe he got tired of her and cut her loose?"

"Would you?"

Rusty glanced at the girl then back at Sarah with an ironic grin. "Not likely."

Sarah hooked a thumb in the back pocket of her jeans and looked around. "What else?"

"Body's cold. She's been here a while." He checked his notebook then glanced at her. "Only took a visual inventory. Thought it best to wait."

"Good. Has the lab been called?"

Rusty nodded. "Took care of that first thing. Well, second to determining the victim was dead."

Sarah wondered if he had pages of the *Fundamentals of Criminal Investigation* stuck in his hip pocket for quick reference. "We'll see what turns up after the techs get through."

A scuff of leather on concrete caught her attention, and she turned to see a figure silhouetted in the sunlit doorway.

"We've got to stop meeting like this." The familiar voice carried the light touch of indifference common to people who are inured to death.

"Only in your dreams, Roberts."

The head of the forensic team adjusted his bow tie and stepped aside to let the techs trundle their equipment into the room. "In my dreams we're high in the mountains of New Zealand, giving the Maoris a lesson in American sex education, complete with a live demonstration."

"Funny. My fantasy has you finding the most incredible piece of evidence so I can hang the guy who did this."

"If you'll clear out and give us room, I'll see what we can do."

Sarah gave Roberts a mock salute, then stepped back into the brilliance outside. "Where's the manager?" she asked Rusty, who'd followed her out.

"In his office. My partner stayed to keep an eye on him. Got Watkins and Hearney to talk to the guests and the lady from housekeeping who found the body."

Rusty nodded toward the two officers Sarah had seen earlier. Notebooks in hand, they were talking to members of the scanty crowd. Most of the people looked like they regretted letting their curiosity draw them out of their rooms, and a dour, fifty-ish woman clung to her cleaning cart as if it could keep her connected to normality.

"You have a camera?" Sarah asked.

"Yes, ma'am."

"Good. Get shots of the spectators. I don't expect much, but you never know." She started to walk away, then noticed the can with cigarette butts just down from the door a little ways. "Wait. Before you do that, make sure Roberts sees this. Never know. The perp might have stepped out for a smoke at some point."

Rusty barely paused to nod before stepping back into the motel room.

Sarah crossed the parking lot to the small building that housed the motel lobby and opened the door. Inside, she saw a petite blond woman in uniform leaning against the counter. When the woman turned, Sarah recognized her. Rita Samuels. A good cop.

Rita nodded at Sarah then jerked a thumb at the man seated in the business section of the registration area. "He's the manager, Ray Timmons."

The man was about thirty-five. Too thin to be healthy, he had trouble keeping his eyes in one place. Sarah dragged the moment out, watching his gaze flick from her to Rita, down to the floor, over to the telephone, then back to Rita. It was like watching a fly on speed.

"Nervous, Ray?"

His attention jumped back to her. "Uh, no."

Timmons repeated his eye performance, making Sarah wonder if he needed a fix or was just coming down.

Whatever the cause, he was so out of it he didn't have the sense to turn on the air conditioning even though it felt like it was ninety degrees in the little room. The plate glass windows acted like solar heaters as the sun streamed in, making sweat bead on Sarah's back in an uncomfortable itch.

"How 'bout we turn on the air, Ray?" she asked.

"Sure. I can do that." He jumped off the stool and went to the thermostat on the wall behind him. When he came back he was a little more settled, as if the official act had been an antidote to his anxiety.

Sarah turned to Rita. "I'll handle this."

Rita nodded and walked to the door. Sarah waited until it had swished shut before walking behind the counter. She leaned against the sharp edge of Formica. "Okay," she said. "I need to know about Tracy Smith."

"You're not supposed to be in here." Timmons lifted the back of his hand as if he could push her back the way she'd come in.

Sarah ignored him.

Timmons struggled with bravado for a moment, then wiped pebbles of sweat from his face. "I don't know nothin' about nothin'."

"How often did she come in here?"

"I dunno."

"How many other girls use this place?"

"I dunno what you mean."

Sarah jerked him off the stool by the front of his shirt, pulling his face within inches of hers. "You'd better start knowing something real quick, asshole. Or I'll have your fuckin' ass in jail for obstructing justice, compounding a felony, and accessory to murder."

"I didn't do no murder." The acrid odor of his fear wafted over her like exhaust from a cheap bar.

"Convince me." She slammed him back on the stool so hard, she could swear she heard his bones rattle.

His voice rattled, too. "I just do what I'm told. The owner says don't ask questions, so I don't. A girl wants a place to rest for an hour or so, she can have it for the forty bucks up front."

"The victim was here longer than that."

"Well, yeah. We don't kick people out."

"Was she a frequent customer?"

Timmons shrugged.

Sarah leaned into him. "You've got to do better."

"Okay. Okay. I never saw her until night before last."

"Nobody checked the room yesterday?"

"The Do Not Disturb sign was on the door. The day guy said housekeeping never showed. So he ignored the room."

"What about last night? You didn't wonder why the girl never came out for almost twenty-four hours?"

"Figured she was having a good time."

Sarah's look froze the smile on his face.

"Hey, I was busy." His voice rose in self-defense. "How was I supposed to know?"

"By doing your job, asshole."

Timmons slumped on the stool. Sarah pulled a notebook and pen out of her jacket pocket. "Okay. Let's go back to the beginning. What time did she check in the other night?"

"About eleven."

"Anyone with her?"

"I dunno. I never paid attention."

"Anybody driving in has to come right past the lobby here." Sarah waved her pen at the expanse of glass. "With this view, you didn't see anything?"

"I wasn't watching."

"Isn't that your job? To keep an eye on things?"

"Not like that. Spyin' on guests." Timmons wrapped thin arms around his narrow chest and held himself tight. "I just sign people in and take care of any problems they call about."

"And the rest of the time?"

"There's records I gotta fill out. An' sometimes I watch a little TV." He nodded toward the set behind him.

I'll bet that's not all you do.

"I'll need a number where you can be reached." Sarah wrote as Timmons dictated, then slapped her notebook closed. "Don't do anything stupid like leave town."

"No, ma'am. I sure won't. I have nothing to hide. And my boss says we gotta cooperate with our friends in blue. You got any questions you just—"

Sarah cut him off with a wave. He was some kind of case. Relief must have given him diarrhea of the mouth, but she didn't have to stay and smell it. She pushed the glass door open and stepped out into the refreshing breeze.

Across the parking lot she saw Angel talking to the two Uniforms who no longer had a crowd to control. Angel dropped her notebook into her brown leather jacket and stepped forward to meet Sarah.

"Sorry I was late," Angel said. "There was an accident and I got stuck being a witness."

"What did the guys get from the people here?"

"Nothing. Everyone took lessons from the Three Blind Mice."

Sarah laughed. The first time she'd felt like it since she'd gotten here. "Did you talk to the woman who found the body?"

"Yeah. She was pretty shook. Has a daughter about the same age. That's where her focus is right now. Not on anything that's going to help us."

Sarah kicked a pebble across the pitted asphalt and sighed, revising her earlier estimate. This was not going to be easy.

"Walt's here," Angel said, leading the way back to the crime scene. "He's about ready to take the body in. Roberts is chompin' at the bit."

Sarah crossed the threshold into the motel room, now lit with powerful artificial light, and saw Walt Henderson's nearly bald head bent over the dead girl. The full glare of neon rendered the scene even more ghastly, and Sarah approached reluctantly, Angel following.

"What can you tell us?" Sarah asked.

Walt removed his latex-protected finger from the side of the victim's neck and looked up. "Prelim' I'd say cause of death is a severed carotid artery. But don't hold me to it until I make it official."

"T.O.D.?"

"Body's cold. Almost completely out of rigor and abdominal swelling is significant. I'm guessing thirty, forty hours."

"Pretty good guess," Sarah offered. "Victim was seen alive at eleven night before last."

"Science is seldom wrong." Walt turned back to the inspection of the body.

"Almost ready to transport?" Angel asked.

"Yeah." Walt straightened again and snapped off his gloves. "Let's bag her hands and take her in."

They stepped aside to make room for Walt's assistants to do their jobs. Sarah motioned for Rusty to stay and accompany the body to the morgue.

Angel touched her arm. "I'll meet you back at the station." Sarah nodded and headed back to her car.

CHAPTER THREE

Angel shrugged out of her jacket and slipped the holster off her shoulder, rubbing a tender spot. She couldn't remember when her jacket had gotten so snug. Must be all those muscles she was building in Tae Kwon Do. *More likely all the cookies you ate over the holidays, girl.*

She was either going to have to consider a diet or a new wardrobe. The diet was more fiscally responsible but lost its appeal when Sarah walked in carrying a paper sack from McDonald's. An enticing aroma of fat and calories drifted from the bag.

"You hungry?" Sarah paused at Angel's desk. "Got some breakfast burritos."

The gesture was as tempting as the food, and Angel couldn't resist either.

For a moment they were just like two fictional cops on TV, sharing an easy camaraderie. It felt so close to normal that if Angel really tried, she could pretend they didn't have a problem.

Sarah licked her fingers, wadded up the paper, and tossed it in the bag. "I'll start the computer checks," she said. "You want to deal with Missing Persons?"

"Sure." Angel dropped her napkin and wrapper in the bag. "Thanks for the snack."

"No problem."

Angel got a cup of coffee then returned to her desk, where she punched the appropriate numbers to reach someone in

Missing Persons. There was no recent report that matched their victim, but officer Pitts took the description and promised to check older ones. He'd get back to her as soon as he could.

Angel cradled the receiver and chewed on the end of her pencil. That girl wasn't going to be on any old report. She was too well-cared-for to have been on the streets any length of time. So they were going to have to pinpoint her identity another way.

Glancing over to Sarah, Angel called out, "Anything?"

"Zip."

"How about I talk to the guys in Vice. See if they have a lead on her."

Sarah pushed back from her desk. "I'll bring the lieutenant up to speed."

In addition to the usual clutter, McGregor's desk supported stacks of file folders that looked alarmingly like paper mountains about to crumble. He glanced up from the yawning drawers of the metal file cabinet standing to one side of the desk as Sarah stepped through the door.

"Cleaning house?" Sarah pulled a plastic chair from the wall and straddled the seat.

"Just making room for this year's mess." McGregor lifted a stack of folders, which miraculously didn't fall when he set them on the floor. Then he swiveled back and faced Sarah. "What do you have?"

Sarah quickly reviewed the few facts while McGregor watched, elbow on the desk and one finger probing the side of his face.

"It's a good guess that Smith isn't her real name," Sarah concluded. "And so far we haven't had any luck making an ID."

"You sure she was a hooker?"

"As sure as I can be without being able to ask."

"What's your next step?"

"Unless Angel gets real lucky in Vice, I guess we go to the streets. Talk to some of the other working girls. I sent a picture of the mark on the victim's forehead over to Sanchez at the Federal Building. He said he'd fax it to Quantico and try to get a quick turnaround. But he reminded me I shouldn't hold my breath. People in the behavioral science group don't take kindly to field agents dictating their calendar. So it could take a few days. Unless there's an outbreak of curiosity."

McGregor nodded. "When's the autopsy scheduled?"

"Walt said he'd try for tomorrow. Late afternoon. He's still backed up from that bus accident on I-30."

"You need Chad in on it yet?"

"Not without any more to go on. No sense in three of us wasting time."

"He could be your pimp. Make you look more legit when you go out on the street."

Sarah remembered the first time they'd tried that and the unexpected hostility it had created in Angel. "No thanks," she said. "We'll just play it straight tonight."

Returning to her desk, Sarah decided to wrap up the paperwork on the Pilcher case and turn it in to be filed. As much as she hated the tedium, it would keep her from calling Roberts only to hear him say he had nothing.

An hour after lunch, which for Sarah consisted of an energy bar and coffee, Angel came back. She plopped into a chair next to Sarah's desk. "Vice was a big fat zero."

Sarah pushed her chair back. "Hope you didn't have any big plans for tonight."

"Don't tell me."

"Yup. Somebody's got to know who this girl was."

Angel pulled herself to her feet. "Better call my mother and cancel out of dinner."

Watching Angel walk away, Sarah fought a surge of resent-

ment. It wasn't her partner's fault she had a loving family and
Sarah didn't.

"I'm going to knock off a little early this afternoon," Sarah
called out. "Want me to pick you up about nine?"

Angel nodded without breaking stride.

Sarah hefted the bag of groceries to her hip and fumbled the
key into the appropriate slot to unlock her door. The side trip to
the store had cost her another half hour after the hour spent
wrapping things up at the station, but it had been vital. This
morning her refrigerator had been dismally bare. The least she
could do was have a decent meal before going out again.

Inside, she pushed the door closed with her foot and headed
toward the kitchen. Cat, curled on the table, looked like a furry,
russet centerpiece. At the sound of her entrance, he roused and
greeted her with a throaty meow, displaying no sign of remorse.

"Get off the table!"

He regarded her with solemn amber eyes, then stood,
stretched, and bounded down. His soft paws brushed sound-
lessly on the tile floor. Every action was underscored with
insolence and prompted a smile as Sarah dropped the grocery
sack on the counter.

Physically, Cat had grown up to his name, but much of his
behavior stayed rooted in babyhood. She couldn't recall exactly
when she'd made the decision to let him stay. Or even if she
actually had decided. He'd sneaked into her life right after
John's death, and her intent had been only to provide temporary
refuge to a starving kitten. But somehow she'd let the months
slip by without taking him to the pound. She'd kidded herself at
first that sympathy for his lot in life prompted her reluctance.
But when she was brave enough to look at herself honestly, she
knew she kept him because his sandpaper affection had been
the only bright spot in that terrible black hole of her life.

Sarah poured some chows in his dish to keep him occupied while she put groceries away. The distraction lasted all of thirty seconds. He sauntered back, then jumped on the counter and sniffed at the frozen dinner she'd left out.

"You can just forget that idea."

His look seemed to ask, "What idea?"

Sarah grabbed the container, tore the cardboard open, and put the dish in the microwave. Then she leafed through the day's delivery of bills and junk mail until she came to a personal letter. Slipping her thumbnail under the flap, she opened the envelope and slid out a small printed card.

Ms. Jeanette Rafferty
requests
the honor of your presence
as she exchanges wedding vows . . .

"Damn!" Sudden, burning tears blurred the rest of the words, and Sarah closed her eyes in an effort to prevent the wetness from slipping out. John had been dead only six months, and Jeanette was getting married again? What kind of loyalty was that?

A rough tongue licked the moisture from her cheek and Sarah opened her eyes. Absently, she stroked Cat's silky fur while she mentally tried to talk herself out of this unreasonable anger.

It wasn't any of her business if Jeanette was ready for someone else. Life had to go on, as the woman had so forcefully reminded her a few weeks ago. But couldn't she even honor her dead husband's memory a little longer?

Or is that just your problem?

Sarah stilled her fingers as the pain of grief washed over her again. Her life, like a kite suddenly without the wind, had spiraled downward since that night her partner had been taken out by a punk's bullet. Even though she tried not to visit the pain often, it was there, waiting like a predator ready to pounce into the slightest opening she gave it.

In the first days and weeks after John's death, she'd found some consolation and stability in the grief she'd shared with his widow. They were like companions rowing the same boat in the same sea of pain. Then Jeanette had told her it was time they moved on. It wasn't healthy to stagnate in misery. She'd sounded like a goddam shrink. And Sarah had told her so.

Then Jeanette had said the most remarkable thing.

That John didn't have two widows.

What the hell had she meant by that?

Sarah wasn't sure if she really didn't know, or if she didn't *want* to know. John had been her partner and probably her best friend for five years, but she'd never thought of him in any other way. Had she?

Rationally she could tell Jeanette that John's fidelity had always been with her, his wife. But even when she said the words, Sarah sensed they weren't entirely true. She was the one he'd talked to the first time he had to use deadly force—because she would understand what it meant and his wife wouldn't. A wife could sympathize. Console. But she could never understand what it meant to take a human life. Or that horrible fear of waiting too long next time. Or the nightmares that screamed in the night. Or the dread that you would never learn to live with it.

Sarah could deny the truth to Jeanette. She could evade it with the shrink at the station. But she couldn't lie to herself. Her relationship with John had been the most solid thing in her life since her grandmother's death, and there had been times she'd entertained the wild daydream of a life with him that didn't end at the station. In her fantasy it would've been perfect.

That thought caught her up short. Isn't that the same fantasy the Pilcher woman had had for her life? And look where it got her.

No. Fantasy is where people go to escape real life. And in real life John would never have left his family for her. He wouldn't have even considered it.

Wiping a tear from her cheek, Sarah silenced the piercing buzz of the microwave. *Don't think. Focus. All you have to do is eat your supper. Nothing else.*

CHAPTER FOUR

Angel tried not to think of the blister burning on her heel, wondering how much longer they were going to stick with this. It was almost midnight, and they'd walked damn near every block in a half-mile radius without finding any girls. "We just going to work clear through until morning roll call?" she called out to Sarah, who was pushing doggedly ahead.

"No. Just this next street. Then we can quit."

Sarah hadn't even lost a stride, and Angel hurried to keep up as the circle of light from a streetlamp cast her partner in sharp relief against the darkness. There was something eerie about the night. The artificial light cloaked Sarah in a yellow pall, blending her hair and her khaki jacket into one flow of color while her jeans took on a greenish tinge. And it was so still. The distant sounds of traffic on Harry Hines, two blocks over, hummed like a bad soundtrack, and nothing disturbed the dank aroma of old garbage wafting from nearby Dumpsters. Where was the night life? Where was the wind?

"Most of the girls don't stand on corners anymore, you know." Angel addressed Sarah's retreating back. "Too dangerous. They cruise now."

Sarah stopped so suddenly Angel almost walked into her.

"You could've told me."

"Thought you knew." Angel pulled her jacket closed against a sudden gust of wind. "You're the homicide dick with all the experience."

Sarah hesitated for just a beat, and Angel wanted to take the words back. Sometimes her own childishness surprised her. If she was so damned concerned about the state of her partner's mind, why did she keep throwing gasoline on the fire? She let out a breath of relief when Sarah bypassed the comment entirely.

"So how do the johns know they're available?"

"It's all high-tech now. They have beepers and cell phones."

"All of them?"

Angel shrugged. "I'm no expert. I'm just going on what Ryan told me."

"Then we'll jst have to assume there's still a few that hearken to the old tradition."

Sarah pushed off again, and Angel followed, thinking the only consolation was not having to get tarted up for this gig. Otherwise, it sucked.

Two blocks down, Sarah rounded a corner and saw three girls huddled against a boarded-up storefront. They ranged in age from early twenties to pushing forty and had that unmistakable air of detached cynicism mixed with guarded hostility. The oldest was puffing heartily on a cigarette, as if somehow under the delusion that its glowing ember could neutralize the winter chill. The youngest, a slight Hispanic cast to her complexion, looked to the third woman for guidance. That one, with skin the color of an antique medicine bottle, stepped forward as Sarah and Angel approached.

"We don't want no trouble," she said in a husky voice that betrayed years of tobacco abuse.

"We just need some information." Sarah flashed her shield.

"Are they going to arrest us?" Anxiety flickered in the young woman's ebony eyes.

The black woman waved a hand to quiet the girl and let an interval of silence dance on the cold wind.

"We're investigating a homicide," Sarah said. "Happened at

the Anchor Inn a few blocks over. You familiar with the place?"

Sarah looked pointedly at the other two, but the black woman maintained her position of leadership. "Couldn't say."

"I came here prepared to be real nice. Treat you with respect and get some answers." Sarah shifted her weight to her toes, effectively cutting into the other woman's space. "And you get all hostile on me. I don't deal well with hostile. Ask my partner." Sarah watched the woman's wary eyes flick to Angel then back again.

"You want to think about this, girlfriend," Angel said. "Yesterday she tried to throw some guy off a bridge. And he wasn't even being rude."

The young girl's eyes widened in fear and she pulled on the woman's sleeve. "Talk to her, Reba."

Reba took a long moment to consider her friend's plea and Sarah's stance. Finally, she dipped her chin in a brief nod.

Sarah pulled a photograph out of the breast pocket of her jacket and handed it over. "You recognize this girl?"

Reba thumbed her lighter to life and tilted the snapshot into the illumination. There was a sharp intake of breath as the woman's eyes rested on the unmistakable picture of death. "What happened?"

"Maybe somebody was disappointed in her service."

"Oh, my God, Reba! Is some maniac after us?" The young woman craned her head over Reba's shoulder to get a better look at the picture.

"You just hush, girl." Reba handed the photo back to Sarah. "I never seen this one before."

"What about you?" Sarah extended her arm toward the other woman who took a break from her puffing to scan the picture.

"Nah." The woman said. "Don't recognize her."

"What if she's new?" Angel asked.

"We'd know," Reba said. "Our man controls this whole area.

Nobody works here 'lessen he sets it up."

"Unless he set something up and forgot to tell you." Angel paused to let that sink in. "Here's my card. You hear anything about a girl coming up missing, call me."

"And why should I be helping you?"

" 'Cause the next body in the morgue could be yours."

Angel lowered her cold, aching body into the comforting warmth of the bath water, stirring the sweet aroma of Natural Wonders Vanilla Orchid. If she closed her eyes she could pretend she was in some luxurious resort being pampered by beautiful young men hand-picked to serve her every need. *Whoa, girl. That's some vision. What would your hardass partner have to say about something so patently feminine?*

Resting her neck against the rounded edge of the venerable claw-foot tub, the only good thing about living in a drafty old house, Angel realized she didn't have a clue what Sarah would think about that or anything else. She wasn't even sure the woman had been doing much thinking at all for some time.

Early in their partnership, Angel had tried to give Sarah some latitude. It couldn't have been easy to lose her partner and kill that kid on the same night. But that had happened months ago, and the woman wasn't getting any better. In fact, her bizarre behavior had escalated. And that trick on the bridge the other day capped it. Angel was glad the guy hadn't ended up as road kill. But still. They all could've ended up as road kill.

Shit.

For the umpteenth time in recent months Angel considered whether to go to McGregor with her concerns, but she knew what could happen if she did. Partners don't rat on each other. Sure, she and Sarah weren't really partners yet. Not in that true sense of unyielding loyalty and trust. And Angel wasn't even sure if it was ever going to happen. But it for damn sure wouldn't happen if she had a chat with the boss.

Should she just ignore it all? It wasn't just her fear for Sarah's life. Hell, she still wasn't sure she liked her enough to even care. But damn, she wasn't going to die along with her. *But damn, you aren't going to talk either, girl. You can't and you know it.*

Angel slid down in the tub, hoping the warm cocoon of water would shield her from her thoughts.

Sarah couldn't remember the last time she'd been to McGregor's apartment. Four years ago when she'd helped him move in? So much for being a supportive friend.

And what the hell was she doing here tonight? If she honestly tried to answer that question, she'd have to admit that Angel's reminder of the incident on the bridge scared her. But it was easier to believe she was following up on a promise so long forgotten it was growing mold.

When McGregor's wife had unceremoniously dumped him and moved back to Ohio with the kids, Sarah had assured him that she would come around now and then. Somehow work and life had always trumped promises, and the two of them didn't really have much in common beyond the occasional drink. Not that either of them needed a reminder that they did a bit too much of that.

Sarah pushed the buzzer on his door and huddled close to escape the chill night air. After what seemed like an eternity, she heard his voice, clogged with what she assumed was sleep. "Who's there?"

"Sarah."

She heard the sounds of the lock being disengaged, then the door opened. McGregor, wearing rumpled sweats, stood on bare feet and ran his large hand over a stubble of beard. "What in the hell are you doing here?"

"We didn't get anything from the hookers."

"That couldn't wait until the morning briefing?"

She shifted from one foot to the other and wondered if she should just turn and walk away. This was a stupid idea.

McGregor sighed and opened the door wider. "Come on in."

Sarah stepped into the entry, waited for him to close and re-lock the door, then followed him into the living room, where the unmistakable odor of sweat and booze lingered in the air. The glow of the television cast a feeble light that barely touched the darkness. It was like walking into a theater after the movie had already started, and Sarah had a moment of disorientation. She stood still while McGregor turned on a lamp. Then he dug in the mess of pillows on the sofa until he came up with a remote control. "Fell asleep watching a movie," he said.

"Happens a lot at my house, too."

He pointed the remote at the television and the screen flicked to black. Then he pushed the pillows and sheet to one corner of the couch and motioned to her. "Sit. You want a drink?"

"Uh, maybe I shouldn't." She perched on the edge of one cushion.

He stopped walking toward a shelf that held bottles and glasses and turned to regard her with a thoughtful gaze. Then he shrugged. "Sure you should. A shot of good bourbon'll take the chill out."

She took the glass he offered. What was she going to do? Argue with her boss? But she regretted her inability to refuse the drink and the impulse that had brought her here.

"So." McGregor sat on the Lazy-Boy across from her. "You still seeing that CPA guy?"

Wow. We really are out of touch.

"No." She took a sip of the bourbon and it slid smoothly down to warm her stomach. "It didn't last long."

"Nothing in life does."

Sarah looked around at the bare walls, the mess on the coffee table, the discarded clothing littering the floor. It wasn't hard to recognize the signs of personal disintegration, and she felt a pang of guilt. She'd been so wrapped up in the mess of her own life, she hadn't thought much about his. "You doing okay?" she asked.

"Dandy." He took a long swallow of the amber liquid.

The ensuing silence was so intense, she could swear she heard the digital clock flash the passing of another minute. "You want to talk?"

He shot her a quick look. "About what?"

"I don't know. Life? Work? The latest Mavericks game?"

He shot her another look, and this one definitely had a "No Trespassing" sign attached.

The silence dripped with tension. When it became unbearable, Sarah set her glass down on a used paper plate and stood. "Just wanted to let you know how we made out."

"Sure." He heaved his bulk out of the chair and walked her to the door.

She touched his arm before stepping out. "Call me if you ever . . . you know . . . want to talk."

"Sure."

The response had been anything but "sure," and a sense of disquiet accompanied Sarah home. If she had the courage to admit it, they were both fucked up royally. And she was an idiot if she thought she could help him. Hell, she couldn't even help herself.

In her bedroom, she stripped off her clothes, slipped naked between the sheets and invited Cat to snuggle in the curve of her stomach. The steady rumble of his purr soothed her jangled nerves. Life would be so much easier if she could just stay here.

CHAPTER FIVE

Fighting the fogginess of not enough sleep, Sarah tried to concentrate on the preliminary report from Roberts. If they ever caught the guy who offed the young prostitute, they had a wide variety of hairs and fibers to try to match. But that would be a challenge. God alone knew how old some of those samples were, cleanliness not being a top priority down at the old Anchor Inn.

Plus, the methodical way the body had been arranged after the deed didn't indicate a doer who was sloppy enough to leave a plethora of evidence among the debris left by the hundreds of people who'd been through that motel room in the last year.

Sarah noted that Roberts did take the can of cigarette butts and would have one of the techs go through them. She shuddered. What a crappy job that would be. Sure, she liked a smoke now and then, but she wouldn't want to sift through a bunch of old butts, especially when doing so might not even get them anywhere with the case.

Swiveling her chair, Sarah dropped the report on her desk and stood up. "When Angel comes in, tell her I've gone over to the morgue," she called to Chad, who acknowledged with a wave.

An acrid, antiseptic odor tingled in her nose as Sarah pushed through the doors leading to the autopsy room. Glad she'd grabbed her jacket, she stepped in where the air registered a cool sixty-eight degrees, a temperature that stayed the same summer or winter.

Walt, who had smothered his wild array of colors in dismal green scrubs, walked around the table, dictating into an overhead microphone. Bright surgical lights illuminated every pore and pimple on Tracy Smith's body.

Watching, Sarah gnawed on her bottom lip. She tried not to think about before; the before when this girl was still breathing, vibrant, and alive, making her deals, maybe even enjoying her work. It was never a good thing to think about the before. That way logic couldn't be clouded with emotion. Better to turn a victim into a case and a corpse into evidence. But damn, this girl had been so young and somehow looked more vulnerable lying naked on this cold, steel table than she had at the motel. Maybe because there she had been covered up.

Walt glanced up and Sarah took a step closer. "Anything?"

"Just got started."

Sarah let her breath out in a slow sigh then glanced over where Chan hunched over a microscope. Something dark and wet she preferred not to identify was in a specimen tray beside him. She turned back as Walt continued the verbal recording of his preliminary assessment.

"Note a laceration on the right side of the neck." Walt paused the narrative to take measurements. "Two-point-two centimeters in length. Fourteen millimeters in depth. Barely deep enough to work, and it might not have in someone heavier. Edges are clean. Cut was made with a sharp instrument."

"Can you narrow the range of 'sharp instruments'?" Sarah asked.

"I can't tell you exactly what it was. Chan will have to do some investigating on that. But how tightly the wound closed up indicates something very sharp. It's like a surgical incision that wasn't retracted."

"You think a doc did it?"

"It's conceivable. It's even possible a scalpel was used. But I want Chan to do his magic before I commit."

"What else can you tell me? Is the laceration the cause of death?"

"Most certainly." Walt shifted his weight to his inside foot and leaned against the edge of the table. "But I'm just talking here for now. None of this is official yet."

"Sure."

"First off, this isn't a regular throat slashing. Wound is too short. Too precise. Almost . . ." Walt paused and leaned closer to the cut, pulling back the edges. "Calculated. Reminds me of the blood-letting I saw in the Amazon."

"Blood-letting?"

"Yeah." Walt faced her again. "Except there the cuts were even shorter. But they had the same look of precision to them. Not like the ones where a guy gets pissed and takes a knife to his woman's throat. He won't stop at almost exactly one inch. He'll damn near take her head off."

He gently touched the thin line on the girl's neck. "Somebody did this very carefully. Like a ritual."

Ritual. It wasn't a word Sarah wanted to hear. It put the murder into that murky realm of psychosis that she hated to have to enter. She preferred a simple drive-by, where the line between motive and result is clear, and the perp is nothing more than a swaggering gangster. Or an old lady tired of her husband's bullying.

"You want to stay for the rest?"

Walt's question pulled her back to the reality at hand. "No. Send the full report as soon as you can. Preferably one that includes the exact murder weapon."

"I'll get Chan on it right away. But the odds are better for winning the lottery than getting an early match."

Sarah took one last look at the remains of Tracy Smith. "Do

what you can."

Outside, Sarah walked for several blocks, oblivious to the gusts of cold wind blowing through the concrete canyons to redden her cheeks and tie her hair in knots. Despite the fresh air, the cloying scent of formaldehyde stayed with her. She had to shake this persistent sense of disquiet that kept punching holes in her professional boundaries. Keeping an emotional distance was the first axiom of good police work, and she used to be able to do that. She couldn't afford to lose it all now.

Detachment. That was the key to survival.

Yeah. Except what if you get so detached you aren't connected to anything?

The question nagged as Sarah stepped into the street. A warning honk propelled her back to the curb, and she paused to let an angry driver finish his right turn after flipping her off. The action was so juvenile, she wanted to laugh.

She wished she could laugh. But she was having a hard time remembering how.

Even the weather was conspiring against her. Today it decided to be January for real, and it was colder than a well-digger's ass. Turning her back to the cutting wind, Sarah headed toward the Municipal Building.

Entering the squad room after a quick stop to grab a cup of coffee, Sarah noticed a young woman sitting next to Angel's desk. A worried frown marred the girl's otherwise flawless face, which was framed by a cascade of honey-blond hair. If she wasn't a model, she should be.

Angel made quick introductions, letting her gaze stay with Sarah at the end. "Pitts called me when Amber came in. She wanted to report a missing friend."

"And the friend's name?" Sarah asked.

"Tracy *Clemment.*" The emphasis Angel gave to the last name left no room for doubt. Next to Trammel Crow, Burke Clemment was the biggest player in real estate development in the city. Sarah recalled seeing the face of a daughter grace the society page of the *Dallas Morning News* a few years ago. Big splash about a sweet-sixteen birthday party. Sarah tried to hang on to a desperate hope that their victim was another girl, but her gut wasn't buying it.

"Did you . . . ?"

Angel shot Amber a quick look. "She just got here."

Sarah pulled up another chair and sat opposite the girl whose blue eyes clouded to violet, then widened in alarm. "Did something happen to Tracy?"

"We don't know if it was your friend," Angel said. "When did you see her last?"

"Couple of nights ago."

"Where?"

"Do I have to say?" Her voice trembled. "She was okay when she left. I know that. So it isn't going to matter, is it? We don't want our parents to find out."

"Find out what, Amber?" Sarah leaned forward with her question.

"What we've been doing." Amber clutched at the front of her loose t-shirt.

Sarah waited out a long moment of silence, hoping the girl would continue. Finally, Angel reached out and stopped the nervous twisting of fingers and fabric. "You're going to have to tell us."

"We thought it would just be fun. Not completely harmless. But okay. You know, legally. So we started to work there a couple of weeks ago."

"Where?" Angel asked.

"The Club."

"Club?"

"You know, The Club."

56

The emphasis registered with Sarah as she realized the girl was referring to one of the exclusive gentleman's clubs. "How old are you, Amber?"

"Nineteen."

Too young to serve liquor. That only left one other job. "You're a stripper?"

"Not exactly," Amber's restless fingers moved to the crease of her jeans. "It's not like those cheap joints."

"You take off your clothes, don't you?"

"Well, yeah."

"Then I don't see a whole lot of difference."

A tear spilled out of the wide, frightened eyes. "Are we in trouble?"

Angel opened a folder on her desk and pulled out a photograph. "This girl was found dead a couple of days ago. You recognize her?"

Amber looked quickly from Angel to Sarah. "There's no way."

"Just look at the picture," Sarah said, attaching her hope to the girl's. She'll look, give a relieved little laugh and say "no."

Amber took the photo in a trembling hand and glanced at it quickly before folding in on herself with a low moan. Sarah stood up and put her hands on her hips. She wanted to kick something, but there was nothing handy. Angel gently pulled the photograph out of the girl's hand. "I'm sorry," she said.

Sarah turned back and took Amber by the arm, helping her to stand. "We'll go someplace private."

They stepped into one of the interrogation rooms. Not the friendliest of places, with its dismal gray walls and battered furniture, but Sarah didn't think the girl would notice. Amber slumped in one of the metal chairs, as if the death of her friend had pulled the stuffing out of her. Even her hair had lost its luster, hanging in limp strands around her ravaged face. Sarah let her cry for a few minutes. Then she poured a glass of water from the pitcher kept in the room, handed the drink to Amber and sat down opposite her. Angel pulled a chair to the end of the table.

"We have a few questions," Sarah said.

Amber brushed tears from her cheek in a quick swipe. "Do I have to?"

"It could help us find whoever did this," Angel said, her voice soft and soothing.

Amber swallowed her tears with a sip of the water and nodded to Sarah.

"How long did you and Tracy work at The Club?"

"Three weeks."

Sarah remembered her impression of the victim as not being a seasoned veteran in the business of selling her body. Amber had the same appearance. Flawless, well-oiled skin without a blemish. Perfect white teeth. Manicured fingers. It just didn't fit, and Sarah couldn't stop the next question, "Why?"

"Why what?"

"Work in a place like that? You don't look like you're desperate for money."

"It wasn't that. We just thought it would be fun."

"Fun?" Angel's outburst made the girl jump, and she turned wide deep blue eyes to Angel.

"We didn't see what it would hurt."

Christ! It killed your friend. Sarah wanted to say the words aloud, but she bit them back. They needed the girl to talk, not dissolve in hysterics. She pushed her chair back and stood up, motioning for Angel to take over. Listening to her partner draw out the story of how the girls had decided to "walk on the wild side" because they found it exciting, Sarah leaned a shoulder against the wall and sighed. They had thought stripping and turning tricks was going to be an adventure, like a bush trip to Africa. How could they have been so naive?

Not that they could have expected the tragic end Tracy had come to. But had they really believed there was no harm in prostitution?

"We weren't going into prostitution as a career choice, you understand." Amber's voice had gained strength with the telling, falling into a manner of expression that reminded Sarah of business women knocking on the glass ceiling. "We just wanted to see what it was like. Sort of like dating. Only for money."

"Did you have many of these 'dates'?" Angel asked.

"No." A bit of Amber's composure slipped. "We didn't have any . . . I mean . . . I didn't have . . . We didn't know how . . . arrangements were made. And we couldn't exactly ask."

"When did you see Tracy last?" Sarah asked.

"That night. When she left to meet someone."

"She had one of those 'dates' that night?"

Amber nodded. "After our last set, we counted our tips together. We always did. To see who got the most. Tracy pulled a hundred-dollar bill out of her pile of money. That was the biggest tip either one of us ever had, and we were really excited. Then she found a note inside the fold of the hundred." Amber paused to take another drink of water. "It requested the pleasure of her company for a private dance."

"In those exact words?" Sarah asked.

"Close. It sounded kind of formal like that and said if Tracy was interested, she should meet him in the parking lot. She was really skeptical at first, but this is what we wanted to try. And I told her it would be okay. I'd already done it once and it was okay. Besides, how could she be worried about someone who obviously had such fine taste and—" Amber clamped a hand over her mouth as her eyes widened in a sudden realization. "Oh, my God! I made her do it. I killed Tracy."

Fresh tears streaked down Amber's cheeks, and her whole body convulsed in a wracking sob. Angel got up, pulled a tissue out of her jacket pocket and handed it over.

Sarah waited a moment for the girl to adjust to her culpability and then pressed on. "What happened to the note?"

"Maybe she took it with her." Amber paused to wipe the mess her tears had made on her face, leaving a slash of mascara high on one pale cheek. Then she blew her nose, daintily, like she'd probably been taught. "I remember she gathered up all the money and put it in her purse."

Sarah remembered the little sequined thing with a gold clasp, but there hadn't been a note in the array of loose bills, tissues, a compact and lipstick. She didn't think there'd been anything higher than a twenty in the purse, either. Could the killer have taken the money and the paper?

"Did she know who had given her the tip?" Angel asked, walking back to her chair.

"She didn't think so. There had been one guy she'd noticed several times. She called him 'the mystery man.' But at the end of the dance when everyone is slipping the money in your costume, you can't tell what any one person is leaving. And sometimes guests will get a waitress to bring the tip up."

"You ever see the guy?"

"Couple of times. He always sat in the back. Away from the large, rowdy groups. He dressed nice and seemed sort of . . . refined. Like an English butler. Wore a suit and a hat."

"Was he there that night?"

"I don't know. I wasn't on the main floor. We had some private parties."

Sarah rolled her shoulders to ease the nibble of pain that had started in the middle of her back. Until that reminder of muscles held too tightly for too long, she hadn't realized that anger still held her in an iron grip—anger at the utter hopelessness of the whole mess. There was such a fine line of demarcation between innocence and stupidity, but neither justified what had happened to Tracy Clemment.

The temptation was strong to take her anger out on Amber. It sounded like much of this had been her idea. But the girl didn't need anyone else piling guilt on her shoulders.

"We appreciate your cooperation." Sarah pushed a notebook across the table. "Give us some numbers where we can reach you."

After making sure Amber had her emotions under enough control to drive home, Sarah and Angel went to find McGregor. He wasn't going to be pleased when they told him the case had just jumped into High Profile.

They found him in the break room eating a microwave pizza and gave him the news while he chewed. When they finished, he wiped the grease off his lips with a paper napkin.

"There's no mistake?" McGregor asked Angel, who poured a mug of coffee and sat down across from him.

She shook her head.

"Damn!" McGregor turned to Sarah. "And they were really hooking?"

"Maybe just flirting with the idea."

"How could they have been so stupid?"

"No telling about people, Lieu. Maybe they thought their social position was a barrier against the depravity of the underprivileged."

McGregor took a hefty swig of his diet cola, then tossed the empty into a plastic bin marked "cans only." "Better find out how the chief wants us to handle Daddy."

"What? He should receive special treatment because he's rich?" Sarah turned so fast, hot coffee slopped over her hand.

"Now who's being naive?" McGregor stood, clearing his napkin and paper plate from the table. "You know how much trouble someone like Clemment can make. Not being treated with the regard he feels he deserves is the quickest way of pissing him off."

Sarah held her tongue and her temper. McGregor was right. But that didn't justify the practice. And she knew Price would have to be involved. He'd give his own little PR spin to things so Burke Clemment's name and reputation could be protected. Wouldn't want one little mention of what his daughter had been doing to hit the press.

"I'll talk to Dorsett and get back to you," McGregor said on his way out the door. "You two have fun at The Club."

If the situation wasn't so distasteful, Sarah would have laughed.

CHAPTER SIX

Seen in the glare of early afternoon sunlight, The Club looked like a high-priced Mexican restaurant. Of course, the owners might not like that comparison, Angel thought as she and Sarah got out of the car and walked to the front door. And the fact that she'd skipped lunch could be influencing her perception. She was willing to admit that. But the Spanish hacienda impression was unavoidable in the thick stucco walls, wrought iron trims, and red tile roof.

Inside, the image changed to swank hotel. Gilded mirrors on the entry walls created an illusion of spaciousness while capturing the glitter of light from exquisite chandeliers. A highly polished marble floor also refracted the light, giving an impression of surround-sight.

A young woman with a dusky complexion sat behind a counter fashioned from a solid chunk of black onyx resting on brass filigree supports. She looked up, her welcoming smile a brief flash of perfect white teeth. When she got close enough, Angel could see that the amber highlights on the woman's braids matched the color of her languid eyes. A hint of mauve on her cheeks was a shade lighter than her lipstick. Nothing as tacky as a nametag marred the sleek lines of the black sheath dress that was as unobtrusive as it was elegant. *Mama always told me you can wear black anywhere, anytime.*

Sarah stepped forward and showed the woman her ID. "We need to see the manager."

The woman's smile didn't falter. "I'll see if he's available."

She slid off the stool and walked with a fluid, feline grace toward the doorway leading to the dining and show area. Watching her, Angel thought it was too bad all that beauty was being wasted in a place like this.

The woman returned a moment later. "Mr. Jeffers will see you now."

She motioned for the detectives to follow her through the plush lounge area where high-backed padded chairs ringed small tables topped with Damask cloths and crystal ashtrays. The look was elegant enough to satisfy royalty.

To her right, Angel heard the clink of glass and glanced over to see a bar tucked in a corner. Along the same wall, but more centrally located, was a stage where a girl with a cascade of blond hair danced. She moved her entire body, matching the rhythmic thump of bass in the instrumental interlude of Al Stewart's "Time Passages." Most of that entire body was nude, and the girl had her eyes closed.

A tickle of titillation surprised Angel. *God, I must be a pervert.* Her self-recrimination was strengthened when she noticed that the men seated at a table in the middle of the room weren't even looking at the girl. But their lack of interest could be due to familiarity. Maybe the act had lost the sense of naughtiness that brought an extra edge of excitement. Looking at dirty magazines when she'd been a kid wouldn't have been nearly as much fun if her mother had given them to her.

That realization only made Angel feel marginally better.

"Some detectives to see you," the young woman said to a slight man seated at a table cluttered with papers, a plate littered with crumbs and a splotch of catsup, and a mug of coffee.

Edwin, "Call me Ed," Jeffers rose from behind the table and offered the women a broad smile. With his hundred-dollar haircut, silk Armani suit, and perfectly manicured fingernails, he could have been a corporate CEO or an elite mobster. "What can I do for you, ladies?"

"We have a few questions about Tracy Clemment." Angel said, taking the soft cushioned chair he offered.

"Who?"

"Girl who was dancing here." Sarah took a chair next to Angel. "Hired on recently."

"You mean Tracy Smith?"

Sarah let the question hang while Jeffers's puzzlement slowly changed to realization. He looked from one to the other. "What the fuck! You telling me I hired Burke Clemment's daughter?" He took another moment for self-incrimination. "Geez. How was I to know?"

"Geez. Checking ID might be a thought."

He shot another quick look from Sarah to Angel. "Certainly you don't think—"

"This is the last place she was seen alive," Angel said. "What do you expect us to think?"

Jeffers rubbed a hand across his smooth chin, letting his fingers rest on his lips.

"How do the girls arrange their dates?" Sarah asked.

He looked at her quickly. "Dates?"

"Let's skip the bullshit."

"I don't like your insinuation."

"Then maybe you should be in another line of work."

That stopped him for a heartbeat. Then he swelled with indignation. "This is a refined, highly respected establishment. We do not pander to voyeurism or sex-for-sale. No one touches the girls. Ever. Any impropriety is handled immediately."

"Do you have many opportunities to refine your 'handling' techniques?" Angel asked.

"No. Patrons know they risk losing their privileges, and the girls will be terminated immediately."

"We'll need a list of members," Sarah said.

Jeffers swiveled his head toward her. "That's not public information."

"We're not with the public. We're with the police."

"Then maybe you should get a warrant."

He made that pronouncement with an air of nonchalance normally used for something as simple as declining dessert. Angel wondered what kind of experience made him so smooth. Could she ruffle him with a threat? "Maybe we'll bring a couple of guys from Vice along with that piece of paper."

"Do what you have to, Detective." Jeffers pulled himself straighter in the chair, as if his posture was somehow connected to his character. "We have absolutely nothing to hide."

Angel glanced at Sarah, who gave an almost imperceptible shrug then turned back to the guy. The long silence tugged at the frayed ends of her nerves, but if he was feeling any anxiety, it was well masked by his casual smile.

"So you'll swear that Tracy didn't have a date with a patron." Sarah posed it as a statement, not a question.

"What the girls do on their own time is beyond our control."

"She made the date before she left the premises."

"And you can prove that?"

Boy, he was damned cocky. There was no way he could know they had no evidence to support Amber's statement. So he had to have balls of steel to invite the possibility. Angel felt a twinge of panic as the advantage went back to his side. "How did you come to hire someone who obviously had no experience?" she asked.

The question broke the momentary impasse, and Jeffers started a little nervous twitch. "I thought you didn't care about that."

"Humor me."

He readjusted his smile and picked up a pen, the click of the retractor button and the little muscle tick in his cheek the only signs that he wasn't cool all the way through. "Tracy had the right look. I was a little disappointed she hadn't danced before, but the other one, Amber, convinced me to let them audition. Amber came out like she'd done it a million times. Worked like a pro. Tracy was different."

Jeffers stilled his nervous thumb and appeared to revisit a pleasant memory. Watching him, Sarah wondered what had precipitated his abrupt willingness to talk. Relief that the focus had shifted away from sensitive areas? Or a clever move to show how cooperative he could be when the right questions were asked?

"She was awkward," he continued. "Unsure of herself. I was ready to tell her to stop when the bouncer said, 'No. Let her finish.' Then he nods toward three guys who've stopped talking to watch her. They were entranced. She had a . . . I don't know . . . innocent quality about her. Like she was untouchable. That made her more appealing."

"So you hired them immediately?" Sarah asked.

"I only wanted Tracy. Pros I already got. But she said no way without her friend. So I signed them both on for the standard month's trial period. Then if we were all still happy, we'd make it permanent."

"Are you going to let Amber continue?" Angel asked.

"If she wants to." He leaned back in his chair and drummed the pen on the top of his desk. "It's the least I can do for her after losing her friend."

Sarah grimaced. *Sure. Because you're such a nice guy.*

Before they left, they got a list of everyone who'd worked that night. Jeffers had decided he wouldn't make them get a warrant for that information. Grotelli would give them the services of a few Uniforms to do some interviewing. Maybe they'd get lucky and find an employee who'd seen something and was willing to talk about it.

Outside, the light was being swallowed by dusk in an abrupt shift that always seemed more dramatic in winter than summer.

"What now?" Angel asked.

"I'll check with McGregor. See where we stand with Clemment."

"Want me to try for the warrant?"

"Sure."

"Who should I call?" Angel asked.

Sarah opened the door to her car. "Danvers. She's a radical feminist. She'd probably get off on giving this guy some grief. We might as well go for employee records while we're at it."

"As soon as I get the warrant, I'll have Grotelli send a couple of Uniforms over to pick up the files."

"That'll work."

Sarah had to keep her accelerator on the floor to keep up with McGregor's LaSabre as it rounded another gentle curve on Marsh Lane. The road cut through two- and three-acre plots of land that some of the city's elite called home. The wide expanse of lawns managed to look sculpted in the dead-zone of winter, a tribute to the meticulous care of well-paid gardeners. Somehow that perfection was incongruous with the image of rural living the residents were trying so hard to establish.

It was late. She'd much rather be headed home than going to tell a man his daughter was dead. But one good thing. She didn't have to do it alone. Helen Dorsett was with McGregor. She figured the rich and famous deserved hearing bad news from the top brass.

Sarah sighed and rolled down her window a few inches. A cool breeze licked across her cheek in a refreshing caress.

McGregor flashed his right turn signal, and Sarah tapped her brakes as he slowed to enter an asphalt driveway that meandered through a canopy of trees. The bare branches stretched dark fingers into a sky graying with dusk, and Sarah could imagine how impressive the trees would be dressed in their summer finery.

McGregor pulled to a stop in front of a massive three-story house that could have belonged to the antebellum South. White pillars supported the third-floor balcony, which curved across the entire front of the structure. Pulling behind the other car, Sarah stepped out and glanced at the front of the house. She wondered if the carved oak doors would be opened by a liveried butler.

"Quite a place," Sarah said to Chief Dorsett, who exited the passenger side of the LaSabre.

"Yeah. Money can't buy a perfect life, but it can sure as hell make what you've got more comfortable."

Sarah fell in step beside Helen, a striking woman with long hair twisted and fastened neatly with a black clip. She wore her authority with restraint, making her the easiest of the brass to deal with.

"I'll take the lead," Helen said, striding toward the door then pushing the bell. "As soon as he's adjusted to the news you can handle the questioning."

The last comment had been directed at Sarah, and she nodded.

A young, attractive maid wearing a simple white apron over a black dress opened the door. Helen told her they were expected and showed her identification. After glancing at it, the maid stood aside so they could enter. They followed the woman to a library where she announced them to the tall, silver-haired man who paced with a crystal glass in one hand.

Sarah visually inventoried the spacious room that obviously doubled as a home office. A massive teak desk dominated one side, resting like an island in a sea of pale carpeting. The top of the desk hosted a computer, a brass desk set, and an array of folders. A printer, copier, and fax machine occupied large compartments in a built-in bookcase to the right of the desk. The matching bookcase behind the desk was filled floor-to-ceiling with leatherbound books.

Sarah shifted her gaze to the third wall, also lined with bookcases. They melted into the mirrors on the fourth wall, creating a sense of endlessness.

The ambiance suited the man, who looked casually elegant in tan silk pants, Italian loafers, and a cashmere cardigan over a turtleneck. He regarded them with cold blue eyes. "This had better be important. I had to cancel a three o'clock appointment."

"We apologize for any inconvenience." Helen stepped forward and offered her hand. "This is a visit we'd rather not be making either."

The energy in the man froze. For one split second he was perfectly motionless, not even the tinkle of ice against glass betraying any reaction. Sarah wondered at his cool control. He didn't even ask the obvious question. Instead, he made some offhand remark about how ominous that sounded.

"I'm afraid it is." Helen tried to steer him to one of the chairs clustered around a low, glass-topped table that was almost big enough to skate on. "Perhaps you'd like to sit down."

Clemment lifted his chin as if disdaining the idea of taking orders from anyone. Helen didn't flinch.

Watching the battle for control, Sarah lost any hope she'd had of being able to like the guy. She'd met few rich people whose humanity hadn't been tainted by their bank accounts, but she always hoped for the exception. Especially now. The questioning would go down easier with a little compassion, but it was going to be hard to garner sympathy for this guy. She exchanged a knowing look with McGregor as Helen told Burke

Clemment that his daughter had been murdered, touching briefly on the details of where and how.

"That's preposterous." Clemment's wild gesture of denial slopped amber liquid on the sculpted Berber carpeting. "My daughter would never be in such a place."

"I'm afraid it's true," Helen said, putting a hand on his arm to guide him toward a chair. "Perhaps you would like to—"

"I will not sit down." More of his drink escaped the glass as he pulled away.

"We're sorry to have to bring you this news." McGregor stepped forward. "But there is no doubt. Her friend gave us a positive ID."

"But Tracy's at school. Her classes at SMU . . ."

"When did you see your daughter last?" Sarah asked.

He regarded her with unblinking eyes. "And you are?"

Later, Sarah would kick herself for giving a pissy response, but now his tone rankled. "I'm the one who's going to find the bastard who carved up your little girl."

Helen shot a quick look at Sarah, but McGregor stopped the chief with a touch of his hand.

Sarah watched the transformation on Burke's face as he processed the reality she'd slapped him with. For a moment his composure cracked, then his face froze in a hard expression. "There's no nice way of doing this, Mr. Clemment. Nothing about it is nice."

She walked over and sank into the plush softness of one of the chairs. McGregor and Helen sat on the other side of the table, leaving the chair closest to Sarah open. She looked at Clemment. "I know this is a difficult time, but I have to ask a few questions."

Clemment lowered himself to the seat tentatively, as if still unsure about relinquishing total control, but he answered Sarah without hesitation or hostility. He hadn't seen or spoken to

Tracy for about three weeks. She had come to the house for a family dinner just before he and his wife left for the Bahamas. They'd only been back a couple of days, and his wife had gone down to Houston to visit her mother.

"Were you concerned about not hearing from her since your return?" Sarah asked.

"No. Katherine and I have been working very hard to respect our daughter's independence." He said it like he expected a medal for superior parenting, and Sarah's sympathy shriveled.

"Anyone she was having problems with? Boyfriend? Another student?"

"Not that she ever mentioned. She didn't associate with the kinds of people who would do something like that."

Sarah waited a moment to let him grasp the absurdity of that comment. "How about not so recently? Anybody have a beef with her in the past?"

Clemment rubbed at the frown line between dark slashes of eyebrows. "One boy was a nuisance last summer. Right after Tracy graduated . . ."

His voice trailed off in the first display of real emotion beyond disdain, and Sarah let go of a piece of her judgment. "From Pinewood School for Girls?" she prompted, remembering that detail from the interview with Amber.

"Yes. All seniors do thirty hours of community service. Tracy did hers at W.T. White. Tutoring."

"The boy?" Sarah prompted again.

"A student she helped with algebra. She felt sorry for him. Even went out with him a few times just to be nice. When she wanted to stop, he wouldn't give it up. Called her incessantly. Sent her letters for several months."

"Did you see the letters?"

"Yes. She was still living at home then. Didn't move into her apartment until classes started at SMU this year."

"Were the letters threatening?"

"Angry. But no specific threat. He accused her of leading him on then throwing him away like a piece of garbage. Said he deserved more respect." Clemment swallowed the last of his drink and put the empty glass on the table. "Tracy was quite upset, of course. She didn't want to hurt the boy. It's just that Katherine and I felt her education was more important."

Sarah took a minute to digest the implication. "You made her break off the relationship?"

"We didn't make her. We simply gave her a choice. There was no way we would commit a significant financial investment for her education if she was wasting her time."

No wonder the girl went to the other extreme. Sarah glanced at Helen, who gave a slight shrug.

"We need the boy's name," McGregor said.

"I don't recall it." Clemment shifted his attention to the lieutenant. "It was something Hispanic." The word shot out of his mouth as if it left a bad taste. Then he turned back to Sarah who still had her notebook open. "But you can find out from my attorney. He sent the boy a letter on my behalf."

Sarah couldn't believe what he'd said. "You had your lawyer take care of it?"

"Of course. That's what I pay him for. To smooth out the little wrinkles in my life." He paused as if giving her time to process that fact of his privileged reality. "His name is Carl Bradshaw. A senior partner at Fritz and Bradshaw. The letter explained the situation to the boy and included modest compensation for his trouble."

Concentrating on her notation, Sarah almost missed the last comment. It registered when Helen blurted out, "You paid the kid off?"

"Not precisely."

"Not precisely? What does that mean?" McGregor asked.

"He never cashed the check."

The kid's right, Sarah thought. He deserves some respect. But she knew she couldn't let her attitude toward Clemment affect her professional judgment. The mere offer of money could have really pissed the kid off. He might have done Tracy just to get back at her old man.

"We'll need to talk to your wife," Helen said. "When did you say she'll be back from Houston?"

"Tomorrow."

"Fine." Helen stood up. "We'll call for an appointment."

Outside, night had fallen for good. Sarah followed McGregor to his car. "You want me to track this kid tonight, Lieu?"

He checked his watch as Helen got in the passenger seat. "Tomorrow is soon enough."

Sarah headed to her car and leaned against the dusty fender of her Honda, listening as the sound of McGregor's car dwindled into a silence so complete, she could hear the wind sigh. She considered the imposing picture the Clemment home presented, finally figuring out what had niggled at her since she'd first seen it. It was like a layout for *Architectural Digest,* not a home. She couldn't recall a single picture that wasn't an original oil worth millions. Where were the snapshots of a happy family?

Likewise, Burke Clemment was a parody of a father. Sure, there was no way to figure how a person would handle shock and grief. But his reactions were all so off base. None of the usual denials of the fact of death. Not one tear. No grasping for the reassurance that his daughter hadn't suffered. No burst of anger at the person who'd killed her. Reviewing his responses, Sarah wondered if he even cared.

That was an interesting thought. Was he just so insulated from the normal experience that he'd forgotten how to behave like a human being? Or was there another reason?

It was worth a little poking into the business and private life of Burke Clemment, but she knew she'd have to be discreet. Price had made it clear to Helen that the family was to be treated with the "utmost consideration." A PR euphemism for "kid gloves."

Opening the door and sliding into her car, Sarah decided she'd watch her step. But no way was she going to ignore a possibility, no matter how far she had to stretch it before it either connected or broke.

CHAPTER SEVEN

First thing the next morning at the station Sarah called Clemment's law firm and got the very important Carl Bradshaw's very busy secretary to give her the information now, not later when she had a free moment. The woman's authoritative voice bristled over the phone at being told what to do, but Sarah finally convinced her that in the time she took to continue the protest, she could look in the file and get the kid's name.

The name, Ricardo Alvarez, came complete with a phone number and address.

Sarah caught up to Angel on the way to the restroom. "I've got something for you to check out."

She brought Angel up to speed on what they'd learned last night, and handed over the address for the boy.

Angel glanced at the address, then back to Sarah. "And what are you up to while I'm driving halfway across Dallas?"

"Ummm. I've got an appointment."

If the evasiveness bothered Angel, she didn't show it. She shoved the paper with the Alvarez information into her jacket pocket and pushed open the door to the restroom.

Sarah went back to her desk and grabbed her jacket.

Along with the name of Tracy's ex-boyfriend, Sarah had weaseled the name of the Clemments' accounting firm from the reluctant secretary at Fritz & Bradshaw. She walked the few blocks to the office building on San Jacinto and pulled the heavy glass door open. She had been here once before, during the time she'd been dating Paul—gorgeous Paul who looked more like a cowboy than an accountant. He had brought her here late one night when the offices had been deserted, and it had been romantic to walk the empty halls hand in hand. He'd suggested they christen the luxurious conference table, but she declined. This had been before she'd given him any part of her body, including her heart, fearing that one day it might be broken.

She'd been right.

Today, daylight streamed through the large front windows and lit her way as she crossed the marble floor to the bank of elevators. Apprehension fluttered in her stomach. Would Paul see her visit as some attempt at reconciliation? Did she want him to? She couldn't deny the surge of longing she felt anytime she thought of their brief fling . . . romance . . . whatever it was.

She had thought of it as more than a fling. A fling was just "let's have fun together for a little while." What she thought she'd had with Paul was stronger, and at one time felt more like forever. Until he made it clear he did not have forever on his mind.

Sarah squared her shoulders and stepped off the elevator directly into the plush entry of Bordowsky, Smithers & Payne. Was this a huge mistake?

Too late now.

Sarah smiled as Paul emerged from a hallway and stopped short. "Sarah?"

"Hello, Paul."

Myriad emotions played across his finely chiseled face, and Sarah wondered which one would dominate. "Sorry," she said. "I should have called first. But I wasn't sure you'd see me."

He adjusted an already impeccable knot in a pale blue tie.

Sarah nodded down the hallway. "Could we go someplace private?"

"Sure." He cleared his throat. "Come back to my office."

Her footsteps whispered on the thick carpeting as she followed him down the hallway past large paintings where cowboys and cattle frolicked. It could have been a wall in a small gallery. And she couldn't help but think it appropriate that a firm handling most of the wealth generated from cattle and oil would have original Remingtons gracing their walls.

She was glad they were headed away from the conference room.

Paul's office was still the same. It reflected his status in the firm with a large teak desk that matched the full wall of shelves and the wide trim around the window. Leather chairs and accessories added the distinct aroma that only the richest leathers can. He walked to a credenza that held a silver coffee service next to a tray of crystal decanters and glasses. "Offer you a drink?"

"Coffee."

"Black, right?"

Sarah nodded, wondering if she should attach some importance to the fact that he remembered.

He motioned her to sit in the leather chair in front of his desk, then carried the mug over. "How have you been?"

"Fine. You?"

"Good. Busy."

He lifted one shoulder in a noncommittal gesture, and Sarah realized they could do this verbal dance forever if she didn't stop the music. "I'm here on business."

"Oh." He lowered his lanky frame into his chair and motioned her to continue.

"We're running a check on Burke Clemment's business."

"Is there a problem?" Paul set his mug on a crystal coaster and sat up.

Sarah took a sip of coffee, stalling while she decided whether to tell Paul about Clemment's daughter. If she did, Paul would realize why she was asking the questions. He was, after all, a very smart man.

"Probably not," she finally said. "I was just wondering if he's had any cash flow problems."

Paul continued to just look at her. She took a deep breath. "We were hoping to do this without the attention of court orders."

"What? You want me to release confidential information just because you asked?"

"Not specifics. Just a general sense of how stable he is."

Paul wrapped long fingers around his mug and lifted it to his lips while his eyes studied her. Sarah covered her need to look away with a sip of coffee, then she dared another glance at him. "I can get this through channels, or . . ."

She let the thought fade as he continued to study her. Then he replaced the mug and leaned back again. "I have your assurance this conversation will never leave this room?"

"What conversation?"

He returned her smile, then sighed. "It's no secret that downtown development's taken a big hit recently. But Clemment's diversified enough that he's riding it out."

Interesting, Sarah thought. But did it mean anything? And did she dare ask anything else? She held his gaze for a moment, then took the risk. "What company holds his insurance?"

"This isn't feeling like some routine inquiry," Paul said. "Is there something I need to know?"

Sarah did a quick mental debate. There was no reason not to tell him about the murder. He'd find out as soon as the media got a hold of the story. In fact, she was shocked it had not been on the morning news. She spoke softly. "Clemment's daughter was killed."

"What?" Paul came out of his chair like a bullet. "And this . . ." He paused as if he couldn't find the words. "Are you

79

investigating him as a suspect?"

"We always look at family first."

Paul braced his hands on his desk and leaned so close to Sarah, she could smell the faint aroma of coffee on his breath. "This is not any ordinary family."

"I'm well aware of the disparity between them and us."

"Is that what this is about, Sarah? You grew up poor so you have this big chip on your shoulder?"

Sarah sucked in a breath. He had been one of the few people she'd told about her past. Now he was using it as a weapon? "I am a professional doing my job."

"This hasn't felt professional since you first walked in here." Paul sat in his padded leather chair and swiveled to face his computer screen. "Next time you come to ask questions about Burke Clemment, you'd better have paper with you."

Sarah stood. She tried to think of something to say, but his posture did not invite any more conversation. She set her cup down on his desk and left.

Outside, where a cold wind blasted around the corner of the building, Sarah couldn't decide if her frustration stemmed from getting nowhere with the case, or the fact that it appeared there was nothing left for her and Paul.

And if word of this got back to Clemment, then to the department, her ass would be in a sling.

Sarah pulled her jacket closed against the gust of wind and cursed the impulse that had sent her here. Even though she didn't dare acknowledge it openly, she knew in that darkest part of her ailing heart that the trip hadn't been pure business. She'd gone with a bit of hope that seeing Paul would rekindle possibilities.

If there'd been any sparks, she'd missed them.

The afternoon sun flirted with the horizon as Angel drove out to the address provided for Ricardo Alvarez. Now she regretted waiting until late in the day to try to connect with the Alvarez kid. Earlier it had seemed like a good idea. Better chance of catching him home from a job late in the afternoon. With the car pointed east on the LBJ Freeway, the sun filled her rearview mirror like a huge ball and cast a golden glow over the entire car. Under different circumstances she might have let herself appreciate the special clarity the light gave to everything it touched. But not today.

Today it was just another irritant, joining the long list that had started this morning when her shower had suddenly turned to ice and she discovered her hot-water tank was broken. Not such a terrible thing, considering her father was willing to come over to fix it. But the grown-up Angel didn't like reverting to the child asking Daddy for favors.

Tilting the mirror to deflect the assault of light, Angel wondered if they'd ever get past the difficulties that had plagued their relationship once she got too big to sit in his lap. She thought it had been better after Alfred's death last summer, but lately little moments of tension had sprung up. They were always especially noticeable after her father listened to the Reverend Billie Norton. That was when he'd revert to his intense distrust of all white folks and expected the family to follow suit.

The sharp blare of a horn broke her train of thought, and Angel realized she'd slowed to the speed limit and a row of angry drivers was stacked up behind her. If she'd been in a better mood, the irony would have amused her. But nothing was very funny right now.

Following the directions on her Mapsco, Angel wound down several side streets in an older section of Garland until she came to a small wood-frame house set back about fifty feet from the curb. The house had been loved a little bit more than its neighbors, the affection reflected in a new coat of paint and an absence of junk in the yard.

Easing her Citation to a stop, Angel opened the door and got out, feeling the chill of approaching dusk in the wind that chased an empty drink cup down the pavement. She hustled to the door and ducked into the protection of the tall pine beside the cement slab of porch.

Her ring was answered by a stout woman with a regal bone structure that declared her Incan heritage. Wariness clouded dark eyes. "*Si?*"

"*No Espanol.*" Angel pointed at her chest. "English?"

"*Si.*" The contralto voice faltered. "Yes."

Angel showed her identification. "I'm looking for Ricardo Alvarez."

"He not here." The woman turned and sent a torrent of Spanish into the dimness beyond her. The only word Angel could pick out of the flood was *policia*. Then a tall, thin man with a drooping mustache stepped up behind the woman.

"What you want with our son?" The man asked. "He good boy. Work hard. Go to school. Not run street like gangster."

"Where is Ricardo?"

Mr. Alvarez consulted a cheap watch with a cracked leather band. "School. He work to three o'clock. Then go to Richland Community College." He proclaimed the school's name with the same emphasis some give to Stanford University, and Angel realized that it carried the same prestige for this couple. A sudden hope that he lived up to his parents' pride threatened her detachment. "Do you expect him soon?"

"No." The woman spoke up. "Eight o'clock."

"He comes home at eight?"

The woman shook her head and then Angel realized what she meant. "His class runs until eight?"

"*Si.*"

"Then he comes home?"

"Mostly."

"When you hear from him . . ." She paused to fish a card out of her wallet. "Have him call. It's important."

The man took the card and looked it over carefully. "You make trouble for my boy?"

"Not if he hasn't already made some for himself."

Angel walked back to her car, then pulled out her cell phone and punched in the numbers for McGregor's office. He agreed that there was no need to try to track the kid down at school. The effort could eat up a lot of time and they might never find him. Better to wait until he was home.

CHAPTER EIGHT

Klieg lights and a bustle of activity transformed the main floor of the Municipal Building into what could have been the set for a movie. A dais, adorned with an array of microphones, halted the steps of curious people who paused to speculate before continuing on to one of the government agencies down the various hallways.

The press conference was scheduled for six-thirty, and all three network stations were represented, along with Fox, the two independents, and the local cable.

Anticipating the crowd that would gather once the video cams rolled, Sarah wished she didn't have to be here. She couldn't think of one productive reason to talk to the press or answer their questions. The commissioner could do his usual schmooze job and leave her out of it. But Price had argued that it was better for her to appear accessible. After all, she was the lead investigator.

He had also insisted that she present a professional image, so high-heeled shoes pinched her toes and goose bumps pimpled her bare legs exposed beyond the hem of her skirt. When she'd gone home to change, she'd found her only pair of pantyhose laced with so many runs the cockroaches could have used them for ladders.

With only five minutes to spare, Price arrived, bringing an entourage from PR to escort Commissioner Hanson forward. Short, with dark hair and a nervous energy that always made him appear to flutter, Price was a perfect contrast to the commissioner, whose flowing white hair and stately manner gave him an air of controlled calm.

Price arranged the participants so Hanson held center stage with McGregor and Dorsett flanking him. Sarah stood on the other side of McGregor feeling about as necessary as a third boob. She didn't even know what to expect since Price hadn't considered it important to include her in the preconference briefing.

In a smooth delivery that could have come from an anchorman, the commissioner read the statement Price had prepared, focusing on the terrible tragedy to a prominent Dallas family and skirting the issue of how little the police knew. Sarah noticed that he also carefully avoided mentioning where the girl's body had been found and her previous association with The Club. He maintained the artful dodge through a barrage of questions, ending with the usual assurance, "We're doing everything we can and are confident that our diligence will bring this unfortunate situation to a satisfactory conclusion."

Bianca Gomaz from WFGA threw the first curve at Price's carefully orchestrated plan.

"Considering Detective Kingsly's past difficulties, do you think it's wise to have her leading the investigation?"

That bitch! A flush burned Sarah's cheeks. She watched Hanson fumble with the papers on the dais as if looking for the appropriate answer, then he turned to Dorsett. "Perhaps the question could best be addressed by the chief of homicide."

Helen stepped forward and faced the cameras. "Detective Kingsly is one of the finest investigators in the department. We have every confidence in her."

"But what about—"

"What happened in the past is just that," Helen said. "We do a great disservice to a grieving family by wasting time with issues that have no bearing on the investigation."

"That's one person's opinion, Chief Dorsett," Bianca said, the challenge inherent in her stance.

"It'll do for now."

Watching the reporter back down from Helen's withering glare, Sarah had to bite her cheek to keep from smiling. Bianca Gomaz was one hell of a reporter. She was also one hell of a pain in the ass. Sarah would be a whole lot happier if the woman got tagged for a network job and got the hell out of Dallas.

Angel sat on her lumpy brown sofa, untouched cardboard containers of sweet and sour pork spread on the walnut coffee table.

The news broadcast had ruined her appetite.

Despite her personal concerns about her partner, no one deserved to have their abilities questioned in a public forum. And Gomaz had the balls to say she had nothing against the department?

But Angel knew it was more than just not agreeing with the reporter's tactics that had ruined her dinner. Even though it shouldn't be debated in every household in Dallas, the question of Sarah's fitness to run the investigation was real, despite Chief Dorsett's on-screen endorsement.

Angel knew from past experience that the chief made sure she knew what was going on with everyone in the department. She was uncanny, a personification of the old joke that mothers have eyes in the back of their heads. Except the chief wouldn't consider it a joke. She'd once said that since all departmental bucks stop at her desk, she damn well better know what was going on. There was no way she wasn't aware that Sarah still walked on the edge. So why keep her in charge of such a sensitive case?

Not that Angel wanted the top spot. It wasn't jealousy twisting in her stomach. It was fear. If Sarah screwed up, everyone associated with the case would take the fall with her.

Sure it's just Sarah's behavior you're worried about?

Angel shoved her chopsticks deep into the box of rice. Why did her conscience decide to get active now?

Can't ignore it, Girl. It's gonna affect the work more and more.

"Okay. Okay." Angel stood abruptly. "I'll talk to her."

Do it now before you chicken out.

Blowing out a breath in exasperation, Angel went into the kitchen and dialed Sarah's number. She probably wouldn't be home yet, but Angel could make an overture. Leave a message on the machine. The next step would be up to Sarah.

After several rings, Angel heard a mechanical voice instructing her to leave a message after the beep. She did, but somehow the act failed to satisfy her conscience. She could hear disapproval thundering in the void left by her now-silent internal voice.

She shook it off and went back into the living room to pack up the remains of dinner.

With no appetite and nothing else to do for the next hour or so before she could expect to hear from the Alvarez kid, Angel decided to go to the Dojo and vent her frustrations on the mat.

Despite the tender bruise on her shoulder from a sparring opponent's side-kick, Angel felt better emotionally when she returned home a little after eight. She dropped her gym bag on the floor next to a small entry table, then went into the kitchen for a drink. Responding to the blinking green light, she pushed the play button on her answering machine then pulled a jug of Rocky Mountain Spring Water out of the refrigerator.

"Tuesday, seven fifty-five P.M.," the voice on her machine intoned. "You have one message."

It turned out to be from Ricardo Alvarez. He was very polite, using her full title, but he was also very adamant. He wasn't going to talk to the police until he'd contacted an attorney. He would call the station in the morning and set a time to come in.

The move was unusual enough to push Angel beyond puzzled to suspicious. Why did he feel the need for a lawyer now? Most people were at least willing to start a dialogue before lawyering up. Maybe the kid wasn't as clean as his folks liked to believe. They wouldn't be the first parents who couldn't see reality even if they tripped over it.

But what if there's another reason?

Recalling the information in the report Sarah had left with the kid's address, Angel drained her glass of water and slid the jug back on the top shelf of the refrigerator. Clemment's high-handed approach to getting the kid out of his daughter's life must've been pretty intimidating to an eighteen-year-old boy.

If Ricardo had seen the same news broadcast most of the city had at six, maybe he was afraid of ending up as somebody's scapegoat. Shit like that happened all the time. Some kid got sucked into a crime he had nothing to do with, just because he was convenient.

She played the message again, listening for inflections in his voice that would indicate his state of mind. No fear or anxiety. Very straightforward and also very determined. Calling him would be a waste of time. There was no way she could talk her way into an interview tonight.

Sarah tasted each component of the delicate blend of flavors on her tongue, the bite of fine scotch, the sweet touch of vermouth with just a hint of lemon. Perfect. Wonder if that's why it's called a Perfect Rob Roy. No. That's too low even for the depths of your drunken nonsense.

There was no doubt she was drunk. She didn't have to count the number of drinks she'd had since she'd escaped the throng at the Municipal Building to know that. Her shrill mental laugh at the stupid pun was evidence enough. But she'd earned the right. At least, that's what she'd been telling herself before her mind went down that quasi-comical path.

Six months of getting beaten up by the press entitled anyone to a good toot.

Leaning against the stiff vinyl of the banquette, Sarah lit one of her rare cigarettes and watched the smoke drift away from her in soft waves. Her mind started playing another silly game, piling all her troubles on the smoke and letting them dissipate along with the blanket of gray.

If only it were that easy, she thought, taking a hefty swallow of her drink.

Her musing was interrupted when McGregor stepped up to her table. He dropped his bulk into the seat across from her and signaled the waitress with two upraised fingers. She brought him Johnny Walker Red on the rocks. Doubled. After he'd downed half of the first one, McGregor looked across at Sarah. "Couldn't wait for me, eh?"

"Didn't know you were coming."

"Figured this is where I'd find you. I do care about more than your closure rate, you know."

"Why can't they just let it go?" Sarah stubbed her cigarette out with a quick, angry movement. "Every time I think I might be able to forget the whole sorry mess, some media wizard has to resurrect it."

"So? Deal with it. But not this way." He made a vague, fluttering gesture. "It doesn't help."

"Outstanding advice from the man who gives such a shining example." Sarah eyed the glass in his hand, and he put it down with a loud clunk.

"I've got it under control."

"Yeah?" Sarah saw McGregor jump as if her word had been a cattle prod. *Damn! When will I learn to keep my big mouth shut?*

McGregor checked his anger with an obvious effort, then slowly lifted his glass, took a swallow of the amber liquid, and put it down before he spoke. "I'm not the one people are watching."

"What are you telling me, Lieu?" Sarah rode her anger like a runaway horse. "That I can't be human. Can't make one fuckin' mistake. Can't let any emotion show. Because some prick with a camera might be there?"

"What I'm telling you is to be a professional. Be human on your own time." McGregor downed the rest of his drink, then stood. "I can't bail you out forever. So you'd better start getting your shit together."

"Is that an order?"

"Does it have to be?"

McGregor dropped a few bills on the table. "Watch yourself, Kingsly."

Sarah danced her glass on the damp cocktail napkin. McGregor was right, even though the pissy side of her hated to admit it. She'd rather hang on to her anger, her grief, and whatever else was driving her to such stupidity. But she'd better start letting go pretty damn quick. Otherwise, she stood to lose the only thing that mattered in her life anymore.

The palatial home, dramatic against the black night sky, filled the television screen. The voice of the reporter started the story as the camera swept the expansive structure. "Today Burke Clemment and his family were notified that their daughter was brutally murdered three days ago. The victim was officially identified late this morning.

"The news rippled through the entire Dallas business community as friends and associates reacted with shock and outrage." The camera angle changed to include the face of Bianca Gomaz in the frame with the house behind her.

The killer drummed close-clipped fingernails softly on the table. This was better than the earlier newscast. Gave the act some dignity and meaning. It would be better if it included why the girl had to die. Then people would understand and wouldn't call it brutal. It hadn't been brutal. Her death had been achieved in the kindest way possible. Done for the right reasons, anything could be an act of benevolence. That's what The Father had always said. The switch wasn't brutal. The nights locked in the closet weren't brutal. The blisters on the fingers weren't brutal. They were all loving acts performed for the sake of discipline.

Only through discipline did one learn to control the deep, dark urges that could thrust a soul into the burning pit of hell.

That was The Father's gospel. The righteous go forth into the world to save those on the brink of damnation. God Almighty decreed this holy work. Holy hands performed the tasks set before them.

It had been the ultimate act of kindness to make that one small cut and let all the evil flow out. A purification. Quick. Painless. Loving.

When people recognized the act for what it was, they would understand why it had to be done. The girl could not be permitted to dance with the devil. She belonged to God. And now she had been returned to Him, her innocence restored.

It had been the will of the Almighty and it pleased Him. People would understand that.

Sarah switched off her television. The news had been depressing. Even though Burke Clemment rankled her every nerve, she still felt sorry for him. Nobody deserved to lose a child, especially not this way.

She took a quick shower and had just invited Cat up on the bed with her when the phone rang. She picked up. "Hello? Kingsly here."

"I told Burke Clemment about your questions."

Despite the coldness of Paul's voice, Sarah couldn't stop the leap of emotion and she wondered why she couldn't be sensible about him. *Because matters of the heart rarely make sense.*

"Fine. I'll deal with it."

"The next time you have questions, they'd better be accompanied by a court order."

Sarah listened to the dial tone for a full ten seconds after he hung up, then cradled the receiver.

Cat unwound himself from his circle of fluff, stretched, and then came to inspect the wetness on her cheek. She pulled him close and let him have his way with her tears. "I really messed up big time," she said.

The soft rumble of his purr was the only response, and Sarah allowed herself a weak chuckle. "You wouldn't want to trade lives for a while, would you?"

He gave her cheek one last swipe with his sandpaper tongue before pulling out of her grasp to reclaim his dent in the covers.

"Didn't think so," she said. "I wouldn't either."

CHAPTER NINE

The phone on Angel's desk shrilled to life, and she dropped the morning comics to answer, surprised to hear her brother's voice. He rarely called her at work except for an emergency. A sudden fear crawled up her spine. "What's wrong, LaVon?"

"Nothing." His voice was calm.

"You scared me half to death. I thought something happened to Mama again."

"I know. I still jump when the phone rings."

In the silence of his pause, Angel heard the faint "ungh" of throat clearing, then LaVon continued. "This is business, Angel. I'm representing Ricardo Alvarez."

"Oh." She pulled her chair forward and leaned her elbows on her desk. She didn't know why she was so surprised. Her brother had a modest, but growing, criminal practice. It was inevitable that they'd come up on opposite sides of the system on one case or another. But she wasn't prepared for it. She didn't know if she could keep the little sister out of the cop's way.

"Angel?"

"Yeah. I'm still with you."

"Okay. Here's the deal. My client will come in and give a statement. We'll be there at two."

She could almost see him ticking the items off on long, slim fingers as he made his points. Didn't leave much room for maneuvering, but then, she didn't feel up to any mental challenge at the moment. "That'll be fine."

"Uh . . . okay."

The slight break in his composure brought a smile to her lips. Maybe she wasn't the only one who was going to find this difficult. She cradled the receiver and retrieved the newspaper.

"You ready to go?"

Angel looked up to see her partner who was adjusting her jacket over her shoulder holster. Sarah could have posed for a dress-for-success ad campaign. Her jacket was the color of rich, dark chocolate, and Angel suspected that the worsted wool would feel incredibly soft to the touch. Winter-white slacks provided the contrast and a persimmon blouse added the color.

"Figured if we're going uptown I could bend to convention," Sarah said. "It's not like I don't know how to do it."

Angel stood and shook her head. Dealing with her partner was like some bizarre twist on the Russian Matrioshka dolls. Except instead of each doll being identical, Sarah was revealing startling different personas, and Angel never knew which one was going to appear.

"You hear from the Alvarez kid?" Sarah asked.

"His lawyer just called."

"Yeah?" Sarah prompted.

"It's my brother."

Sarah gave her a sharp look. "You okay with that?"

"Sure." Angel heard more confidence in her voice than she felt.

"Okay, then. Let's head out to the school." Sarah moved toward the door. "I'll get us a car from the pool and pick you up out front."

Before leaving, Angel stopped at the restroom, ran a comb through the thick cluster of curls framing her face. Some white gene in the family history had blessed her with smooth hair that curled instead of frizzed. Of course, Daddy denied that their heritage was tainted with white blood. How could he hate whitey so if whitey was one of his ancestors?

Angel chuckled and shook her head. Then she applied a touch of lipstick and tucked her shirt into her gabardine pants. Her concession to the "uptown" look.

Rebecca Modine, looking every inch the well-turned-out lady, from the hint of lace at the collar of her navy suit to the severe twist of dark hair at the nape of her neck, sat behind a pristine desk made of cherry wood. A small digital clock sat on one corner of the desk and the other sported a roughly carved figurine that could have been a dog. Sarah wasn't sure. In between were a fancy pen holder and a notepad.

Sarah wondered how a woman could run such a large, busy school without creating a mess. Or did being headmistress allow her to delegate all the work so she would be free to present a tidy image of life at Pinewood School for Girls? That image included this lavish office with heavy, dark wood paneling and prints of Old Masters on the walls. Or maybe not prints. Sarah reminded herself they were among people who could afford the real deal. That rough little carving might very well be some priceless work of art.

"Appreciate you taking time to see us," Sarah said.

"Not at all." Rebecca gestured to the plush chairs across from her. "Please have a seat."

Sarah glanced toward Angel, then settled into the soft embrace of the nearest chair. "As I said on the phone, Ms. Modine, we just have a few questions about Tracy Clemment," Sarah said. "Did you know her very well?"

"I know all my girls." Despite the voice inflection, the woman's face remained impassive. It was a posture so like Burke Clemment's, Sarah wondered if all the rich folks learned how to do it right after mastering which fork to use for the shrimp.

Maybe it was even taught right here in these hallowed halls. But then, Amber hadn't cloaked herself in affectation. The awareness of the difference hadn't surfaced until right this minute, but Sarah found it interesting enough to pursue.

"What can you tell us about Amber Robinson?"

The abrupt detour seemed to surprise Angel as much as it did Rebecca. Sarah felt a stir of curiosity from her partner, but what she felt even stronger was a ripple of unease from the woman across from her. It was childish to derive such perverse pleasure from rattling someone's cage, but Sarah enjoyed being a child now and then.

"She was a moderate student."

"How do you mean?"

"She never excelled in anything. But then, that wasn't surprising, considering . . ."

"Considering?" Angel prompted.

Rebecca kept her gaze leveled on Sarah as if she had asked the question. "She was one of our scholarship students."

"I don't understand," Sarah said. "Aren't scholarships given to the best and the brightest?"

"Normally. But we're required to give one each year based on need. Some federal regulation we have to satisfy to keep our accreditation."

Interesting, Sarah thought again, ignoring Angel's rustle of impatience. The physical impression Amber had given was that she had come from the same pampered background as Tracy. Wonder how her commonness sat with Daddy Mega-Bucks?

"Were Amber and Tracy close friends all through school?"

"Yes. Naturally, Mr. Clemment tried to discourage the association."

Naturally, Sarah thought, watching Rebecca search for the right words to continue. "But the friendship appeared harmless.

And the Robinson girl did catch on to proper deportment rather quickly."

Sarah squashed a surge of anger. If the woman got any more condescending, she'd get a nosebleed.

"Did Tracy have other associations at the school that weren't so friendly?" Angel asked. "Something that could point to a motive for murder?"

The woman took so long to answer; Sarah was surprised by the terse response, "No."

"What about friends outside the school? Boyfriends?"

"I wouldn't know about that."

"You weren't aware of her involvement with Ricardo Alvarez?" Sarah didn't try to hide the note of skepticism.

"Mr. Clemment would prefer I not talk about that. He said he settled the matter with you yesterday."

Whoa, deep pockets create very long arms.

"Let me see if I understand." Sarah leaned forward. "You won't answer certain questions because Mr. Clemment told you not to?"

"That is not what I said. He assured me the former business had no bearing on the present. It would serve no useful purpose to keep bringing it to the table."

"When did you have this conversation with Clemment?" Angel asked.

"This morning. Shortly after you called to make the appointment to visit with me," Modine said. "I figured I owed him the courtesy."

Sarah fought an urge to stand up and slam her fist on Rebecca's desk. Anything to shake the woman out of that controlled delivery. But caution held her back. She couldn't afford to alienate the entire upper crust of Dallas.

Angel broke the tense silence. "We'll determine what has relevance and what doesn't, Ms. Modine. So if there is anything you can tell us about the Alvarez situation, we need to hear it."

Rebecca allowed her gaze to flick from Angel to Sarah, then back to Angel, as if measuring the benefits of continuing the bluster. "Very well," she finally said.

The edge of haughtiness tempered into a dry, factual delivery of the program that paired students from Pinewood School for Girls with those from public schools.

"Tracy's involvement with Ricardo went beyond tutoring," Sarah said. "Was that usual?"

"It happens. Not with every student. But some. Young women can sometimes be carried away by zealous idealism, believing they can save every lost soul."

"Was Ricardo a lost soul?"

"I'm sure Tracy saw him that way. She felt sorry for him."

"How did she react when her father bought him off?"

"Tracy was quiet. Remote. She didn't want to talk to me about it, but then, she had been confiding in me less her senior year than in the past. Part of exerting her independence. I understood that."

"Did Ricardo cause trouble after the break-up?"

"Not really. He did come to the school a few times. Stood outside to try to talk to Tracy. We had our security people escort him off the premises."

"He go willingly?"

"There was nothing in the reports to indicate otherwise."

"So you don't know if he could be mad enough about the whole thing to kill her?"

"How absurd. One would have to have a better reason than that. Don't you think?"

Sarah paused to absorb the comment. Did the woman believe that murder was okay as long as the reason was good enough? Or was it just one of those inane remarks people make when they are trying to put the act within the parameters of their own lives?

"Did Tracy have problems with anyone at the school?" Angel asked.

"Of course not." Rebecca shot her a quick look. "We're like a family here."

"Families have problems."

"Not the kind that lead to murder."

"Actually." Angel leaned forward to keep her visual hold on the woman's attention. "Family members kill each other with some regularity for all kinds of reasons."

A long silence followed. Sarah realized they could spin their wheels here for another hour or go do something more productive. She closed her notebook and fished a card out of her pocket.

"Give us a call if you think of anything that might be of help." Sarah dropped the card on the desk and stood up.

Angel and Sarah wove their way around clusters of students moving from one class to another, accompanied by a hum of conversation that was so low it could have been mechanical.

Stopping for a second, Sarah looked at the orderly procession of students, finally realizing what was missing. Chaos. Noise. The clang and bang of lockers. Whoops and whistles to get someone's attention. People pushing and shoving each other. She leaned closer to Angel. "This isn't how I remember high school."

"Me either."

Outside, a cool breeze toyed with the bare branches of trees on the school grounds. Crossing to the parking lot, Sarah breathed deeply, exhilarating in the fresh air that was such a relief after the inside atmosphere.

The bland, unmarked Buick from the motor pool contrasted financially with the Lexus and BMW it was squeezed between.

Sarah's experience with cars that cost more than some houses was limited, but she had ridden in a Jaguar once. They'd confiscated it from a drug dealer, and Sarah had talked McGregor into letting her drive it back to Impound. For one brief moment, she'd played with the fantasy of actually owning a piece of that kind of luxury.

It could happen.

If she won the lottery.

"I was hoping to get something to use in the Alvarez interview this afternoon," Angel said over the roof of the car as she opened her door.

Sarah paused on the driver's side. "What did you think of the Modine woman?"

"About what I expected."

"Really?" Sarah leaned her elbow on the roof and propped her chin with her fist. "I had a feeling there was something just a bit off, and it finally came to me."

"Would you care to share this insight?"

"She was emotionless about the death. Like the father. Not expressing all the things we're used to hearing from victims' families."

"Maybe she wasn't that close to Tracy."

"Okay. So she's not going to wail and weep. But how about some anger? Some moral indignation that something so horrible happened to a young woman she knew for four years."

"What are you saying? You actually think there's something suspicious about that?"

"No. Just trying to figure out what makes the upper echelon tick. They certainly are an odd lot." Sarah opened the car door and slid in. "You think it's the money that makes them act that way?"

"How rich could she be?" Angel hooked her seat belt. "Certainly not in a league with the clientele of the school."

"She could be. Could have come from money and just decided she liked to work." Sarah started the engine and put the car in gear. "Or maybe she got that way by hanging around money."

"Maybe."

CHAPTER TEN

When they got back to the station, Chad told Sarah that McGregor wanted to see her ASAP, so she hustled down to his office. The minute she saw his face—it was not a friendly sight—she knew some kind of shit had hit the fan.

"You checked up on Clemment?"

She was glad he jumped right to it. This way she didn't have to stand here wondering if he was going to kill her or just yell at her.

"I tried to be discreet."

"*Discreet?* By going to his CPA?"

She pulled a chair over and straddled it so she wouldn't feel so much like a little kid standing before an angry father. "I take it Burke called."

"The chief. And the commissioner. And the mayor." McGregor rocked in his chair. "Surprised he didn't call the president."

"Clemment's a supporter?"

McGregor glared.

Sarah took a deep breath and blew it out slowly. "Would it have been good police work not to check him out?"

It was McGregor's turn to sigh. "What did you find out?"

"Not much. But business hasn't been great. He could have a cash-flow problem. And I'm guessing he has hefty insurance policies on his family."

McGregor looked at her like she'd just slandered the pope. "Building a house of cards, Kingsly?"

She had the good sense not to answer.

"Unless some piece of concrete evidence comes in tying the father to the scene, you back off. Got it?"

She nodded.

Relieved that the lieutenant hadn't torn her a new one, Sarah left his office and started back to the squad room. Then a rumble in her stomach reminded her she'd missed lunch. She turned and headed toward the break room, needing a brief reprieve as much as she needed food.

No one else was there, so she quickly scanned the contents of the refrigerator, hoping for something she could "borrow" without the absence being noticed. Single servings wouldn't do. She moved a couple of plastic containers and saw a bag that looked like it held more than one sandwich.

At the sound of the door opening, she forced herself not to whirl in panic. How do crooks keep their cool? Taking a moment to still the wild beating of her heart, she glanced over to see Simms and Burtweiler head for the coffee pot. They weren't even paying any attention to her. She kept her back to them and pulled one sandwich out of the bag, dropping a dollar in to ease her conscience. Then she walked toward the door, hoping her larceny didn't show.

"Eating on the run again?" Simms asked.

Sarah nodded as she opened the door to step out.

"You're gonna get an ulcer," Burt called.

Sarah ate the sandwich in the hallway, then went into the restroom to wash off any tell-tale odor of tuna. She got back to her desk in time to see Angel greet her brother and his client, a tall, rangy Hispanic man with short black hair and a closed expression on his finely sculpted face.

She pulled Angel aside. "Chad better help me with the interview. If this guy's our doer, we don't want to screw it up with any taint of conflict of interest."

Angel nodded and Sarah stepped toward the two men, offering her hand to LaVon. She'd forgotten how tall he was, but not the striking planes of his face or the faint scent of Stetson.

"Nice to see you again, Counselor."

LaVon gave her a firm handshake. "Never did thank you for bringing Angel to the hospital that day."

He didn't specify what day. Didn't have to. Sarah remembered the day when his mother had almost died. She knew what that kind of loss felt like. "Didn't notice an oversight."

A quick smile softened his serious expression, and Sarah watched the smile touch his light brown eyes. It was an expression that suited him better than "business." It was also easier to handle than the anguish she'd seen when his mother was so critical. She returned his smile then switched her attention to Ricardo, whose stillness was so complete, he could have been a mannequin. "You understand this is not a formal interrogation?"

His brief head bob dropped a dark curl onto his forehead and made him suddenly appear very vulnerable.

Good. Maybe I can use that.

Motioning for the men to follow Angel, Sarah hung back. She crossed the room to Chad's desk where he was talking on the phone. She gave him a "hurry up" sign, and he acknowledged with a wave.

After Chad hung up, Sarah briefed him, then he followed her to the interrogation room. LaVon and Ricardo were seated on one side of the wooden table. Two empty chairs flanked the other side.

"Eric's on his way," Angel said, catching Sarah's eye as she stepped into the room with Chad behind her. "There was no objection to a video record."

"Thanks." Sarah moved away from the doorway to let her partner go out. A moment later, Eric bustled in. He wore what appeared to be the same jeans and vest he'd had on the other day. She hoped he'd at least showered since then and perhaps had a different shirt on. Otherwise, this session could turn unpleasant in more ways than one.

Eric hoisted the camera to his shoulder and positioned himself for the best angle. Sarah sat in one of the empty chairs and Chad leaned against the wall.

"I'll be making my own tape," LaVon said, opening his leather attaché and pulling out a small cassette recorder. "And we've prepared a statement."

LaVon dropped a folder beside the recorder on the scarred surface of the table. He took a moment to make sure the machine was working, then slid a piece of paper across to Ricardo. LaVon looked at Sarah. "Whenever you're ready."

She signaled Eric to roll tape and verbally established the salient facts of the interview.

From the time he'd entered the room, Ricardo Alvarez had sat with his hands in his lap, eyes downcast. "Ricardo?" Sarah waited for him to look at her. "You understand you're not being charged at this time."

He nodded.

"So tell me, why the lawyer?"

"Wait a minute!" LaVon slapped an open palm against the table. "That's an improper question. The right to legal protection is not an indication of guilt or innocence."

"Innocent people rarely call an attorney." Sarah maintained her composure and her eye contact, waiting out several tense moments.

"Let's just hear the statement and go from there," Chad suggested.

LaVon glanced at the other detective, appeared to consider his words, then nodded to Ricardo. The young man picked up the paper and read the prepared text in a soft monotone with just a hint of an accent. The statement was brief, laying out the facts in chronological order, starting with when he met Tracy the previous February and ending with the last time he'd gone to her school to see her.

"I have not had any contact with Tracy Clemment since June when she called to apologize for her father's actions a few weeks before that." He carefully lowered the paper to the table and looked at the detectives, the tension in his dark eyes belying his outward calm.

Sarah held his gaze, giving him nothing in her expression. She was rewarded with a bobble of his prominent Adam's apple before he tilted his head away from her. The whole thing didn't feel right. The attorney. The nervousness. What was he hiding?

"We've heard Burke Clemment's version of events," Sarah said. "And unfortunately, Tracy can't give us hers. So tell us your side of the story."

Ricardo glanced at LaVon, who nodded permission. "It was just before graduation. Tracy sent a letter saying we couldn't see each other anymore."

"Did she say why?"

"That it wouldn't work out. We couldn't overcome the cultural barriers."

"The break-up was her idea?"

"I thought so at first. Then I tried to call. I wanted to hear her say that. I just couldn't believe it. She was never available, so I went over to her house. Her mother told me to leave. That Tracy didn't want to see me. I still couldn't believe it." A note of defiance put an edge in his voice. "I went over to the school and tried to talk to her. They had security keep me off the grounds.

"Then I got the letter from that lawyer." He dipped his head again, as if somehow shamed by just being associated with someone else's nefarious conduct. "And the check."

"Mr. Clemment said you never cashed it."

"I tore it up." Anger lifted his head and twisted his face into an ugly grimace. "He thought he could treat me like some cheap *puta.*"

"It made you angry." Sarah made it a statement. Not a question.

"You're damn—"

LaVon reached out a restraining hand to keep Ricardo in his seat, then looked at Sarah. "Please don't bait my client."

His voice was soft, almost like a caress, and Sarah felt a rush of heat.

"Certainly Mr. Alvarez was angry about the check," LaVon continued. The overhead light reflected on his glasses, making it impossible for Sarah to read his eyes. His posture, however, was controlled and commanding. "It's a normal reaction to the indignity of the act. But I fail to see what is accomplished here by rehashing old history."

"Motive, Counselor. Motive."

"You said my client was not a suspect."

"We said we weren't charging him," Chad put in. "Not that he wasn't a person of interest."

"Then this interview is over." LaVon swept his papers together and put the folder in his attaché case.

"We still have the right to ask him where he was on the night Tracy died." Chad motioned to Eric to keep taping. "Unless you'd like us to charge him now with impeding an investigation."

LaVon paused with the recorder halfway to his case. Then he put it back on the table and pushed the "record" button. "Okay," he said to Ricardo. "Tell them where you were. But don't answer any question not connected to your alibi."

"In the afternoon I studied for a history exam. Then I went out for a hamburger. Later I decided to go to a movie. Got home at eleven and went to bed."

"Can your parents verify the time?" Chad asked.

Ricardo shook his head. "They were in Chicago visiting my grandmother."

"You have the movie stub?" Sarah asked.

Again he shook his head, and Sarah blew out a breath in exasperation. "Help us out here, Ricardo. Your claims are going to be damn hard to prove."

"It's the truth."

Sarah noticed LaVon start to reach over to touch the young man, then apparently change his mind. "What movie did you see?" she asked.

"Fringe."

"What theater?"

"Twenty Grand in Plano."

"Why so far away from home?"

"Because it was spur of the moment. Figured with so many screens there I could find something starting around the time I arrived."

"Did you meet anyone? Talk to someone who might remember you?" Chad asked.

"I said 'thank you' to the girl who gave me the ticket. And again to the one who sold me popcorn. But would they remember me?" He shrugged eloquently.

Sarah's mind swam with the enormous problem of trying to check his story. Was it even worth going out there with his picture? Yeah. They'd make the effort. The system was a long way from railroading some guy just because he didn't have a convenient alibi. At least the part of the system she was connected to.

"Any objection to us taking a picture?" She directed the question to LaVon, who shook his head. Then she nodded to Eric who put the video camera down and pulled a Polaroid out of the canvas case strapped across his back. After the picture was snapped, she stood up, offering a hand to LaVon. "Thank you."

He pushed his chair back, touching Ricardo on his shoulder. "Let's go."

At the door, LaVon paused and looked at Sarah. "You will contact me first should Ricardo be elevated from 'person of interest.' "

There was a slight questioning inflection to his comment, but she recognized the inherent demand.

"Of course, Counselor."

At five, Sarah walked into the conference room feeling like she'd been rode hard and put up wet. Rusty and another uniformed officer she didn't recognize were stacking portable file boxes on a long table against the wall.

"This the stuff from The Club?"

"Yeah." Rusty glanced at her and dropped a box, the loud *whoomp* attesting to its weight. "We've got ten in all."

"That's a lot of records," Sarah said. "Didn't know there could be this many employees for one small club like that"

"We got some financials and customer records, too. Apparently the DA found a judge who was very sympathetic to our cause."

Sarah laughed. "Great. Thanks."

"Yes, ma'am." Rusty wiped a bead of sweat from his face. "You need anything else, just call."

The bright neon lighting cast his face into sharper planes, and Sarah saw a hint of the strength that would soon emerge when he outgrew his boyishness. She wouldn't be surprised to see him out of uniform in a year or two if that was what he wanted.

Pulling out a chair near the front of the room, Sarah rolled her shoulders to ease the tight knot in the middle of her back and sat down. She was glad the files were there. They represented the only concrete sign of progress so far. Nothing had come back from Quantico yet, and they had a long way to go to make anything stick on the Alvarez kid.

Angel came in and sat next to Sarah as the room started to fill up with detectives and a few Uniforms. McGregor strode to the front of the room, an armload of papers hugged to his side. The coffee in the Styrofoam cup he carried sloshed with each step.

"Okay, children. Make Papa's ulcer go away." McGregor dropped his papers on the dais, took a sip of his coffee, and surveyed the assembled officers.

"We collared that Blanket Rapist," Burtweiler said, a grin cutting through the wrinkles on his face. "Geronimo tracked him."

Sarah glanced quickly at Simms, who gave a slight shake of his head to accompany a wry smile. Anybody else, and he would've been all over him like hot grease. Sarah knew. She'd seen him take on a whole bar full of rednecks. And Burt had been right there beside him. Maybe that's why he could elicit a smile instead of a black eye when he made a racist comment.

The sound of Burt's voice detailing the apprehension of the rapist who had been terrorizing North Dallas for a month drew Sarah away from her musing. "We found the 'souvenirs' at his crib. The guy's going away and won't be back until he qualifies for Medicare."

Applause and whistles followed that pronouncement. McGregor raised a hand to quell the outburst. "Good job, guys." He gave the two detectives a nod. "Until something more pressing comes in, you can give Kingsly and Johnson a hand. They've got a paper avalanche to go through."

McGregor turned to Sarah. "How's it shaping up for your suspect?"

"Pretty weak alibi. And he could have a motive."

"Enough for a search warrant?"

"Not yet." She leaned forward and rested an elbow on the table.

"We should have a better idea by morning," Angel said. "I'm checking the story tonight."

"Okay." McGregor finished his coffee and set the empty cup down. "If the alibi doesn't wash, we'll see about the warrant."

McGregor regarded Sarah again. "Anything from Roberts?"

"A lot of hairs and fibers. No big surprise, considering. But he's sure if we get the perp, he can put him at the scene." She checked her notebook. "Roberts also has someone checking a pail of cigarette butts found near the scene on the off-chance the perp had a smoke while he was there. We might get some DNA."

"Is he going to start testing them all?" Angel asked.

"No, he already told me there are too many, so he can't justify the expenditure. Right now his guy is just sorting them according to brands and keeping them for future reference."

"Does this Alvarez kid smoke?" McGregor asked.

Sarah looked at Angel, who shrugged.

"Find out," McGregor said. "If he was there at the motel, maybe his bad habit will nail him."

"And if he wasn't?" Angel asked.

"Let's just pray that he's our doer," McGregor said. "We need a quick end to this."

As the meeting broke up, Sarah felt another twinge of discontent with how this case was coming down. McGregor was obviously feeling the pressure from the Suits, and she hoped it wouldn't push them all into a preemptive move that would eventually bite them all in the ass.

CHAPTER ELEVEN

After leaving the station, Angel stopped at Luby's for a salad, a concession to her impulse to diet. She could have gone to her folks' house for supper. Her mother always liked her to drop by, even if her father grumbled about grown children still mooching off their parents, but the prospect didn't hold its usual appeal. Maybe because she wasn't ready to talk about what was bugging her, and her mother would certainly ask. Wasn't much Angel could hide from that woman.

So she sat in a stiff plastic chair next to an elderly couple who ate an entire meal without speaking. Angel wondered if it was because they didn't have anything else to say after all the years together. Is that what happens?

She thought about her grandparents, picturing them at their old Formica dinette the last time she'd been down to the Valley to visit them. They'd talked then, but was it only because they had company? If she hadn't been there, would they have shared silent meals, too?

Funny, Angel thought, pushing her plate away and finishing her water. You never know what people are really like because you only see what they want you to see. Which meant her impression of the Alvarez family could be all wrong. Maybe they weren't really the respectable, concerned people who'd stood on the porch the other day. And maybe the only reason she was thinking the kid couldn't have killed Tracy was because his parents wanted so badly to believe in him.

Angel glanced again at the old couple who were now sharing the same piece of pie, utilizing a system of dips and pauses that appeared as well worn as the nubby knit sweater draped around the woman's shoulders. The man noticed Angel watching and smiled, the action creating folds of wrinkles that almost swallowed his eyes.

Angel smiled back. You are getting far too cynical for your own good, girl.

The Twenty Grand was doing a brisk business when Angel got there. She went inside, trailing a group of teenage girls who were trailing a group of disinterested teenage boys. The giggles were loud and self-conscious and renewed Angel's relief at being a long way from fourteen.

Zack, the manager, offered her a quick smile and a willingness to check his employment records to see who'd been working three nights ago. Angel followed him to a small office. "What time are you interested in?" he asked, running stubby fingers through thinning blond hair.

"Evening shift. From about seven until whenever you closed."

He checked a paper tacked to a corkboard. "Okay. I had four guys taking tickets. Two of them are here tonight. The concession's going to be harder to pin down. We normally have eight servers in the big one. Then we've got the small stations."

"How many girls?"

"About half." He grinned. "We're an equal opportunity employer."

His good mood was infectious, and Angel felt marginally better as he checked the records for that night.

"Okay. There were five girls here. Three in the main concession area, two in the other ones. And you're in luck. They're all here tonight."

"When can I talk to them?"

"Let's see." Zack flicked his wrist for a quick look at his

watch. "We've got about five minutes until the main draws will all be rolling. That'll clear out the lobby."

The first two kids Angel talked to couldn't say for sure whether Ricardo had been there, but they also pointed out they couldn't say he hadn't been. As one boy put it, "Hordes of people go through here in an evening. How can we remember one face?"

One young girl, who could have been Angel's kid sister, hesitated over the picture. "He's cute."

Angel sighed. "My question was 'have you seen him in here?' Specifically, Sunday night."

"Can't say for sure." She handed the picture back and continued wiping spills and fingerprints from the counter.

"Since he's so cute, wouldn't you remember him?"

"Not if he came through before the movies started. We're so busy then, I wouldn't notice Will Smith." The girl paused and smiled. "I shouldn't say that. I think Will Smith would stop me cold."

"So you can't say that this man was here? Or that he wasn't?"

The girl shook her head. "Sorry."

Double damn! Angel didn't know whether she was disappointed that nobody could place Ricardo at the theater or that they couldn't. Either way wasn't helping the case. A good defense attorney—LaVon—could make a lot of mileage out of the ambiguity.

Angel thanked the girl, then on impulse bought a box of Jelly Belly candy. She might as well have something to show for her trip here. On her way out, she stopped to thank the manager for his help and hesitated briefly when he offered to comp her to a movie. Then she decided why not. It would be a small measure of consolation for a totally frustrating day. And she had the candy already.

The alarm rang at six. Sarah reached a hand out of the warmth of her covers and pushed the button to shut it off. Six o'clock already? It couldn't be. A temptation to stay in that cozy place halfway between asleep and awake tugged at her, but discipline overcame the urge. She pushed the blankets back and made a dash to the bathroom, dancing on the cold tile. Maybe the apartment manager had the seasons mixed up and the air conditioning was on instead of the heat.

She pulled on the cleanest pair of sweats she could find, tied back her hair, and laced up her running shoes. Cat hadn't even budged from his nest in the middle of her comforter. "You're going to get fat just sleeping all day," she said, giving him a pat. He opened one eye, stretched, then became a russet ball again.

Sarah laughed and shrugged into her light jacket, deciding it was all she needed over a sweatshirt.

The outside air wasn't much different from that inside her apartment, which confirmed her earlier suspicion regarding the heat. Of course, she could be more understanding of the manager's difficulty in knowing whether it was going to be sixty or thirty degrees on any given day in January in Texas. But she had the same problem in reverse on summer days. Sometimes Sarah swore the manager was a sadist.

She walked to the end of the sidewalk, then paused to stretch before starting her normal circuit, which would take her about four miles in just under an hour.

Sarah started off with an easy lope, then increased her speed until the rhythmic flop, flop, flop of rubber on cement reached the tempo that felt right. She let her body work on instinct while her mind wrangled pieces of the case.

Ricardo was looking better as a suspect, especially after Angel called last night to say his alibi didn't hold up. Nobody could put him at the theater, which made it more possible that he'd lied. Maybe he'd lied about everything. Just because he seemed like such a nice young man didn't mean he was beyond murder. Some people had thought Andrew Cunanan was a nice young man until he went on a nationwide killing spree.

But she did agree with Angel that they needed stronger evidence to actually file charges against Alvarez. No matter how much pressure was coming from up high to close this case, the DA couldn't act on nothing more than a weak alibi.

The time flew by with the miles, and Sarah turned up the sidewalk to her apartment, exhilarated by the run.

After her shower, Sarah decided that her favorite jeans and t-shirt were probably a step below what was appropriate to meet Mrs. Clemment this morning. She should probably try for an uptown look again. Or maybe federal? She took her one good suit out of the plastic wrap from the cleaners, amazed at how different she felt in pinstripes. Even Cat gave her a funny look. Then she remembered she hadn't given him breakfast. That oversight could account for his attitude. But then, he was the one who chose to stay in bed all morning.

In the kitchen, she dropped a frozen waffle in the toaster and ran the hot water tap for her instant coffee. Quick. Easy. No deep attachments. Not even to a coffeepot.

Sarah stirred the foamy brew and contemplated her solitary lifestyle. Basically, it sucked. She tried to convince herself that the freedom, the independence, was worth whatever loneliness she experienced, but the conviction never got much deeper than her intellect.

Last year when she'd met Paul, she'd thought the relationship was going to go somewhere. Not only did he stir enough chemistry to fill a lab, he was smart, unaffected by his looks, and sensitive. He'd been there with her during the havoc following John's death and seemed to understand how painful everything had been for her.

It hadn't been the same as having John back, but good enough. From the very first she'd thought the initial attraction was developing into something stronger. Then suddenly he'd pulled back. Said things were going too fast. Shocked the shit out of her.

But more than that, his desertion cast her loose without an emotional anchor. *And that's why you're so mad at Jeanette, isn't it? You're jealous.*

What an absurd—

Sarah pulled away from that unwelcome thought and pushed the lever to make her waffle pop up. She slathered it with butter and grape jam, then folded it over and ate it, leaning one hip against the counter.

"What do you think?" she asked Cat, who was licking the trickle of butter running down her hand. "Should I go out and find me another man?"

Cat cocked his head, regarding her with a steady amber gaze. Sarah recognized that the question already had an answer. Maybe she was just looking for validation in this crazy world of sex-for-fun and disposable relationships. Was she too naive to think there should be something more? Yet she didn't want a man just for the equipment he had.

She'd gone down that road a few years ago. Actually, more than a few years ago if she was honest. It was just around the time that AIDS brought promiscuity to a screeching halt for some folks. But she'd grown tired of the whole routine of pick-up, romp, and not really liking herself much the next day. The disenchantment had been reason enough to quit, and then she didn't have to worry so much about health concerns.

She'd wanted more with Paul. Maybe a real relationship. That's what she'd hoped she was developing with him. Mutual caring on a deep level. Trust. Respect.

Then she'd let her hormones take over.

Damn!

Sarah finished the waffle, filled Cat's food dish and left.

Angel was going to meet her at the Clemment home. The appointment was for ten. When Katherine Clemment had called to make the appointment, she'd sounded like a gracious hostess arranging a brunch. Not a woman verifying a meeting with homicide detectives. Sarah looked forward to seeing what kind of woman could be that cool after her daughter's brutal murder. She was also eager to see what type of person would be married to the esteemed Burke Clemment. She hoped her preconception would be shattered.

Angel looked in her rearview mirror and saw Sarah's Honda pull up in a cloud of white dust. She waited for the powder to settle, then stepped out and walked with Sarah to the porch, trying her best not to look like a rube in Manhattan for the first time. The television cameras had failed to capture the sheer size of the house and surrounding areas that included garages and other outbuildings. Angel's entire neighborhood could probably fit on the grounds.

"Pretty impressive, huh?" Sarah gave her a sideways grin as she reached for the bell.

"I don't think it's quite me."

The ring was answered by a young woman in a standard maid's uniform, and Angel felt a twinge of satisfaction that the woman was white. She knew she probably shouldn't. If she was truly as free from prejudice as she wanted to believe, the woman's color wouldn't matter.

"The missus will see you in the parlor," the maid said, leading them through the magnificent foyer to a door that opened on the left. The parlor? Even my mother stopped calling it that a long time ago.

A petite woman, stylishly dressed in a dark flowing skirt and ivory silk blouse, rose from a sofa to greet them. Her short hair just covered her ears in soft, platinum curls. Gold bracelets jangled on her outstretched arm. Makeup didn't quite mask the ravages of grief, but the woman was doing her best to project the proper image. At least that's what Angel guessed she was doing—out of bed and all gussied up twenty-four hours after hearing her daughter was dead. Angel didn't know what it was like to lose a child. She didn't even want to know, but she remembered the day after almost losing her mother. She'd never gotten out of her robe all day.

"We appreciate you seeing us," Sarah said.

"Anything to help catch—" Katherine bit her lip, then appeared to garner strength from somewhere. "Burke said it was necessary."

Interesting, Angel thought. Would she have refused to talk to them if Hubby hadn't insisted?

"Please. Sit down." Katherine motioned toward two Queen Anne chairs that flanked a table across from the sofa. "Would you care for refreshments? I can have Tilly—"

"No, thank you." Angel shot Sarah a questioning look, which was answered with a shrug.

Sarah began the questioning, covering most of the ground they were already familiar with. Angel was content to sit back and let her partner do the work, noticing how Mrs. Clemment recited her answers almost as if she was reading from a script. Had Hubby prepared her?

The first falter came when Sarah asked about Burke's business.

"I'm, uh . . ." A hand went to the delicate string of pearls at her neck. "He doesn't usually discuss that with me."

"What about finances? Cash flow?" Sarah asked. "Certainly he talks to you about the household budget."

"I fail to see that this is any of your concern."

"Under normal circumstances, you would be right." Angel kept her voice soft, calm, a soothing balm to Mrs. Clemment's agitation. "But murder changes that."

Angel paused at the woman's quick intake of breath, then added. "We will be discreet."

"Well, my husband did say our trip would be the last big expenditure for a while. But I'm sure that has nothing to do with a business or financial problem."

"He keeps you on a pretty short leash, doesn't he?" Sarah asked.

"I don't think I like your insinuation."

"We're not insinuating anything," Sarah said. "The more information we get, the greater the chance of finding your daughter's killer."

Katherine slumped as if the harsh words had softened her spine, and Angel almost felt sorry for the woman. Nervous fingers looked for something to do, flitting from her hair to her cheek, then finding the pearls again.

"We find it curious that you stayed in Houston for another entire day after your daughter was identified," Angel said. "Under the circumstances, I'd think a mother would rush home."

The color drained out of Katherine's cheeks and her chin quivered, but the look she gave Angel carried a hard edge. "I am not accustomed to explaining myself. But since you insist." She paused, as if waiting for them to demur.

They didn't.

She cleared her throat and continued. "There was no purpose to be served by my early return. As my husband explained to your chief, I had family business to conclude. It was best that I finish and return as scheduled last night. That hardly casts me as an uncaring mother."

The little speech apparently stiffened her spine and Katherine sat straighter, her hands folded neatly in her lap, pale against the dark fabric. Angel cast a mental net for some other avenue of questioning, but it came back empty. She leaned forward. "We appreciate your cooperation, Mrs. Clemment." She paused to get a card out of her pocket. "Call if you think of anything that would help."

Katherine took the card, glanced at it briefly, then laid it on the teak coffee table. The maid appeared, as if on cue, and escorted the detectives to the door.

Outside, Sarah whirled on Angel. "Don't you ever do that again."

"What?"

"Close down an interview before I'm done."

"We weren't going to get anything else."

"That was my decision to make."

"Not alone. Last time I checked the duty-board we were still partners."

Angel regarded the crimson flush that crawled across Sarah's cheeks, a familiar signal of impending eruption. Her first impulse was to push a little harder and have it out right here, right now. But the potential repercussions of two detectives duking it out on the grounds of the Clemment estate held her back. She turned and headed toward her car.

"Where are you going?"

"To do my job." Angel got in and slammed the door.

Sarah watched the Citation slew across the gravel as Angel pulled away. *Of all the stupid, childish . . . Is that a judgment of her or yourself?*

"Oh, shut up."

After getting in her Honda, Sarah started the engine then sat there for a moment. She pulled her mind away from the things she didn't want to think about and responded to the nagging feeling that something wasn't quite right with the Clemments.

Mrs. Clemment was as much an enigma as her husband. On one hand, she came across as a docile corporate wife who didn't even take a piss without consulting the husband. But she did have a little steel, even though it had been obvious she wasn't accustomed to using it. Was that because she didn't dare let it show to her husband? He certainly impressed Sarah as a type capable of a pretty volatile reaction to someone disagreeing with him.

Teenagers were noted for being disagreeable. Had Tracy stirred a few of Daddy's embers?

Sarah started the engine and drove slowly out the circular drive, pondering the wisdom of even following that train of thought. In a normal case, checking out the family was standard, but this was anything but normal. Word had already come from the commissioner that Burke was not to be treated as a suspect unless something very convincing pointed at him.

Since a gut feeling wasn't particularly convincing to a jury and never was of much interest to McGregor, Sarah wondered if she dared do any more discreet probing.

Chapter Twelve

The first thing Angel noticed was the contrast to Pinewood School for Girls. W.T. White High School resounded with noisy students banging locker doors closed before hustling to class. A boy with dreadlocks and a Marilyn Manson t-shirt bumped into her in his haste to escape the office area. He mumbled something that could have been an apology as he passed her, and Angel chose to believe it was.

Lines of tension narrowed the eyes of the woman at the information counter, and she glanced at Angel impassively. "Yes?"

Angel showed her identification. "I need to talk to the principal."

"He's busy." The woman's manner suggested they were all too busy to bother with unscheduled interruptions.

"I'll wait."

A half an hour later Angel was introduced to Mr. Kevin Reynolds, a diminutive man who didn't appear to hold himself in the same regard as the receptionist did. The coffee he poured was fresh, and he was happy to talk about Ricardo Alvarez.

Angel sat in a comfortable padded chair, and Reynolds settled in a swivel chair behind the desk, offering her a pleasant smile. "May I ask you why you're investigating Ricardo? Is he in trouble?"

"Nothing official. We're just getting some background on him."

"I see." He appeared to take the deflection pragmatically. "What can I tell you?"

"Basically what kind of student he was. Any trouble he might have had." Angel took a sip of her coffee and put the cup on the edge of his desk between two stacks of folders.

"Well, he didn't start his high school career with a bang. Ninth and tenth grades were almost a wipeout. Poor grades. Breaking rules. Fighting. Junior year he did a little better, then he really knuckled down last year."

"Pretty typical for high school students, isn't it?"

"Perhaps I should be a little more specific. The first two years Ricardo probably got suspended ten times for smoking on campus, and his absences put him on probation. Even when he was here, most of the teachers wished he wasn't."

"Why?"

"We're not an inner-city school, but we do have our share of gang rivalries. Wish I could say that prejudice isn't a part of it, but it is." Reynolds picked up a pencil and tapped the eraser on his desk in a staccato rhythm. "Ricardo was on in-school suspension for three months his sophomore year for fights."

"Any criminal activity?"

Reynolds regarded her with soft hazel eyes for a moment before answering. "He was in a gang. He didn't get there by being a choir boy."

Angel recognized an almost noble streak that seemed to be holding the man back from cynicism in the face of a system floundering in a sea of problems. She was sure his vague response was carefully chosen to avoid dredging up an unsavory past that was best forgotten. She admired him for that, and she'd bet a month's pay that Ricardo wasn't the only student who'd benefited from Reynolds's approach.

But feelings aside, she still had a case to solve. "That hardly sounds like the college student his parents are so proud of."

"He was a different kid then."

"What precipitated the change?"

"This is a real tug-your-heartstrings story." Reynolds leaned back in his chair. "We were about to suspend the kid for good. Most of the teachers, the counselor . . . we were all ready to dump him. Then one of my teachers appealed to give him another chance. Said Ricardo was much too bright to just toss away. Let her work with him in her summer at-risk program.

"I was pretty skeptical. He had known gang connections and a bad attitude. Turning him around was going to take more than a smile and a conviction."

Reynolds paused to rub his chin with thin fingers, and Angel waited for him to continue. "I don't know what she did to him, but after that summer he came back with a whole new attitude. Still struggled academically, but he worked. And avoided trouble when he could."

"A model student?" Angel finished her coffee and set the cup back on the desk.

Reynolds laughed, a remarkably hearty sound from a man so small. "I'm not sure what a model student is. Did he get in trouble again? Yes. But it wasn't as bad as his first two years. A few detentions for being late. Some for disrupting class. But he broke his connection to the gang and started planning a future that didn't include jail or the morgue."

"Did you get to know Ricardo well?"

"Yeah. He was in here a lot." Reynolds waved his hand to encompass the room.

"How far would he revert if he was really angry at someone?"

The principal's smile faded. "That's a pretty direct question for a non-specific investigation."

Angel let his comment slip into silence. He waited out a few awkward moments, then leaned forward. "I don't want to think that Ricardo could ever harm anyone. I prefer to look at the innocence of youth. But unfortunately, that isn't the reality of teens today. Most of these kids haven't been innocent since third grade. So, to answer your question, I really don't know."

"Or are you just afraid to say?"

"I'm afraid of high places and wild animals." He held her in an unwavering gaze. "Not much else."

Angel had asked the question hoping to provoke an uncensored comment, and his response rattled her for a moment. She could feel the power behind his words and wondered how many other people were misled by his appearance. Reynolds was only a small man in size.

His next comment surprised her even more. "What do *you* think of Ricardo's capacity for violence, Detective?"

After a moment's hesitation, Angel said, "I honestly don't know."

Reynolds smiled again. "Then we're even."

"I guess so." She returned his smile. "Thank you for your time."

Reynolds rose to walk her to the door. "Is Ricardo in serious trouble?"

Angel hesitated a moment, then decided, what the hell. Reynolds deserved the truth. "Maybe."

"I hate to hear that. I really thought we'd made it with this one."

Stacks of papers covered the entire conference table as Sarah, Burt, and Simms dug through the boxes that had come from The Club. Simms was going through the employees' records, making a likely list to run through the NCIC. Sarah and Burt shared the daunting task of sifting the membership lists.

"Now I know why they rejected my application," Burt said. "I don't run with the right crowd."

"You don't run with any crowd," Simms countered. "Besides,

you couldn't afford the fees."

"But Mr. Burke Clemment could." Sarah waved a paper at the other detectives.

"No shit! He was a member where his daughter was stripping?" Burt grabbed the paper. "How come he didn't drag her ass home?"

"The bigger question," Simms said, "is how she had the nerve to work where her father might see her."

"Daddy was out of town for almost three weeks," Sarah said. "Which may answer both questions. Unless Tracy didn't know about her father's peccadilloes."

"What the hell does a piccolo have to do with anything?" Burt asked, a scowl crossing his well-lined face.

Simms exchanged a glance with Sarah. "That's why we now only accept college graduates."

"You can kiss my Kosher ass."

"Okay, guys." Sarah held up a placating hand. "I can't even think here. Fight some other time."

"This is no fight," Burt grinned at her. "A fight is when we mean it."

Before Sarah could respond, McGregor stuck his head in the door. "Sanchez is here. Brought our very own expert from Quantico."

Sarah got up. "Sorry, guys. You know how I hate to run out on you like this."

"Sure, sure." Burt waved her away.

Sarah followed McGregor to his office where Sanchez waited with a man who had large unblinking eyes, thinning blond hair that receded from a high forehead over a thin slash of nose and a wardrobe that could have been an ad for mediocrity.

"Detective Kingsly. Nice to see you." Sanchez stood and offered a firm handshake. "This is Victor Peeples."

"Dr. Peeples," the man clarified, limply accepting Sarah's hand.

Sarah glanced at Sanchez and caught the brief flicker of amusement in his black eyes. "Victor was intrigued by your pictures. Wanted to come and give his report in person."

If Peeples objected to the use of his first name, he gave no indication, but Sarah guessed that she wouldn't get away with doing the same thing. She wiped the residue of moisture from his handshake on her jeans and sat down. "We appreciate you coming all this way."

"Not at all."

When everyone was seated, Peeples delivered his report in a clipped, emotionless tone. "Your killer is a white male between the ages of twenty-five and forty-five. Probably closer to the high end. He's had some years to perfect his craft."

"You mean he's done this before?" Sarah asked. "We haven't had any other cases with the same MO."

"Maybe you just haven't looked in the right places."

Sarah bit her lip hard. What a pompous ass.

Peeples continued, obviously unaware that he came up seriously short in the social graces department. "Everything about the crime indicates planning and organization. Things he learned from experience. But what is particularly interesting about this killer is that he breaks out of the usual modality. By this I mean he doesn't hate women. Most psychotic killers work out of some childhood trauma that usually involved their mothers. That's why they mutilate. Their actions are spurred by rage and hate. But your victim was treated with a macabre sort of tenderness."

Macabre is right, Sarah thought. But remembering the careful way the body had been arranged, she knew Peeples was right. She didn't have to like him to give him that.

"What about the mark on her forehead?" McGregor asked.

"Could be religious," Peeples said, the first sign of a smile softening the deep lines on either side of his mouth. "In fact, my first look at the picture made me think of ashes."

"Ashes?" Sarah leaned forward, puzzled.

"You're not Catholic?"

Sarah shook her head.

Peeples let the smile come to full bloom. "When I was a child we always spent Ash Wednesday with a smudge of dirt on our forehead. It was supposed to be the sign of the cross. But it always smeared. I wanted to wash it off right after church but my mother told me I'd burn in hell if I did."

"So our perp is Catholic?" Sarah asked.

"Not necessarily. Other denominations use ashes, too. But the mark, the total covering of the body, and the lack of any sexual abuse suggest a strong religious influence. Something old and traditional. Roman Catholic or one of the other mainline sects. Not that the killer is himself particularly religious. But he could have come from a strict, dogmatic environment."

Sarah tapped her thumbnail against her lip, digesting the information. The religious angle could fit the Alvarez kid. From what Angel had said about the parents, they could have deep ties to a traditional church. And maybe Ricardo couldn't live up to a moral standard they'd set out for him. But he didn't fall into the age parameters Peeples had laid out. Did she dare ask if he could be wrong about that?

McGregor beat her to it. "Our best suspect so far is a nineteen-year-old," he said. "Any chance the low end of your estimate is off?"

"As you know, what I practice is not an exact science." Peeples made a minor adjustment to the lapel of his gray suit. "But I would be skeptical of one so young. Simply not enough time to gain the experience evident at this crime scene."

After Peeples and Sanchez left, Sarah looked at McGregor.

"That doesn't mean he didn't do it."

McGregor leaned back in his chair, bracing his head with his folded hands. "Let's keep after him until something conclusive shows up either way."

"I'd like to look a little more at the father, too."

"What?" McGregor came forward so fast the edge of the desk cut into his ample stomach.

"You saw how he was the other day. And the interview with the wife was like an instant replay minus the intimidation."

"Need I—"

"No." Sarah stood. "I'm well aware of his powerful connections and his influence. It just burns my ass that I can't conduct this investigation the way it should be done."

"After you've been in the game as long as I have, you'll develop scar tissue."

"Is that supposed to make me feel better?"

"No. Consider it career guidance."

After leaving McGregor's office, Sarah stopped in the break room for coffee and found Angel there banging on the side of the pop machine. "Practicing your karate?"

Angel glanced at her for a moment. "It's Tae Kwon Do. But no. The damn can is stuck."

She turned her attention back to the machine. A powerful kick dislodged the can, sending it rattling into the opening.

"Remind me never to piss you off," Sarah said.

Angel grabbed the can and pulled the tab with a loud hiss that sent foam sliding down the side of the can. She licked her fingers, then looked at Sarah. "Found out Ricardo was less than a stellar citizen before last year."

"Really?" Sarah took her coffee to the table.

"He was in a gang." Angel pulled out another chair and sat down. "The principal wouldn't be specific, but it was clear that the kid came from a potentially violent background."

"Murder wouldn't be too big of a stretch?"

"Probably not." Angel took a swallow of her soda.

Sarah condensed the report from Peeples into a few brief statements, then asked, "What do you think? Does that fit with the kid now?"

"I don't know about the profile. Except that there's always room for error. But I'm liking Alvarez more since my talk with the principal. Given the right circumstances, a kid like that can revert. And being dismissed by the girl, humiliated by the father. Those are pretty strong circumstances."

"But if Peeples is right about this being the work of an experienced killer . . ." Sarah stopped, not sure how to voice the little niggle of doubt.

"Maybe he's wrong," Angel said. "Wouldn't be the first time they missed a call."

Returning was a risk. But only a small one. Here anonymity ruled and one could sit quietly to savor the offerings with no interruptions, except for a nagging conscience.

Watching the girl on stage move her hips in quickening thrusts created a flush of heat and engorgement. This was naughty, but not evil. Not like the other. For this weakness of watching The Father would be displeased. He would not, however, be angry. There was a difference. Anger brought the swiftest, most vile consequences. Displeasure manifested itself in brief periods of pained silence. But they were bearable. An hour of penance on aching knees brought forgiveness.

And having these occasional moments of pleasure was worth whatever penalty had to be paid. These visits were the only opportunities left anymore. Contact was no longer possible. Not since—

No. Don't even think it. Put it far away from you so your thoughts won't draw them.

A swallow of smooth scotch quieted the erratic heart. *There. That's better. Stay calm. There's nothing to be afraid of.*

Then a swell of music filled the room as lights slowly rose on the center stage. A girl stepped into the halo of light and recognition cut swift and deep.

No! Why is she doing this? She shouldn't be here. Oh, Father in heaven, help me. She didn't listen. Why didn't she listen?

The flickering stage lights played tag with the bronze highlights in Amber's hair as it swayed in a sensual wave, following the moves of her dance.

Why was the lesson lost to her? Doesn't she know she has to stop or she will be forever lost? *Please, God, make her stop. I don't want to . . .*

But it was impossible to tear hungry eyes away from her.

The little slut. What is it going to take . . . ?

Calmness reigned again as the answer fought its way out of the murky depths.

Yes. Of course. It's the only way.

CHAPTER THIRTEEN

Chad felt a quickening of excitement as he looked at the dead woman tangled in the dirty motel sheets. The MO wasn't a carbon copy of the Clemment case, but there were enough similarities to warrant that surge of adrenaline.

Pulling out his cell phone, he dialed Sarah's home number. "You might want to come and look at my DB," he said in response to her hello.

He walked away from the cloying smell of death and answered her question. "The Cameo Motel. I'll leave a light on for you."

He didn't get the laugh he was fishing for.

After Sarah hung up, Chad dialed Angel's number and gave her the same invitation. He wasn't pretending that he had to call her. Sarah could have done that. But he still played with the hope that Angel would someday change her mind about him. It didn't hurt to constantly remind her that he still existed.

He went outside where the roof lights of two cruisers slashed the night with intermittent flashes of blue and yellow. The crime-scene tape cordoned off a section of the walkway leading to the room, and the wind lifted the yellow plastic with a slight rustle.

Chad stepped under the tape and pulled a thin cigar out of his jacket. A whine from the neon lighting played treble over the bass rumble of traffic on the nearby expressway, and the music almost muted the murmur of voices belonging to a patrol officer and the night manager.

The officer took a step forward and introduced Mr. Stevie Wonder.

"Not to be confused with the singer," the stout white man said, offering his hand. "I'm not blind."

The attempted joke fell like a rock, and Stevie dropped his hand just as quickly. The patrol officer shook his head and walked away.

Chad took the unlit cigar out of his mouth and deposited it in his pocket. "Tell me what you saw."

"Nothing. I, uh . . . Do you mean before or after I found the body?"

"Both."

"Okay. Let's see. She came in about seven. Took the room for two hours."

Chad flicked a wrist to check his watch. Almost midnight. "And you just now got around to checking on her?"

"What's wrong if I cut her a little slack? She was a good customer."

The manager's beady eyes got even smaller as he appeared to realize his mistake.

Chad smiled. "She was a regular?"

Stevie's head bobbed once.

"She usually overstay her payment?"

"Some. Not that often."

"You got some reason to dance around the questions?"

"Well, you know." The man shot quick looks at the other officers.

"We're not from Vice, Stevie." Chad pulled his jacket against a blast of cold air. "So why don't you answer the questions. Then we'll let you get back to work."

"That's reasonable." Stevie ran chubby fingers through his sparse hair.

A flash of headlights washed over them, and Chad recognized

Angel's Citation as it pulled from the darkness into the glare of neon that boasted the amenities of the Cameo Motel. He deferred his next question until she joined them.

Chad made the introductions, and this time the manager didn't attempt his joke. Maybe he was intimidated by two black faces looking at him.

"He was telling me about the dead woman," Chad said. "We were just getting around to a name." He looked back at Stevie and made it a question.

"Uh, Rosie. Her name was Rosie."

How appropriate, Angel thought. Hookers were never named Mary or Nancy or Laura. Or maybe they had been in some former life.

"You want to look at the crime scene?" Chad asked. "I'm almost done here."

"Don't want to walk all over your case."

"It may not be exclusively mine anymore. That's why I called you and—"

Before he could say her name, Sarah pulled up in a rattle of loose car parts and a whine of rubber. Angel took a step back as the car came to within a foot of plowing into them.

Her partner got out, slammed the door and walked over. Near as Angel could tell, Sarah didn't show a glimmer of remorse or embarrassment for almost knocking them down.

"What do you have?" Sarah addressed her question to Chad without acknowledging the presence of her partner or the manager.

Angel was tempted to turn around and go home, but she didn't have a baseball bat to take with her. Besides, she was really trying to get past such childish reactions.

"Dead hooker in there." Chad inclined his head toward the doorway behind the fluttering yellow tape. "This here's the motel manager, Steve."

"Stevie, actually." The man stuck out his hand to Sarah. "Stevie Wonder."

The slightest smile touched the corners of Sarah's mouth, and Angel wondered if her partner found it equally difficult to manage the juxtaposition of mental pictures.

"Chad was explaining why he called us out in the middle of the night," Angel said. "The MO on the dead girl has some similarities to our vic."

"Come on," Chad said. "I'll show you."

The air inside the motel room hung heavy with the stench of death, and Angel's stomach protested as she looked at the brown body tangled in the sheets. Used, abused and discarded like a piece of trash.

"Isn't that one of the hookers we talked to the other night?" Sarah asked.

"Yeah. The smoker." Angel turned away. "None of them thought it could happen to them."

"They never do."

Angel watched her partner step closer to inspect the body. How long did it take to achieve that level of dispassion?

Chad stepped up to the other side of the bed. "Thought it had enough similarities to be worth your time."

Angel forced herself to look at the gaping cut on the side of the dead woman's neck and the pool of congealed blood haloing her head. "If it's the same perp, why leave this one in such a mess?" Angel gestured to the blood splattered on the headboard and wall.

"Maybe she fought more," Chad said.

"Could be," Sarah said. "But the autopsy report on the first victim said there were no defensive wounds. Nothing under her nails. She didn't fight at all."

"Are you thinking it isn't the same guy?"

"I don't know. Could be. But there are some things that

don't fit. Looks like this girl was slashed, not carefully cut the way Tracy was. If one person is responsible, why did he change the MO? And why go from high-class to street hooker?" Sarah stopped and looked at the body again. "We're either dealing with two different perps, or Peeples is right and we're facing one highly complex son of a bitch."

"I can buy the Alvarez kid doing the other one," Angel offered. "But not this."

"I agree."

"The forensic team's on the way," Chad said.

"Good," Sarah said. "We'll leave this in your capable hands." She turned to Angel. "We can go for another midnight walk."

They found Reba huddled near an outdoor phone booth at a gas station. She had her hands wrapped around a steaming cup of coffee as a heater.

"It would help if she put some clothes on," Angel commented as they approached.

"Yeah." Sarah noted the expanse of unclad legs and wondered how the woman tolerated the cold wind night after night.

"Get outta my face," Reba said, turning a shoulder to them. "Ain't got nothing to say."

"Where are your friends, Reba?" Sarah asked.

"I don't know. Around."

"One of them isn't around anymore." Sarah moved so she was in Reba's line of vision. "She's down at the morgue."

The hooker graced her with a full gaze. Her expression didn't change, but her eyes narrowed. Perhaps an effort to stop the brief tic of fear. Sarah waited for the question that never came.

"It was the older one," Angel said.

Reba turned her attention to the other detective but still didn't say anything. "We need her name," Angel said.

"Rosie."

"Not her street name."

Reba sighed, then gazed off into the distance. "Shauntay."

"Last name?"

"Brown."

Reba took a sip of her coffee and Sarah noted that the woman's hands shook. She appeared controlled on the surface, but something had been rattled deep inside.

"We also need your pimp's name," Angel said.

"He ain't gonna like this."

"He doesn't have to."

"Shauntay didn't deserve to die." A shudder shook the woman, and Sarah didn't know if it was from the cold or the reality. "How'd it happen?"

Finally the question.

"Someone cut her," Angel said.

This time coffee slopped over the edge of the cardboard cup.

"His name is Jingo."

"Full name?" Angel asked.

"He never did tell us."

Sarah paused a moment, wondering what it must be like to do this kind of work. And for someone who doesn't even tell you his name. She shook her head. "You think he killed Rosie?"

Reba took a long moment. "Had no reason."

"That you know of."

Angel's pronouncement seemed to startle the woman. Sarah watched guarded eyes flick from her partner back to her. "Was he ever violent with you?" she asked.

Reba shrugged. "The usual."

"Which was?"

"Making sure we never forgot who was boss. But he never marked us."

Sure, Sarah thought. Don't damage the merchandise. "So he just slapped your hands now and then?"

Sarah didn't hide the sarcasm, and Reba gave her a sharp look.

"I said he never hurt us, and that's what I meant."

"Never?" Angel's question insinuated disbelief. "He never got high and lost it with one of the girls? Must be the perfect boss."

Reba pulled her fur jacket closed and turned out of the scant protection of the kiosk. "I don't have to talk to you."

"Actually, you do," Sarah said. "And I'd rather not mess with all that paperwork at the station."

Reba paused but didn't look back.

"Just tell me the truth," Sarah said. "Did he ever cut any of the girls?"

"You need to talk to Gloria." Reba faced the detectives. "She wanted to get into another line of work and he convinced her not to."

"Where can we find her?" Angel asked.

"She moved to Frisco a while back."

"San Francisco?" Sarah asked.

"No. That city way north past Plano." A brief smile flashed white against the woman's face. "She thought she could find respectability in the burbs."

Chapter Fourteen

Angel stopped at a grocery store and bought a dozen red roses and a cinnamon streusel coffee cake. After she'd gotten home in the wee hours of the morning, she'd remembered the date and felt a sudden stabbing pang. When she'd almost lost her mother back in the summer she'd sworn she'd never forget her birthday again.

Well, hell. Nobody's perfect. She hurried across the parking lot, the asphalt glistening in the light drizzle. Would her mother see through the charade of the early-morning surprise party?

Pulling into the driveway in front of her parents' small brick house in Garland, Angel checked her watch. Eight-thirty. Her mother would be up.

She grabbed her packages, shielding them from the rain in the folds of her brown trench coat, and hurried up to the porch. She fumbled her key out of her pocket and unlocked the door, pushing it open. "Hello. Anybody up?"

"We're in here."

Angel followed the sound of her mother's voice to the kitchen. Her parents sat at the small oak dinette with cups of coffee and a light breakfast of scrambled eggs and toast. Never ones to be caught lounging, they were both dressed, and her father was cleanly shaven.

Handing the flowers to her mother, Angel bent to touch smooth cheeks with a light kiss. "Happy Birthday."

"What a nice surprise." Martha turned to her husband.

"Look, Gilbert. It's been years since I've had such pretty roses."

Gilbert made a noise that sounded suspiciously like a snort, and Angel wondered if it was in response to his wife's unintentional criticism. Or was it because he recognized the charade?

"Can you stay?" Martha asked. "I could make up some more eggs."

"For a bit." Angel hung her damp coat on a peg next to the back door. "I brought some cake."

"For breakfast?"

"Why not? It's a special day."

Her father snorted again, and this time Angel didn't have to wonder. He knew this was a last-minute scramble.

Balancing three plates with generous slices of cake, Angel walked to the table, carefully avoiding a direct look at her father. "Do you have something special planned for today?" she asked her mother.

"Your daddy's going to buy me a big juicy steak." Martha paused to take a bite of pastry. "We're meeting LaVon at Austin's about seven. You're invited."

"Can't promise anything. We're really putting in long hours right now. Didn't get home until after two last night."

"You working on that Clemment thing?" Gilbert wiped cake crumbs from his lips and regarded her with an unreadable expression.

Angel nodded.

"Got a suspect?"

"Nobody solid."

"You gonna look at the father? Or is it only rich black folks what get accused of killing the ones they love?"

Angel put her fork down and looked directly at him. "Are you serious?"

"Look what happened to O.J."

"Daddy! That's ridiculous. That was a long time ago and a

totally different situation. Right now there's no reason to suspect Clemment of killing his daughter."

"Why not? Don't cops always look at family first?"

"Yeah. When we've got some evidence of motive."

"And you'd only have that if he was black?"

"You know what, Daddy? I'm tired of these discussions that never get past the color of someone's skin."

Martha put a restraining hand on her arm. "That's no way to talk to your father."

"Well, Momma. I can't just be quiet anymore." She turned to her father. "You're making me crazy. I can't tell the difference between a real racist incident and my own paranoia anymore."

"Watch your mouth, girl."

"Oh, right. I forgot. You're the only one entitled to an opinion around here."

Her father stood quickly, the wooden legs of his chair scraping loudly across the tile. His liquid brown eyes held hers in a narrowed gaze. "My opinions were just fine when you wanted me to tell you about Selma, Alabama."

"I was a child then, Daddy. I wouldn't have disagreed if you'd said the sky was green. But I'm grown up now. I should be allowed to think for myself."

"The truth is the truth."

"Is it? Or is it just the latest propaganda?"

Her father grabbed her arm and rubbed so hard she could feel the burn. "Daddy! What the hell are you doing?"

"Just checking to see if you still black."

Angel pulled her arm out of her father's grasp. He glared at her for a moment, then whirled and left the room.

Cradling her throbbing arm, Angel turned to her mother who sat frozen in her chair. "I'm sorry. I didn't mean for this to happen."

"What did you mean?"

The question rattled Angel. "I don't understand."

"You pushed him." Her mother stood and started clearing dishes from the table. "You know better than that."

"But I'm right."

"This ain't about right. It's about respect."

"It's disrespectful to disagree with him?"

"No." Angel's mother paused and held her gaze. "It's disrespectful to talk hateful to the man who provided for you all these years."

Angel slammed her chair into the table and stomped over to get her coat. "I hoped just for once you'd take my side."

"Oh, baby." Her mother stepped up and put a hand on her shoulder. "Taking sides don't work in families. You know that."

The silence that followed made Angel ache, but anger held her from reason or comfort. She shrugged out from under her mother's hand and put her coat on. "I'm sorry I ruined your birthday."

Outside, Angel lifted her face to the full force of the rain. It was an adequate punishment for messing up. Plus, she could pretend those weren't tears on her cheeks. Damn her father for being wrong, and damn her for being right.

She didn't doubt the wisdom of her mother's last comment. That philosophy of never drawing lines in the dirt had brought a lot of harmony to the Johnson family. But Angel had always hoped for something more. Maybe on the level of "we can agree to disagree." That way she would have felt like her ideas were worth thinking about and perhaps even consideration, especially with her father. She couldn't remember ever feeling like anything she thought ever mattered to him.

Sarah grabbed a cup of coffee to fortify herself after a night's sleep that hadn't been as satisfying as some of her naps. Chad was already in the conference room with McGregor when she stepped in. He sure looked bright this morning.

"We're going to run these cases together for a while," McGregor said by way of greeting. "At least until we can determine there's no connection."

Sarah set her coffee on the table and pulled up a chrome and vinyl chair, looking at Chad. "What did Walt have to say last night?"

"Enough similarities to consider it close. And the blood on her forehead could have been an attempt to mark her like the other one was. He'll have more after the full post."

"Will that be today?" Sarah asked.

Chad nodded. "He'll let me know what time."

McGregor turned to Sarah. "What's your take on it?"

"If they're connected, that supports the fibbies' theory, but it just complicates ours. I can buy the Alvarez kid doing the girl. But the hooker?"

"Unless he's a serial killer," McGregor said.

"You've got to be joking," Sarah said. "He's just a kid. You can't seriously think he's been on a spree."

McGregor ran a hand across the stubble of beard on his chin. "I don't know what to think right now."

"Maybe the kid's clean," Chad offered. "You find out anything from the other hookers?"

Sarah opened her notebook and condensed the information they'd gotten from Reba.

"Think we got a pimp going over the edge?" McGregor asked.

"That'd work for the hooker," Sarah said. "But not for Tracy."

"Unless the girl was more into the business than we thought," Chad said. "Maybe got mixed up with the same pimp."

"The girlfriend said they weren't."

"So she lied."

Sarah took a sip of her coffee and thought about it. Then she put the cup back down. "It's worth considering. Let's haul in the pimp. Lean on him a little and hope something good comes out."

Chad touched his forehead in a mock salute and stood up. "I'll get right on it, boss-lady."

His smile assured Sarah that he was just having fun, and she waved him away. Then she swallowed the last of her coffee, which was now cold, but, hey, it was caffeine.

Back at her desk, Sarah found a copy of a report from Simms. He and Burt had finished going through the boxes from The Club and had come up with a list of employees who'd scored high on the NCIC scan. Sarah read the names, twenty in all, surprised that a small private club employed that many people. Well, actually more, since this list held just those who had criminal backgrounds. She called Grotelli and asked him to assign a couple of Uniforms to do the preliminary legwork. Then she called ADA Jessica Franklin. She always managed to be on the good side of Judge Danvers.

Hanging up, she saw Angel enter the squad room and weave her way to her desk.

Noticing the dark, damp spots on Angel's coat, Sarah momentarily regretted not assigning herself an indoor task. Slogging through the rain was not her idea of a good time.

She got up and went to meet Angel. "You want a cup of coffee before or after I tell you we have to go out?"

"Either way."

The vague response surprised Sarah and she noted the tight lines of tension in her partner's face. "Something wrong?"

Angel shook her head and stepped closer to her desk to leaf through some loose papers. "Where are we going?"

"The Alvarez crib."

Angel looked up. "We getting a warrant?"

"Yeah."

"Maybe I shouldn't have missed the briefing this morning."

"It's okay. Whatever you had to do must have been important."

Sarah waited for Angel to respond to the implied question, wondering why her partner was having so much trouble with eye contact.

"It was nothing." A tightness in Angel's posture labeled her a liar.

"You sure?"

The sharp smack of papers on the top of the desk made Sarah jump. "I said I'm fine. Just back off."

"Okay." Sarah held up a placating hand. "Why don't you talk to Ryan. See if he can get us a lead on the pimp. We'll leave after I hear from the ADA."

"Fine."

Sarah pulled to a stop in front of the Alvarez house and tugged the collar of her coat around her neck before stepping into the rain. Without waiting for Angel, she sprinted to the small porch and ducked under the eave that offered meager protection. She mashed the doorbell, then pounded on the door.

"That's not going to bring them any faster," Angel said, stepping up beside her and shaking water off her jacket.

"You never know."

At the first sound of life behind the door, Sarah pulled her ID out of her inside coat pocket and held it in front of the oval window in the wooden door. "Police."

Mrs. Alvarez opened the door a crack and Sarah was struck with how tiny the woman was. And how much fear was reflected in her coal black eyes. *"Si?"*

"Is your husband home?" Angel asked.

"Si."

"I'm Detective Kingsly. You remember Detective Johnson?" Sarah paused until the woman nodded. "We have a search warrant. You have to let us in."

"No comprendo."

"Just get your husband," Angel said.

The woman turned and Sarah pushed the door the rest of the way open. She stepped into a small entry that hosted an antique table as the base for a shrine to Our Lady of Guadalupe. Sarah pointed it out to Angel. "I'd say this qualifies them as highly religious."

Angel's response was cut short as Mr. Alvarez bustled forward. "What you do in my house? You have no right."

"Yes we do." Sarah handed him the warrant. "That says we can come in and search."

"What for?" The tall man held the paper in trembling hands and looked at it.

Angel spoke up. "Your son is a suspect in a murder investigation."

Alvarez narrowed his eyes and slapped the paper with an open palm. "Why you do this to my boy?"

"Please let us do our job." Sarah pushed past the man and motioned to his wife. "Which room is your son's?"

In a move as quick as a lizard snatching a fly out of the air, the man reached out and grabbed Sarah's arm. She spun, pulling free, and shoved him against the wall so hard, a picture clattered to the floor. "We can easily make it a cell for two."

Mrs. Alvarez stepped forward. "Please. No hurt my Jorge."

Sarah held the man until she could feel his hard muscles relax. When he made the decision to back down, she could see it form in his eyes, but she didn't know if acquiescing was motivated by his wife's distress or his own common sense. She maintained eye contact for one more long moment. "Don't interfere."

Alvarez gave a quick nod and Sarah turned back to the

woman who had tears streaking down amber cheeks. "The boy's room?"

Mrs. Alvarez led them through a cluttered living room and turned into a hallway. She stopped in front of the last door on the left.

"He's not home?" Sarah asked.

The woman shook her head.

"I'll start on the other side of the house," Angel said.

Sarah nodded and opened the door.

A musty smell of old sweat greeted Sarah when she stepped in. She pulled on latex gloves and looked around. The room was small and rather barren with just a rumpled twin bed, a tall bureau, and a desk. Dirty clothes decorated the floor and hung over the back of the desk chair. No mystery where the odor came from.

Mr. Alvarez stayed in the doorway but Sarah didn't protest. She felt better knowing where he was and what he was doing.

Haphazard piles of books and papers cluttered the desk, reminding her of the mess on McGregor's. She walked over and started sifting, careful not to knock anything to the floor.

Most of the papers were related to school; notes from classes, research, and rough drafts of reports. Sarah was about to dismiss the whole mess when a folded, dog-eared sheet of loose-leaf paper caught her attention. She opened it to find what appeared to be a poem. The title made her heart race—BROKEN HEART . . . HEARTLESS BITCH.

What followed was poorly written but Sarah wasn't reading it to give a review. The message chilled, plunging to the depths of a very angry young man "at the mercy of a woman of stone . . .

". . . she doesn't know the pain cutting deep within my soul

". . . if only she could feel the pain

". . . she needs to feel the pain!"

Sarah pulled a plastic evidence bag out of her pocket and slid the paper into it. Then she signed and dated it. It wasn't a confession, but it went a long way to showing motive.

Nothing else of interest turned up until she found a pair of lacy black panties in a dresser drawer. They were tucked under a stack of BVDs. How appropriate. Sarah slipped the scrap of lace into a second plastic bag and took one last visual sweep of the room. It was plain, almost austere, lacking the posters of rock groups and sports stars she was accustomed to seeing in a teenager's room. The only attempt at decoration appeared to be the model planes suspended from the ceiling by thin wires. The heat kicked on, and a black stealth bomber gently rode the wave of warm air.

Sarah turned to the father. "Did he do these?"

"*Si.*"

Looking back at the models, all dancing lightly on the breath of air, Sarah wondered at the patience needed to create the replicas of fighter planes from the early bi-wings to the F10s. It seemed incongruous with the history of short-tempered violence the young man had lived.

She found Angel in the living room. A shake of her partner's head answered the silent question. No matter. She'd found something.

Turning to Mr. Alvarez, who'd followed her down the hall, Sarah asked. "Where is your son?"

"At work." His clipped response underscored his resentment.

"Okay. Stay here with your wife." Sarah motioned for Angel to follow her into the kitchen.

"You look like a kid who just found his first dirty magazine," Angel said.

Sarah showed Angel the two bags of evidence. "This should be enough to bring the kid in again. Get on the horn to McGregor. I'll keep an eye on the parents."

Hostility permeated the air as Sarah walked back to the living room. Mr. Alvarez obviously hadn't missed the significance of the kitchen conference. His dark eyes flashed, and a muscle in his jaw beat in a rhythmic tic. He had one arm around his wife, who had that scared-rabbit look of impending bad news.

Sarah reminded herself that she wasn't responsible for their pain. She might be the messenger, but Ricardo was the cause.

CHAPTER FIFTEEN

There was no way they could keep the arrest of Ricardo Alvarez out of the media blitz. Channel Nine News must have stationed someone at the courthouse, just waiting for the felony arrest warrant to be filed. Bianca Gomaz and her minions met them at the Municipal Building with mini-cam whirling. Angel hustled Ricardo through the throng and made it up the steps. Sarah wasn't so lucky. Bianca shoved a microphone in her face.

"Detective Kingsly. Will the DA seek the death penalty for this heinous crime?"

Sarah stopped and gave the reporter a withering look. "The man hasn't even been arraigned."

"Well, certainly under the circumstances—"

"What circumstances are those, Ms. Gomaz?"

Sarah didn't have to ask. The entire city clamored for a swift conclusion to the Clemment case. It was the least they could do for the revered Burke Clemment. But the question did effectively silence the reporter for the moment. Sarah seized the advantage, pushing past Gomaz to open the front door.

Inside, she was met with another air of expectancy. But this one was different. The room resounded with the professional hope that they could give the DA a tight case and the good guys would win one.

Angel had already stashed Ricardo in one of the interrogation rooms, and McGregor met them in the hallway. His excitement rolled him forward on his toes. "Good work." He directed the comment to both of them, then turned to Sarah. "You going to have a go at him?"

"He wants his lawyer."

"Damn."

"We better let him make the call," Angel said.

"Can't we keep our window of opportunity open a little longer?" McGregor asked.

What the hell? Sarah shot him a quick look. *Is he gonna risk blowing the whole case?*

McGregor avoided her eyes, but not before she noticed that his were unusually bright, the whites laced with red rivulets. She'd seen those ravages of drink before. She just wasn't used to seeing them this early in the day. She touched his arm. "I'm not a stickler for the rules, Lieu. But we better play this one right or we'll all end up back in blues."

"You're right." He wiped a massive hand across the pebbles of sweat on his forehead. "We got enough for an indictment?"

"Looks good so far. A motive that just got stronger. Opportunity. His alibi is nebulous at best." Sarah moved to let Chad pass them in the narrow hall. "But the ADA would like to see some piece of concrete evidence that would put him at the scene."

"What about the murder weapon?"

That's when an elusive something that had niggled at her at the Alvarez house clicked. Modelers often used X-acto knives. Walt had said they should look for a very sharp instrument with a narrow blade. Another nice little detail of evidence to shore up their case, except they hadn't found a knife in the kid's house.

Time to assign some Uniforms to do a detailed search, including the garbage. The kid wasn't the brightest bulb. It's possible he threw the knife in his own trash.

A disturbance at the other end of the hall drew Sarah's attention, and she looked around McGregor's bulk to see LaVon. The attorney personified agitation as he moved toward them, a briefcase in one hand, the other swinging in a brisk tempo that matched his stride. *This is not a happy man.*

"Guess we don't have to make that call," Angel said.

"Please tell me you questioned my client without me being present." LaVon's gaze flashed on each of the detectives in turn. "I'd love solid grounds for a dismissal of charges."

Angel wasn't sure, but she felt as though his eyes lingered longer on her and burned deeper than usual. She took a half-step back. Personal and professional had to have a huge gap here.

"Counselor." McGregor turned to face LaVon. "You overestimate our stupidity."

LaVon directed another smoldering look at Angel. "You had no right to search my client's residence without notifying me."

At least she could stop wondering how he knew Ricardo was here. The father must have called. "No charges were made before the search," Angel said. "You had no legal grounds to prevent it."

"But I could have been there. I should have been there."

"No, Counselor." Sarah stepped forward. "We were not bound by law to notify you in advance. It's unfair to insinuate otherwise."

"Fair? Are you prepared to be totally fair in these proceedings?"

The question hit a raw nerve. Was he just posturing, or was the department on the verge of another racial incident, but instead of "poor black boy," it would be "poor Hispanic boy"?

Or was that just her paranoia?

She searched the lawyer's chiseled face for some indication of how far off she was. LaVon held her gaze and gave no clues.

"Do you doubt our ability to treat a suspect without bias?" she asked.

"Is that a rhetorical question, Detective?"

"It wasn't meant to be."

His coal-black eyes held hers, and she wasn't sure if it would be wiser to just end the discussion before the hole got too deep.

McGregor ended the silent debate. "I think we've heard enough, Counselor," he said. "We can either keep sparring here in this hallway or we can all get back to our jobs."

"You're right, of course. This is a waste of time."

Sarah was still trying to figure out LaVon's last statement when he turned and walked briskly away. Initially, she hadn't pegged him as a rage-filled black man, but she'd been wrong on other initial assessments. She glanced at Angel, raising an eyebrow in question.

Angel shrugged, but before she diverted her gaze, Sarah saw anxiety reflected in the tight lines around her partner's eyes. A pang of concern grabbed her. She didn't envy Angel's precarious position between her brother and their case.

Angel sat in the semi-darkness of Pete's Bar & Grill, an out-of-the way place she liked to come to when she didn't feel like hanging with cops. A TV screen was mounted above the bar, and the bartender switched from ESPN Sports to the local news. The broadcast led with a report on the arrest. Bianca imbued the story with her own brand of drama that practically had Ricardo tried, convicted, and fried. Angel watched from a stool halfway down the bar. She didn't have to worry about not being able to hear. A hush had fallen over the sizable crowd as soon as the report started. Not even a tinkle of ice against glass disturbed the broadcast.

Listening to the report, Angel wanted to feel relief. She wanted to celebrate the fact that they were on the brink of closing the case so she could join her fellow drinkers in the cheers. And she couldn't figure out why she didn't. Unless it was because she knew she should be at another place with another crowd of people celebrating something else.

She'd thought about going to Austin's despite the blow-up this morning. There had been other occasions when family members had all behaved for the sake of her mother's feelings. Times when they were polite, smiled, and pretended nothing was wrong. But she didn't know what kind of a tear LaVon would be on tonight. His attitude at the station earlier had left an unequivocal impression. He was disappointed that she was not his ally in this. *But how can he expect that when there's a legal line drawn between us?*

And her father would support LaVon's stance. To hell with what protocol dictated. He would insist that she should have given her brother extra consideration and called him before they searched the Alvarez house. After all, they were blood. And they were on the same side of the cause.

Except that's what Angel wasn't so sure of anymore. The cause wasn't as clearly defined in her mind as it seemed to be for others, like the Reverend Billie Norton.

Angel finished her beer and dropped a five on the counter. She'd had enough of the news and her own discouraging thoughts.

When Angel pushed through the heavy door and stepped outside, it was into a darkness so complete she had to take a moment to let her eyes adjust. Couldn't the owner spring for one more light in this lot?

Walking toward her car, she heard a faint scrape of metal on metal. She stopped to see where the sound was coming from. That Camaro over there, three cars up from hers. Maybe somebody too drunk to get the key in the lock?

She eased around the trunk and saw a shadowed figure

hunched by the driver's-side door. She was about to ask if he needed help when she realized he was breaking into the car.

She teetered in indecision. Her phone and her gun were locked in her car. She was officially off duty and had planned to stay that way. Should she go make a call for help? Or nab him before he got away? The click of the latch erased her indecision and she stepped into view. "Hold it right there. Police."

The perp looked at her, glanced quickly to his left for a way to escape, then turned dark eyes back at her. "What you gonna do, bitch? Shoot me?"

His verbal challenge stunned her for half a heartbeat, and he took that moment to charge, throwing his weight into her shoulder to push her aside.

Another instinct, honed by hours on the mat, kicked in and Angel took his charge, grabbing his arm. She let his momentum pull him past her, then twisted his arm and held it in an arm-bar. The pain pushed him to the ground, and she followed with a knee in his back.

"Hey, bitch. You can't do this. I got rights."

Angel lifted him, then slammed him back down. "You want to know your rights? You have the right to have your face shoved into this concrete. You have the right to try to fight again and I'll break your fucking—"

"What's going on? You okay, lady?"

Angel looked up to see a middle-aged man running across the parking lot. "Police," she said. "You got a tie?"

"What?"

"A necktie." Angel nodded to the thief's arm still twisted across his back. "I can't hold him like this forever."

"Oh, right." The guy dug in the side pocket of his suit coat. "Came here right after work."

Angel took the tie and bound the perp's hands. Then she stood and motioned to the civilian. "Watch him. If he twitches, stomp on his head."

The man took a half-step back. "Is that legal?"

"I don't see a judge, do you?"

Leather heels scraped on concrete as the man danced from one foot to another, and Angel realized it wasn't because he was cold. "It'll be all right," she said, purposely dropping the semi-bantering tone she'd used earlier. "He's not going to move."

"Sure." The man bobbed his head and ended the dance.

Hurrying to her car, Angel unlocked the door and grabbed her cell phone. As she walked back to relieve her impromptu deputy, she connected with Dispatch. After giving the pertinent information, she closed the phone and nodded to the business-man. "Where should I send the tie?"

"Never mind." He was already backing away. "I got a million of them."

Within moments, the wail of a siren indicated a response to her call for assistance. Then the headlights and flashers of a patrol car sliced the darkness.

"He's over here," Angel said to the officer who emerged from the driver's seat. "Book him for attempted auto theft. Assault. Resisting arrest. And generally being a scumbag. And don't forget the *Miranda*. He's real interested in his rights."

"You coming in for processing?"

"I'm in no mood. You can have the collar. And the tie if you need one."

The officer gave her a puzzled look then walked over to the guy on the ground. Angel heard a light chuckle as the officer pulled his handcuffs.

After the perp was stashed in the squad car, Angel started to tremble. Holding herself around the middle, she leaned against the bed of a pickup. What the hell had she been doing? Talk about being on the edge. This was as bad as any stunt Sarah had pulled.

Angel relaxed her death grip from her stomach and looked at her hands. Smears of blood were barely visible, but she knew they were there. She'd scraped her knuckles on the pavement along with the perp's face. She fumbled an old tissue out of her pocket and carefully wiped her palms, her fingers, the backs of her hands.

A month ago. A week ago. Hell, even an hour ago, she'd have sworn she would never be capable of something like this. This kind of brutish behavior was reserved for thugs who became cops because they liked wielding power. She couldn't believe she'd allowed her personal frustrations to make her lose control like that.

Is this what it's like for Sarah? The question surprised her almost as much as her behavior did. She'd been so sure of things before. Sure that it had to be some personal defect that caused such erratic behavior. But here she was teetering on her own precipice. And now things weren't so black and white. No pun intended.

"Screw it." Angel turned and went back into the bar for another beer. It was going to be a long night.

A flicker of light from the TV was the only illumination in the room. It was easier to hide in the dark. And it was necessary to hide. The burning need to purify one more was growing stronger.

The news report had gotten it all wrong and time was suspended between relief and anger. Why is it so hard for them to see? To understand? It isn't about love lost. Or jealous rage. It's a holy order of salvation. And there's no way a mere boy can grasp the deeper meaning of that. Let alone carry it out.

The messenger is as important as the message. Redemption is not a deed acted upon impulsively. It has to be planned, prayed over, and carefully executed. Not a thoughtless act born out of passion.

Yes, my child. You are exalted among men.

"Silence, you scourge of hell."

But the truth shall set you free.

"I know the truth. 'Do not put yourself above the Lord thy God.' "

Because he wants all the glory for himself. And what reward do you get?

"He has promised—"

Ha! Words. Empty words. You are his puppet on a string.

"Be gone with thee, Satan! I will not be swayed from this Divine mission. Speak no more!"

The voice stilled.

And out of the ensuing mental quiet new direction emerged. They could punish that boy if that was their desire. It didn't matter. The Holy order of things would continue regardless of what those sinners did. And there was no doubt they were sinners. All of them.

But that was not the concern this day. Only one sin mattered. The one that had launched this Divine Mission. And the mission had not been completed yet.

CHAPTER SIXTEEN

Sarah was surprised by the knock on her door. The last time it had happened had been a surprise, too, and she'd been so delighted at the rare occurrence that she'd bought six boxes of Girl Scout cookies.

Leaving the security chain on, she cracked the door open and felt the blood drain from her face when she saw Jeanette standing on the welcome mat.

"You haven't returned my calls."

"We've been swamped . . . You know . . . Big case and all." Sarah glanced at Jeanette, then at the streetlight over the woman's shoulder.

"Can I come in?"

"Oh. Sure. Sorry." Sarah stepped aside and caught a whiff of a pleasant, light perfume as Jeanette stepped through the doorway.

"Would you like something to drink?" Sarah asked. "Coffee? A beer? Soda?"

"A beer would be good."

Sarah could feel Jeanette's eyes on her as they walked into the kitchen. I guess ignoring the problem was not the way to go. She opened the refrigerator and pulled out two Miller Lite longnecks. "You want a glass?"

"The bottle's fine."

Back in the living room, Sarah wondered how much longer they could pretend this was just another casual visit. It was small consolation, but she did notice that Jeanette wasn't as composed as Sarah had first thought. Dark green eyes had difficulty resting on any particular thing, and Jeanette twisted a strand of her russet hair around a finger.

Absently stroking Cat, Sarah mentally scrambled for something harmless and inane to say. "So how are things?"

Jeanette shot her a quick look. "Why don't we get to the point?"

The challenge made Sarah squirm.

"Come on." Jeanette leaned forward, setting her beer down on the coffee table with a loud thunk. "Don't try to pretend that you're not royally pissed about something."

"I'm not pissed."

"Oh, yeah? I'm supposed to believe that you haven't called in nearly a month because you've been too busy?"

Sarah surged to her feet, sending Cat flying. "What do you want?"

"The truth."

A heavy silence filled the room, and Cat beat a retreat to the bedroom. Sarah could hear the blood roaring in her ears like a wild surf. Jeanette sat, unmoving and unwavering, her face lifted in challenge.

"Okay . . ." Sarah took a deep breath and let it out. "I can't believe you're getting married again."

"So you decided to punish me?"

"I'm not."

"Then what are you doing?"

Sarah averted her gaze, pacing behind her recliner. That was a very good question. She wasn't sure about what was driving her. On one level, she realized she was acting like a spoiled child who wasn't getting her way. But self-justification kept her from going there too often.

"This is pretty quick." Sarah purposely gave her voice a hard edge. "Aren't you afraid you're jumping into something?"

"It's always a bit of a leap, isn't it? Relationships, I mean."

The calm response rankled. So did the veiled implication. But Sarah didn't want to open that box either. A defensive position was never an advantage. "So you're going to marry some guy you just met?"

"He's not 'some guy' I just stumbled across. He's been a good friend for years."

"And you had the balls to challenge John's fidelity?"

"You bitch!" Jeanette rose in one swift movement and leaned into Sarah. "Don't you ever question me like that. Whatever I decide to do with my life now takes nothing away from John. Or my loyalty to him."

Jeanette's breath tickled across Sarah's cheeks, and it took every ounce of strength she had to resist slapping the face looming into hers.

She swallowed, once, twice, then found voice for her words. "You're right. I was out of line."

The other woman took a step back, but kept her gaze fixed on Sarah. "You've been doing a lot of that lately."

"What do you mean?"

"I hear things. You're not the only connection I have to the department."

Sarah turned away. "That's none of your business."

"Oh. You're the only one who can butt into other people's lives. Pardon me. I must have failed to get your memo on that."

Jeanette grabbed her jacket from the end of the sofa and pulled it on. "It's no wonder you don't have any friends."

The words reverberated in the room long after the last echo of the door slamming. *The nerve of that woman. How could she? I have half a mind to—*

What? Anything you can to avoid looking at the truth?

"Fuck you!" Sarah's cry sent Cat on a dive back down the hall.

After a moment of feeling like she'd entered some bizarre otherworld with herself as the chief alien, Sarah followed Cat into the bedroom. He was nowhere to be seen, so she dug through the pile of unfolded clothes on her bed, pulling out a pair of jeans and an Aggies sweatshirt. No way was she going to stay home and listen to her conscience.

Sensing a presence at her desk, Angel dropped the report she was reading and looked up. Ryan O'Donnell gave her a crooked grin. "Still getting all the high-profile cases, I see. Maybe I should come in out of the cold."

Angel shook her head. "You're much better off where you are. Believe me."

Ryan leaned a hip against the edge of her desk, and Angel found his proximity as unsettling as it was the last time she'd seen him. *Wouldn't Daddy have something to say if he knew what I was thinking about this white boy.*

"Hello? Detective?"

A flush of embarrassment warmed Angel's cheeks when she realized he'd been talking to her. "Sorry. I was . . . distracted."

"I'm crushed." He overplayed a pained reaction. "You found something more interesting than me?"

"Well." Her gaze strayed to the smooth pull of denim over his thigh.

A discreet cough pulled her attention to his face, and she realized that he knew exactly where she'd been looking. She felt another rush of heat, thankful that her coloring made it hard to detect a blush. One of the few items she could put in the positive side of being black.

His deep blue eyes sparkled with suppressed laughter and

Angel sighed. "Do you think we could just start over?" she asked.

"Certainly." He wiped a hand across his face and the smile disappeared.

Angel recognized the move. "Martin Riggs, right? I love that man."

"You do?"

Angel tried to be stern, as much for herself as for him. "Are you flirting with me?"

"You started it."

Laughter escaped before she could prevent it. Then Chad walked into the squad room. Angel saw a quick flash of dismay cross his face as he looked from Ryan to her, then back to Ryan. The smile he attempted was as unnatural as the makeup in a B movie.

"I thought we were going to interrogate the suspect," Chad said.

"Suspect?" It was Angel's turn to look from one to the other.

"Yeah." Ryan slid off her desk. "That's what I came here for. We got that pimp."

"Great." Angel stood and straightened some papers on her desk to cover the awkwardness of the moment. She could still feel Chad's gaze on her, and there was no doubt he'd read the situation accurately. *Can't fool a cop.*

A tall, thin black man sat at the table in the interrogation room. His blazer, chinos, and silk shirt weren't what Angel expected the well-dressed pimp to wear. He didn't have a gold chain in sight. Watching him through the one-way glass, she noted that he seemed very relaxed. He leaned casually against the back of the chair, raising the front legs a couple of inches off the floor, took a swallow of Coke, then looked directly at her and winked.

Angel turned to Ryan who was on her left. "I take it he's well acquainted with the mirror."

"He's got a few frequent-flier miles."

Chad touched her arm and motioned toward the door. "Let's go."

Angel followed him into the interrogation room, where a sweet smell of cologne almost choked her. Jingo took a sip of his drink, then gave her an insolent grin.

Chad stepped forward. "Heard you've had a little dent in your business."

"Not that I'm aware of."

"You should keep better track of your girls," Angel said.

"They're fine."

"Rosie wasn't so fine last time we looked."

Jingo swung his gaze toward her, and Angel was pleased to see the flash of alarm.

"Didn't you miss her the last couple of days?" Chad asked.

"I give my women a lot of freedom."

"That's not what we heard." Angel stepped closer. "They were feeling downright constrained the other night."

Jingo sat mute.

"Is that why you offed Rosie?" Angel continued. "To teach the girls a lesson?"

"Rosie's dead?"

"Don't play dumb with us," Chad said.

Angel stepped closer. "What about Tracy Clemment?"

"Who?" For a moment, the man looked truly confused, then he bolted out of the chair. "Wait a minute. You talking about that rich bitch that was killed? I had nothing—"

"Sit down." Angel rocked forward to enforce her command, and Jingo slowly eased his weight to the edge of the chair.

"Let me see if I've got this straight," Chad said, hitching one hip on the corner of the table. "You didn't know Rosie was cut up like a side of beef. And you don't know Tracy Clemment."

"I know about her. I can read."

"Was she working for you?"

"No."

"Where were you last Sunday night? Around midnight?" Angel asked.

"Don't remember."

"Would a first-degree murder charge refresh your memory?" Chad asked.

Jingo wiped the sheen of moisture from his face with long, slender fingers. "I think it's lawyer time."

Angel shot a quick, irritated look at Chad, then strode toward the door. In the hall, she saw Ryan still standing before the glass. He gave her an understanding nod. "Hate it when progress comes to a screeching halt."

"Think he did them?"

"I don't know." Ryan looked back at the window, and Angel stepped next to him.

"He's good for the second vic," he continued. "But I don't have a good feel for the girl."

"Why not?"

"He doesn't run unseasoned girls. Prefers experience." He faced her with a shrug. "Don't see him breaking pattern like that."

"We should drop him as a suspect for the Clemment girl?"

"Nope. Just don't be disappointed if he doesn't pan out."

"Damn!"

"You still got the kid, don't you?"

"Yeah. But if both women were killed by the same guy, tying the kid to the second vic is a bigger stretch than trying to connect Jingo to the girl."

"Don't force it. If it's going to fit, it'll happen naturally."

His voice was so soothing, Angel turned toward the comfort, sensing, more than seeing, encouragement in the depths of his eyes. She felt a sudden urge to touch him, to connect with his confidence. He smiled and the invitation was unmistakable—an invitation she didn't dare accept.

She took a step back. "Got to report to McGregor."

"Sure." Ryan shifted his weight away from her, then smiled again. "See you around."

Angel watched him go, part of her wanting to call him back. But damn! This wasn't a complication she needed in her life right now.

Chapter Seventeen

"A moment, Detective?"

Sarah looked up to see Quinlin, duly authoritative with his dark suit and somber expression. His presence had not been missed by the other detectives, and the usual cacophony of noise stilled. Sarah stared at Quinlin. What the hell did the head of SIU want with her? Her gut had an answer but she didn't want to hear it.

"This isn't a good time." She motioned to the spray of folders across the top of her desk.

"It'll have to do." Quinlin took a step away. "If you'll come with me."

A stir of unease from the other detectives rippled across the room as Sarah rose and trailed Quinlin toward the door out of the CAPERS department. He led her through a labyrinth of halls until they came to his office, the door marked boldly SPECIAL INVESTIGATIVE UNIT.

Inside, she declined his offer of coffee, sitting stiffly on the wooden chair he cleared for her. He sat down behind his desk, regarding her with unblinking brown eyes. It was a strange moment of déjà vu, taking Sarah to another time she'd faced his scrutiny, and she forced herself not to break eye contact.

"We're looking into a report about McGregor," he said.

Sarah bit her tongue to keep from asking "what report?" It's what he wanted her to do, to open the line of dialogue, but she wasn't going to fall into his trap. She sat on her curiosity and met his gaze.

He waited her out for a heartbeat, then opened a folder. "What do you know of his drinking?"

The question shattered her calm. Quinlin had a way of doing that. Of going for a direct attack that kept a person off guard. No little pleasantries or small talk first. Not trusting her voice, she answered with a shrug.

"Don't compromise yourself to protect him."

"I wasn't aware he needed protection."

Quinlin rested his chin on his fingers and regarded her. Sarah held herself still by sheer effort of will until he picked up a paper from the desktop. "This goes back to the screw-up on the Alfred Thomas suicide. Lloyd has asked for a review."

In a flash, Sarah remembered. Almost like she was looking at a spread of crime-scene photos.

Alfred standing on his porch with a gun to Angel's head.

The SWAT team in place, Lloyd hell bent on taking him out.

That stupid reporter walking into the street. Talking to Alfred.

The sudden explosion of a gunshot.

Angel, covered with blood and bits of bone, collapsing in her arms.

It had only been later that Sarah realized the blood belonged to Alfred. If there was a screw-up that day, it wasn't McGregor's.

She swallowed hard and held Quinlin's gaze. "That matter was settled six months ago."

"Don't worry, Detective. This isn't about you."

"So Lloyd just now decided there was something wrong with McGregor?"

"No. He just now decided it was worth taking formal action."

Bullshit. Something else was going on here. "Can't help you, Lieutenant." Sarah rose. "You'll have to hang him with someone else's rope."

Quinlin gave a slight nod. "Rest assured we'll do that."

Sarah left the office feeling like a bug some sadistic cat was toying with. She let the frustration propel her out to the parking lot, where she dug in the glove compartment of her car for a crumpled pack of cigarettes. She lit one, choking on the stale tobacco, and leaned against the door. What the hell did McGregor think he was doing? Didn't he care about who else might get stung if he kept pissing on the hornet's nest?

"Ever consider that might be bad for your health?"

Sarah turned to see Chad approaching across the asphalt. "This job's bad for my health." She field-stripped the cigarette and dropped the butt in her pocket.

He gave her a thoughtful look. "What's up?"

"The sun. The moon." She moved toward the building. "And the fuckin' SIU."

"Quinlin strikes again."

The words stopped her and she turned to look at him. He lifted one shoulder. "We had a 'visit' the other day."

"About?"

"McGregor." He hesitated ever so briefly. "And the bottle."

"Damn." Sarah fished the butt out of her pocket and relit it, blowing a furious stream of smoke. "What'd you tell him?"

"Nothing."

"What do you think?"

"Nothing."

"Bullshit."

"He gets the job done."

"So you don't worry just a little bit."

"Nope."

She considered his reserve for just a beat, then stubbed the cigarette out on the tray of the large metal trash container beside the door. Was he really so sure?

"Come on." She motioned to Chad. "We've got a briefing."

Angel was already in the conference room with McGregor

when Chad and Sarah stepped in.

"This isn't a fuckin' social engagement you can be fashionably late for," McGregor snapped.

"Sorry." Sarah slipped into a chair next to Angel.

"The ADA just called," McGregor said. "She's worried. The Alvarez arraignment didn't go well. The judge drove his SUV through the holes in our case."

"What about the poem? The panties?" Sarah asked.

"Clemment swears his daughter never had any underwear like that," McGregor said. "And even if she bought the panties after she started dancing, there is no way to prove when the kid took them. Hell, we really don't know they *are* hers."

"Maybe we caved into the pressure to arrest too soon," Angel said. "We still haven't located a murder weapon. Plus there's no physical evidence the kid was at that motel room, and now we've got the pimp to look at."

"What'd the ME say about the second vic?"

Chad pulled out his notebook. "Cause of death, severed carotid artery. Similar to the girl. Could've even been the same blade. But Walt won't swear to anything. Too many little inconsistencies."

"Forensic?"

"A print at the Cameo puts Jingo there sometime," Angel said. "But nothing to prove it was that night."

"Witnesses?"

McGregor directed that question to Sarah who shook her head. He sighed. "Great. Two suspects with barely a scrap of evidence between them."

"How do you want us to proceed?" Sarah asked. "Build a case on the kid or the pimp?"

"Keep going on both. Sooner or later we gotta get lucky."

Yeah, Sarah thought. Luck was about the only thing that'd pull them out of this hole.

When Amber opened the door, Sarah stepped in and stopped short. The small living room was decorated like a shrine to Hollywood and Marilyn Monroe, and Sarah was practically face-to-face with a life-sized poster of Marilyn in the infamous street-vent pose.

"This was my grandfather's," Amber said. "He was not-so-secretly in love with Marilyn."

"I must admit this is the last thing I expected to see in your apartment."

"Yeah, well, I loved my grandpa."

The wistful tone in the girl's voice tugged at Sarah. She knew what it was like to love a grandfather that completely, but she didn't want to share her own emotion with this girl. She didn't want to share anything with this girl who didn't have the good sense God gave a tick.

Amber had called a half hour ago, frantic about a message she'd received at The Club. Sarah's first impulse was to shake her into sensibility, but she wasn't here to discipline a child.

"Where's the paper?" she asked.

Amber pointed to the mess on a small coffee table where an unruly pile of money spilled over onto a paper plate stained red from some previous meal. A small, folded rectangle of white paper rested next to the money.

Sarah leaned over and lifted the top flap with her pen. The message was a variation of the invitation Tracy had received.

"Why didn't you call last night?" Sarah asked.

"I just checked my tips a little while ago." Blue eyes widened in fear. "Could it be the same guy who left the note for Tracy?"

"I don't know." Sarah released her frustration in a long breath and swept a hand toward the array of money. "Why are you still

172

doing this?"

"Isn't it obvious?" It was Amber's turn to nod toward the money.

Christ. Would she ever learn? Sarah shook the angry thought away. "Last night. Did you see anyone who was there the night Tracy was killed?"

"I don't know." The reminder seemed to sober the girl. "With the stage lights and all, it's hard to see faces."

Sarah slipped the paper into an evidence bag and sealed it. "This might not be related to what happened to Tracy. But maybe you should stay with your parents for a while."

Watching Amber adjust to the implications, Sarah fought another impulse to mother her. Did the girl think anything good would come from staying here and continuing to strip?

"That's not going to be possible."

An undercurrent of helplessness in the girl's voice took the edge off of Sarah's anger. "Why not?"

"They said I have to live with the consequences of my choices."

Sarah was so stunned she couldn't speak for a moment. "They cut you loose?"

Amber nodded, and Sarah took a deep breath to keep from screaming. She'd never understand what drove some parents' behavior. "Listen to me, Amber," she said when she had control. "Working at a place like that is not safe. Do yourself a favor and quit."

"And do what? Flip hamburgers?"

"You might live longer."

Amber held Sarah's gaze for a moment, then looked at her fingers that were pleating the fabric of her lounge pants. "I'll think about it."

Sarah shook her head, stashed the evidence bag in the pocket of her blazer and stood. Amber didn't move, so Sarah walked to the door and left. She didn't know if the girl would take her advice or not, but she felt marginally better for giving it.

Back at the station, Sarah showed the note to Angel. Later she'd give it to Roberts for testing, but for now, she wanted her partner's take on it.

"Could be the same guy," Angel said, handing the plastic bag back.

"Yeah. But did he want more from the girls than just a little romp at the 'No-Tell Motel'?"

"We might never know."

Sarah leaned back in her chair and put one foot up on her desk. "Too bad they don't have security cameras inside The Club."

"Tight security's bad for business."

"Yeah. But the lack of security is bad for us." Sarah rocked for a moment, then looked at Angel. "Maybe we should spend a little time at The Club."

"Going to run this by McGregor?"

Sarah dropped her foot to the floor and sat up. "He won't have a problem with it. Anything to get the brass off his ass."

Angel nodded and Sarah thought for a moment before asking, "Quinlin talk to you?"

A paper on her desk seemed to command Angel's attention. Sarah sighed. "What did you tell him?"

"That Lloyd is full of shit."

The response was so unexpected, Sarah couldn't stifle the laughter. "Did you mean it?"

"Yeah." Angel looked up, a hint of a smile touching her lips. "The whole thing was a major screw-up, but not McGregor's."

"Then you're okay about . . . everything?"

Angel found the question absurd. Nothing was okay. She still had nightmares about that awful day, and it would be a relief to divert responsibility from herself or Alfred. It would also suit the esteemed Reverend Norton. He'd been trying to slap a racist label on the incident for months.

"Angel?"

The question pulled her out of her contemplation and she regarded her partner, wondering if Sarah filtered everything through a colored lens the way she did. What would life be like not to have to do that?

"You know we never did talk about it much," Sarah said.

"That's okay. I'm handling it."

"You sure?"

"Yeah." Angel stood and grabbed the plastic evidence bag. "I'll get this to Roberts."

Out in the hall, an unexpected urge to pound the wall nearly overcame Angel. She stopped walking, ignored the stares of passing officers and tried to assess the origin of the unrest. Was this what it was like for Sarah? That awful gut-wrenching dichotomy between duty and heart? Did they maybe have more in common than she thought?

Angel still felt responsible for Alfred. He was her best friend's father. She should have been able to talk him down. Instead, he had blown his brains all over the porch where she used to play as a child.

CHAPTER EIGHTEEN

McGregor unbuttoned his suit coat, watching Helen balance the phone between her shoulder and ear while making notes on a small pad of paper. He knew why she'd called him in. At least he hoped he knew. It had to be about the case. She was probably getting all kinds of heat from the commissioner. He wished he had something to tell her. He also wished he had a drink to soothe the ache in his gut and the tremor in his hands.

When had it gotten so bad? He wasn't stupid enough to think he could escape the scrutiny of the department for long, but he'd hoped to avoid it long enough to get some control before his drinking blew up his career. Had he waited too long?

Helen cradled the receiver, then looked at him for a long moment. "Do I need to relieve you of the Clemment case?"

The question confused him. Why would she say that? "I trust you to do what's best." He forced his body not to squirm.

"I got a very disturbing report from SUI."

A fist of pain grabbed his stomach. "Sarah's okay. She's just—"

"Not about Kingsly."

McGregor couldn't find a safe place to let his eyes rest.

"We've been friends a long time, Tom. Don't make me do something I don't want to do."

He wanted to respond to the kindness in her voice, but he didn't know what to say. He didn't even know how deep the shit was.

The silence was worse than her words.

"Anything official?"

"The only part that is, I can quash." Helen slid a paper across the desk to him. "A complaint filed by Lloyd. From the Thomas case. The guy who shot himself in that mall murder case."

"I remember." McGregor picked up the paper, damning the soft rustle of sound as the page shook. He put it back on the desk and scanned the words, almost wanting to laugh at the absurdity of the report. He hadn't even been drinking during the day then.

Helen must've sensed his mood. "Don't treat this lightly. He's well connected. Makes it easier to stir the shit."

He risked meeting her eyes. "How far is this going?"

"It can stop here." She held his gaze. "Everyone knows he's a whiner. And the whole incident was thoroughly investigated when it happened."

He waited out her pause, knowing there was more.

"About the other. That's up to you."

"What 'other'?"

"Cut the bullshit." The harsh words accompanied by the slap of her hand on the desk raised him an inch off his seat and set his heart pounding. "You've got a serious problem."

"I'm okay."

"You want to lie to yourself. Okay. But don't try it with me."

McGregor regarded the tight lines on her face and realized he'd pushed her beyond the bounds of their friendship. She'd go to the mat for him for a lot of things. He knew that. But he saw the line she'd drawn in the dirt here. "I'll take care of it after—"

"You'll take care of it now."

Stifling a flare of anger, McGregor nodded. But he had no idea how he was going to take care of it. His sensible side told him every day that he needed to quit drinking. Go to rehab.

Join a group. But the sad, lonely, miserable part of him wasn't ready to give up the bottle.

He stood and walked out on shaking legs. Maybe if he made some small effort. Cut down. Stopped bringing a flask to work. Go to a couple of AA meetings. Helen would note that effort in his file and the inquisitors would go away.

Sarah cast another glance around the dimly lit room that was lightly populated with patrons for the late show at The Club. She didn't hold out a lot of hope that their current effort would net results, but it was better than nothing.

Lights flashed, drawing her attention to the stage where she saw a young woman, draped in layers of filmy material, step into the spotlight. The woman looked like Amber, and Sarah studied the face, hoping that she was wrong. Hoping that the girl had taken her advice. But hoping didn't work.

She leaned closer to her partner. "I am not believing this."

Angel shrugged. "No accounting for stupidity."

The music began, the bass setting a slow, seductive beat, and Amber started to dance, discarding pieces of her costume in diaphanous puddles on the stage floor. Sarah noticed an immediate effect on the mood of the room as the hum of conversation quieted and the soft rustles of movement ceased. Even Chad seemed to have forgotten they weren't here for the entertainment.

Watching until Amber was naked except for a small triangle of gold *lame*, Sarah vacillated between titillation and anger. She knew where the anger came from. She couldn't believe the girl was still doing this after all that had happened. Like an irate mother, she wanted to yank Amber off the stage. But where did that other response come from? If she was a straight heterosexual woman, the sight of a naked female body shouldn't excite her, should it? Or was it just the atmosphere of raw sexuality dressed in country club finery that was getting to her?

Sarah turned her mind from the questions and her eyes from the stage. She wasn't here for self-exploration. Doing a quick scan of the room, she mentally cursed the dim lighting that cast most of the tables in shadows. She couldn't see a bloody thing, but she did get a whiff of cigarette smoke. She nudged Angel. "Do you smell cigarette smoke? I thought smoking wasn't allowed indoors anymore."

"Maybe nobody here complains," Angel said.

Setting her glass down, Sarah pushed her chair back and stood. "I'm going to have a look around."

"Want company?" Chad asked.

"Think it should be female. Men don't often walk their dates to the restroom."

Chad smiled, then turned his attention back to the stage. Angel rose and followed Sarah through the narrow pathways around tables.

Heading toward a lighted sign that announced REST-ROOMS, Sarah caught a stronger whiff of smoke and followed the smell to a table near the arch of an alcove. A lone man sat there, a cigarette burning in the ashtray. She couldn't see the face below the brim of his fedora, but his general appearance raised a little alarm. He had a very refined look, just like Amber had described.

Sarah nudged Angel and gave a discreet nod in his direction.

As they neared the table, Sarah glanced at the man, who met her gaze for a moment, then turned away. Features weren't distinct, but there was something about the eyes. Hostile, almost feral. Forcing her feet to continue toward the alcove, Sarah fought an impulse to confront him directly. Better to formulate a plan first.

When the door closed behind them, she turned to Angel. "You see that guy we passed? The one with the hat?"

Angel nodded.

"Could be the guy Amber told us about. Go tell Chad to cover the hall to the back entrance. Then work your way toward the front." Sarah checked her watch. "In two minutes I'll come out and approach him."

Angel nodded again, then left. Sarah tried not to count the seconds as they ticked away, but adrenaline made her aware of every beat of her heart and kept her feet moving like a boxer warming up. After what seemed like an hour, it was time. She burst out of the ladies' room and immediately regretted not composing herself better. The man looked up as she stepped through the archway and something in her manner spooked him. He pushed away from the table and rose in one fluid motion.

"Stop!"

The command drew the attention of nearby patrons but didn't slow the man's steps. He pushed roughly past a waitress, upsetting her tray and sending drinks crashing across a table of four. One man stood abruptly. "What the hell!"

Wiping at spots on his dark jacket, he stepped into Sarah's path.

"Out of my way," she said, trying to get around him.

He didn't budge. "Look what you did."

Sarah shifted to her right to get past him, but he cut her off again, still wiping at the jacket. "Costs a fucking fortune to get this cleaned."

"Move!" Sarah had half a mind to deck him, but the arrival of the bouncer stilled the impulse.

The young man fixed cold blue eyes on her and rolled shoulders as wide as a stock car on a train. "What's the problem?"

Sarah caught a glimpse of her quarry just clearing the last cluster of tables. Angel wasn't close enough to catch him, but

Sarah urged her on with a broad sweep of her hand.

Angel followed her partner's wild gesture and saw the mystery man stride toward the front door. She took one more glance at her partner, who was still talking to the hired hulk, then took up the pursuit.

As if sensing her presence, the man shot a quick look over his shoulder, then bolted into the glittering entry. Angel saw the heavy outside door open as two men in evening finery stepped through. The mystery man brushed past them. She ran, heels skittering across the polished marble. Then she kicked off her shoes and sprinted the last few feet to the door.

Outside, shadows reigned and Angel ran blindly down the cold concrete steps. The lights of the parking lot shone like beacons and she headed in that direction, wincing when her foot landed solidly on a small stone. She faltered for a few steps as her instep adjusted to the pain, and she saw a dark car back out of a parking space. She wasn't close enough to distinguish the make, but it looked like a luxury sedan, and she caught a fraction of the plate number before the driver turned glaring headlights in her direction. The blinding light effectively killed her night vision as the car veered to her left with a squeal of protest from rubber. It was out of the parking lot without giving her a chance to see the rest of the plate.

Damn!

"You dropped something."

Angel turned to see Chad. He gave her a crooked grin and held out her shoes. "Might be better to wait a few months for barefoot walks in the moonlight."

She grabbed the shoes and tried to stuff her sore foot into the stiletto heel. Her foot didn't want to be stuffed anywhere. Chad leaned closer. "You okay?"

"Yeah."

"Fucking moron didn't believe I'm a cop." They both turned

to look at a breathless Sarah as she scanned the parking lot. "He still out there?"

Angel danced on the cold concrete. "Split."

"Son of a bitch!" Sarah looked at her partner, noticing the bare feet. "Put your shoes on, girl."

"Can't."

Chad burst out laughing.

Sarah looked from one to the other, then shook her head. "Let's go talk to some folks."

The manager, Jeffers, was not any more help tonight than he was the first day the detectives interviewed him. He did not know the name of the man they'd chased out of the club, and no, there were no receipts. The man had paid cash. He always paid cash.

"How long has he been coming here?" Sarah asked.

Jeffers shrugged. "I don't count their visits. Just the money."

"You son of a bitch." Sarah took a step toward Jeffers, but Chad stopped her with a touch of his hand.

"You don't want to do that," he said.

"Yes I do." But she backed off and took a deep breath before facing Jeffers again. "We need to talk to the waitress who worked that section." Sarah pointed to where the mystery man had been seated.

"You've disrupted my business enough for one evening, Detectives."

"Okay, now I really am going to hit him."

Sarah took a step forward and Chad grabbed her arm again. "What's gotten into you?"

"This sleezeball acting all high and mighty." Sarah pulled out of Chad's grasp.

"Well, this sleezeball has rights. And if he doesn't want us to talk to his help that's one of those rights."

"He also has the right to help us find the other sleezeball

who killed one of his girls," Sarah said. "But I guess he forgot about that one."

Jeffers smirked, but Angel gave a soft chuckle as she pulled Sarah toward the lobby. "Let's go outside where you can cool off."

"I've got something I need to do first." Sarah pushed past Jeffers and went to the table where the man had been sitting. The cigarette was still there. She grabbed a napkin and folded the cigarette into it.

Back in the lobby, she looked at Chad. "You got an evidence bag?"

He nodded and pulled one out of his suit coat pocket.

"Here." She handed the napkin over. "Get this to Roberts. We need to find out who that guy is."

The door opened behind her, and Angel started to step aside, but recognized the woman who entered as the one who had introduced them to Jeffers the first time they'd come to The Club. She touched the young woman on the arm. "Excuse me," she said. "Do you have a minute?"

The woman nodded, but a frown of puzzlement crossed her nearly flawless forehead.

"We met you the other day when we came in to talk to the manager," Angel said.

"Oh, right." She gave Angel a brief smile, then glanced at Sarah and Chad, letting her gaze rest on him for several seconds before her smile widened and she offered her hand to him. "Chantell Duffy."

"Detective Chad Smith." His smile almost matched hers in intensity, and Angel didn't know whether to laugh or slap the bitch for making a move on him. That little twinge of jealousy caught her up short. Hadn't she pretty well told him to shove off?

Before Angel could even think about sorting that all out,

Sarah stepped forward. "Do you work the evening shift very often?"

"I work the evening shift most of the time," Chantell said. "I was just here that afternoon you came in because Melody was sick. She normally takes care of the daytime clients."

"Do you get to know the men who come in frequently?" Sarah asked.

"Some. Not all of them." Her smile dimmed and she looked intently at each of the detectives in turn. "What is this about?"

"The dancer who was killed," Angel said. "Did Jeffers tell you about it?"

She shook her head. "He plays things pretty close to his chest."

"It's possible that a patron of The Club is responsible for the murder," Chad said.

Chantell let her gaze rest on him for a moment again, but this time there was nothing flirty in the look. "That can't possibly be."

"Actually, it can," Sarah said. "A few minutes ago there was a distinguished-looking man in a dark suit and gray fedora who bolted when we showed some interest in him," Sarah paused for a beat to let Chantell get her mind around that fact, then continued. "Amber, one of the dancers, described someone like him as a guy who had a special interest in Tracy."

Again Sarah paused to give the girl time to process. "Does anyone come to mind?"

Chantell shook her head slowly. "A lot of men wear hats and dark suits. I think they use them like disguises. So if their wives come in they won't recognize them."

"If he always sits in the same area, would one of the girls know more?"

"I don't know." Chantell started to shrug, then glanced over Sarah's shoulder. "Mr. Jeffers. I'm . . . uh . . . Just let me put

184

my things away and I'll be ready to work."

"Detectives." He gave them all a cold look. "Unless you have some papers to keep you here, I'll ask you to leave."

Sarah pulled a card out of her pocket and handed it to Chantell. "If you can help, call me."

Chantell snatched the card and moved off. Sarah hoped the woman listened between the lines, so to speak. It could be very helpful to talk to one of the waitresses. She gave a curt nod to Jeffers, then led the way out the door.

The next morning, Sarah noticed the slight gimp in Angel's stride as they neared the door of the conference room where McGregor waited for the early briefing. "How's the foot?" she asked.

"Protesting." Angel pulled a tissue from her pocket. "And I think I caught a cold."

"At least we caught something."

Angel grimaced as they stepped through the doorway, and Sarah realized her attempt at a joke did nothing to improve her state of mind either. It didn't help that she was running close to empty on her sleep tank. They'd been at the club until nearly two in the morning, managing to talk to one waitress in the parking lot as she was leaving. Then Sarah had gone home to a play-deprived Cat, who wasn't the least bit interested in sleep until nearly three-thirty. Did she dare add that extra hour to the overtime?

There was a small measure of consolation in the tight lines she saw squeezing McGregor's eyes. At least they weren't the only ones being pulled through the wringer.

"We got anything to make any kind of case on anybody?"

Sarah slumped into the chair next to him. "How about a third suspect?"

"I don't want to hear it."

"Lieu, these cases have more complications than Trump's love life."

McGregor took a deep breath and leaned back in the chair. "What's the latest?"

Sarah gave him a condensed version of the events at The Club, omitting the details of her confrontation with the hulk and Angel's barefoot romp.

"What did you find out about this guy?"

"Nothing." Angel said.

He looked from one to the other. "Nothing?"

"*Nada*. One waitress said she thought he's only been coming there for a few weeks. At least she hadn't seen him before that. But he could have come in on her days off. Manager said they didn't have a paper trail on him."

"You mean he just walked in there?"

Sarah shrugged.

"Probably happens a lot," Angel said. "They don't have security at the door."

McGregor rocked the chair on the back legs for a moment, then let it fall forward. "He ever approach any of the other dancers?"

"Amber wasn't even sure he was the guy who slipped Tracy the note. Just thought he could be," Angel said.

"So maybe he isn't."

"But maybe he is," Sarah said. "Let's not forget the fact that he ran."

"Might have been a politician running for his reputation."

The comment brought a laugh that relieved some of the tension, and the muscles in Sarah's neck unwound a bit.

McGregor turned to Angel. "What did Roberts get on that message to the other girl?"

Angel pulled out her notebook. "Plain bond paper. Sold in thousands of outlets to millions of customers. No prints. It was done on a laser printer. Probably a pricy one."

McGregor drummed stubby fingers on the table and chewed the inside of his cheek. Sarah watched for a moment, then turned to Angel. Where the hell could they go from here?

As if responding to the silent question, Angel cleared her throat. "We've got to be real careful, Lieu."

McGregor looked at her and she continued. "It's tempting to push facts together to end this mess. But we can't make something out of nothing."

The voice was different, but the wisdom was John's, and Sarah wondered if she'd been underestimating her partner all along. Before she could explore that thought, Angel continued. "We're a little thin on hard facts in these cases and no real evidence to speak of. I think—"

She was interrupted by Grotelli, who strode through the open door, a plastic evidence bag in his hand and a big grin on his face. Sarah could see a small metal object inside the bag.

"Ladies and gentlemen, I have good news," Grotelli said. "One of my guys just nabbed this out of Alvarez's trash. He would've brought it in himself, but he didn't smell so good. My guy, not Alvarez."

Sarah fingered the bag that Grotelli dropped on the table until she could see the object clearly. It was a blade from an X-acto knife.

McGregor stood and leaned over to get a closer look. "Hot damn!" He glanced at Sarah. "Get this over to Roberts. Then to Walt."

"Should we notify ADA Franklin?" Angel asked.

McGregor shook his head. "Nothing's solid yet. Let's just talk to the kid and see what he has to say."

CHAPTER NINETEEN

Sarah threw the bag with the knife blade on the table. Alvarez gulped, looked at LaVon, then back at her.

"It has your prints on it," Sarah said.

The kid swallowed again.

"And a trace of blood." Sarah leaned a hip against the table. "Figure that probably belongs to Tracy. But we'll know soon enough when the lab results come in."

"I didn't kill her."

"Why'd you throw the knife away?"

Alvarez turned to LaVon, who nodded.

"It had blood on it," Alvarez said, fingering a puff of white scar tissue on his palm. "I cut myself."

"You throw away a perfectly good knife because you got a little blood on it?" Sarah asked. "Couldn't you just wash it?"

LaVon cleared his throat. "Don't bait my client," he said. "He explained the blood on the blade, and it doesn't matter why he didn't wash it."

Sarah pulled out a chair and straddled it. "Okay. Here's the deal. We can do a DNA test. Prove the blood was yours. But say that test doesn't come out the way you want it to. Then we don't even have to talk. We've got you on murder one. Big case like this, the DA'll probably go for the needle."

"I didn't do it." Alvarez came halfway out of his chair, and LaVon held him back.

Sarah ignored the outburst. "But if you could say how maybe

you didn't mean to do it—"

"Don't be absurd, Detective." LaVon's voice was deceptively soft. "I've read the crime scene report. No way can we put a 'crime of sudden impulse' spin on this."

"You saying your client meant to kill her?"

Lavon smiled, and Sarah had a hard time getting past the way it transformed his whole face. Made it softer, friendlier. "The boy didn't do it."

Man. He's good. If I was on the jury I'd vote not guilty.

"And it's way too soon to fish for a deal." LaVon put the cap on his pen and closed his notebook.

"When a DNA test comes back, it may be too late," Sarah said, standing up.

"When the test comes back, we won't have to deal."

"Pretty confident there." Sarah pushed the chair up to the table. "For the sake of your client, I hope you know what you are doing."

"I always know what I am doing."

"Does that include allowing your client to give us a DNA sample?"

LaVon had a brief, whispered conference with Alvarez, then nodded.

Sarah picked up the evidence bag and motioned for LaVon and Alvarez to follow her. She took them to the lab, where a tech did a swab inside the kid's cheek.

"Can we go now?" LaVon asked.

She had nothing to hold Alvarez on, so Sarah nodded. "Make sure your client stays in town."

LaVon smiled again. "I didn't think cops really said that except on TV."

Sarah kept her expression impassive as she motioned them toward the door. She was far too familiar with the ploy of a disarming smile to fall for it here. She escorted them out, dropped the evidence off with Roberts and returned to the squad room.

Angel was at her desk, and Sarah wondered if she had spent the entire morning helping Simms and Burtweiler go through more of the records from the club.

Angel looked up. "How did it go with Alvarez?"

"Wish I could get a minute with him without his lawyer."

"I take it the interview wasn't fruitful."

"I did get a DNA swab," Sarah said. "That was worth something. But if the blood on the blade turns out to be his and not Tracy's, I think we can scratch him off our suspect list."

"Here's a little tidbit of information that can muddy up the waters some more," Angel tipped back her chair and smiled up at Sarah. "The esteemed Burke Clemment has a membership at The Club."

"You're kidding."

"Nope. And apparently he goes there frequently."

Sarah pulled up a chair and straddled it. "That may not mean anything."

"But what if it does? What if Daddy went to the club and saw his darling daughter dancing. Confronted her and then lost it?"

"But that would be a crime of passion. Peeples said it didn't look like a crime of passion."

"Clemment could have killed her in the heat of passion, then 'arranged' her afterward. The way she was covered could have been done by someone who loved her and couldn't face what he'd done."

Sarah shook her head. "I don't know. We could apply the same rationale to the Alvarez kid. And neither of them fit the profile Peeples gave us."

"True. But while we're waiting to see if the lab is going to clear Alvarez, it might be worth looking at Clemment's financials. See if we can put him at The Club sometime after Tracy started dancing."

"What about his alibi? The trip he was on when Tracy got killed. That seems pretty solid."

"There are ways around that," Angel said. "Maybe he hired it out."

"But the scene? That didn't look like a hired hit. Most of them are staged to look like an accident."

"True. I'm just saying."

"We go after Clemment, the commissioner's going to blow a gasket."

"That might be fun to watch."

Angel smiled again, and Sarah swore she saw a hint of mischief in her partner's dark eyes. "I thought you were the one who's supposed to keep us out of trouble," Sarah said.

Chad walked in, carrying what looked like a ream of paper. "Got this from the DMV," he said. "They ran the partial against registrations of large luxury vehicles. There's a bunch of them. It's going to take us a month of Sundays to go through all this."

"You can do that while we're in church," Sarah said.

"I didn't know you . . ." Angel stopped, then laughed. "Yeah. Right."

Chad just shook his head, walked over and dropped the papers on his desk.

"Let's take them to a conference room," Sarah said. "There's nothing else we can do until the results come back from the DNA test."

Chad raised an eyebrow in question, so Sarah filled him in on the developments with the Alvarez kid.

"So he's looking pretty good?" Chad asked.

"I don't know," Sarah said. "It would be nice if it was him. We could put this one to bed and move on. But there are too many loose ends that wouldn't be tied up with him."

"So we keep slogging until everything is nice and neat," Angel said.

Sarah nodded. "We keep slogging."

"And what is it that we are slogging for here?" Angel asked, nodding to the box of papers.

"Anything that pops out at us," Sarah said. "For starters, we could compare luxury car owners to the list of patrons who frequent The Club."

Two hours later, Sarah dropped the paper she had been looking at. It joined the others that were strewn across the conference table like a poorly dealt deck of cards. "I am done, done, done."

She stood and stretched, hearing little pops as vertebra clicked into place. "Going to go out for a good stiff drink, then head home." She paused and glanced at Chad and Angel. "I'm open to company."

"Can't tonight," Chad said. "Got plans for later."

Sarah didn't miss the little flicker of interest that crossed Angel's face, and she had to suppress the smile that threatened. "Angel?"

"Uh, no. Thanks."

No explanation. Just no, thanks? Sarah swallowed her irritation and headed out. Every time she thought things were getting better between them, Angel got all snarky on her.

Outside, a cold wind blew down the nearly deserted downtown streets. It had been almost balmy when Sarah came to work, so her light jacket was hardly protection at all. She hustled to the parking garage and opened the trunk of her Honda. A real Texan knows enough to keep a heavy coat handy in the winter, and Sarah had lived here long enough to be considered a real Texan. She traded coats, then got in the car and drove to her favorite watering hole.

Once inside, she shrugged out of the coat and hung it on the back of a barstool. She caught the bartender's eye and motioned for a drink. He didn't have to ask.

While she waited, Sarah glanced around the half-empty room, noting a couple of uniformed cops who must have just ended a shift. She gave them a nod before turning back to catch a bit of the late news playing on the TV above the bar. The bartender had switched channels from the local news to CNN after he brought her drink, and she was glad that she didn't have to watch the DPD being raked over the coals by their favorite reporter.

"Thanks." Sarah raised her glass and the bartender nodded. She took her first sip and it went down smooth and cool. She shifted on the bar stool when she sensed movement beside her, then glanced up to see LaVon as he straddled the stool next to her. She gave him a wary look. "Counselor."

He nodded briefly, then motioned to the bartender. "Ballantines. Neat."

"Sorry, sir, we don't carry that. I can offer you Chivas or Dewars."

"Dewars, then."

The bartender set a glass in front of LaVon and poured. Sarah took a sip of her Rob Roy and waited out the silence. When the other man moved away, LaVon picked up his glass, gave her a slight salute with it and swallowed half the contents. "I hate having to accept a substitute," he said.

"I gather you are particular about your scotch."

"Actually, Ballantines is one of the finest whiskeys made. Dewars is a scotch whiskey."

"Oh." Sarah took another swallow of her drink. "How edifying."

LaVon smiled, and again Sarah was struck at the transformation on his face. The smile softening the lines around his mouth made him much less formidable, and she wondered if he knew that. Used it to disarm a jury. Then she realized she was silly for even wondering. He was a successful attorney. He didn't get that way by not being aware of his effect on people.

"Can we talk?"

Sarah raised her glass in a "go ahead" gesture.

"Are you seriously going to charge my client? Or was today just a fishing expedition?"

"That's up to the DA."

"You need to look elsewhere."

Sarah just gave him a look.

"The kid is innocent."

Sarah laughed. "That's what they all say."

"He really did love her."

Sarah laughed again. "And nobody was ever killed by someone who loved them."

"Touché." LaVon finished his drink and motioned for another. "You want one?"

Her first impulse was to decline, but then she thought, what the hell. She nodded and LaVon caught the bartender's attention and pointed to her glass.

"What do you have if the DNA test shows the blood on the knife doesn't match the victim?" LaVon asked after the drinks were poured.

"That's getting a little too specific, Counselor. We shouldn't be discussing the case."

"Consider it part of discovery."

Sarah took a hefty swallow of her drink, then set the glass down. "I'm not comfortable with any of this."

He took a deep breath, glanced away, then back at her. "Of all people, I thought you would understand."

"Understand what?"

"What it feels like to be falsely accused."

She took a moment to assimilate his words and all they

implied. "Word was, you thought I was guilty of murder."

"Angel tell you that?"

Sarah nodded.

"I never said you committed murder." LaVon shifted on the stool. "What I said was innocent black boys don't need to be shot."

"And that's not the same thing?"

"No. 'Cause I don't think you meant to kill that boy."

"You might have said something while the Review Board and the good Reverend Norton were all over my ass."

"And incur my daddy's wrath?" LaVon shook his head. "I'm sure Angel told you about him, too."

Sarah laughed. "She did, yes. But she didn't have to. I got a pretty good sense of what he thought of me that day in the hospital."

"Yeah, well, we were all under a bit of a strain."

"Angel says your mother is recovering well."

"She's better. Lots better. But she will never fully recover."

A hint of sadness washed over his face, and Sarah fought an impulse to touch his cheek in a gesture of understanding.

"I'm sorry," LaVon said. "I shouldn't have—"

"It's okay."

The subtle shift in the atmosphere was both scary and exciting. Sort of like standing at the edge of the high dive and wondering how cold the water is.

Sarah could empathize with him. She'd been through enough sickness and loss to know what he was feeling. But this . . . whatever it was . . . was also opening a door she never thought would be opening.

"Do you like to ride?"

The question stunned her. "What?"

"Horses. Do you like to ride horses?"

"I don't know. Never did it."

"You should try it sometime." He took a sip of his drink. "Great stress reliever."

She laughed. "Not sure that would work for me. Just trying to hang on would cause me as much stress as the job."

"Nah." He smiled. "I could get you an old nag that wouldn't have the energy to throw you."

The banter was light and breezy, but the look in his eye was anything but. "Are you asking me out, Counselor?"

He shrugged. "Only if you're interested."

Whoa there, hormones.

"What would Daddy say?"

"Daddy doesn't have to know everything I do." He paused for a beat. "Neither does Angel."

Sarah glanced quickly away and made a big production out of folding a napkin and putting it under her glass. He was serious, and she shouldn't just leave the question hanging. But what could she say? There were a million reasons she should say no, starting with her partner. Angel would blow a gasket. But then, LaVon was right. Angel wouldn't have to know.

He touched her arm. "Let me make this easy for you. I understand your reluctance."

She searched his eyes, wondering if he thought her hesitation was based on something other than professional ethics or the wrath of her partner. "It's not—"

"No need to explain."

Something in his tone told her she should. "This is awkward, but not because of this . . ." she touched his cheek. "There are professional boundaries we should probably not step over right now."

"Of course." He seemed to gather himself tighter and pulled slightly away from her. "I should never have . . ."

Sarah waited for him to finish, but he just shrugged. In the mirror behind the bar she could see him looking at her. She leaned into him. "Maybe when the case is finished you could . . . or we could . . ."

He didn't respond. He dropped a couple of bills on the bar and left. Just like that. Walked out. *What is it with this family?*

Sarah nursed the rest of her drink, wondering if she should have ignored professional ethics and just said "yes" to the man. God knows, she had been sorely tempted. No matter how hard she tried, she couldn't ignore the fact that he had an appeal that was speaking directly to her. In addition to being incredibly attractive, he was smart, funny and kind. She had seen the kindness at the hospital, and she'd even seen it in the way he treated his client. There was definitely a tender side to this man.

And he's black.

That thought caught her up short. She'd never before thought about crossing racial lines. That was part of her Deep South upbringing. And was that really the reason she hesitated in her response?

She sighed. It didn't matter now. He would probably never ask again. And maybe that was for the best.

CHAPTER TWENTY

After roll call the next morning, Sarah looked at more of the reports from the DMV. It was the tedious kind of police work that sometimes made her mind turn to mush, so it was a relief when Gladys called to say someone was there to see her. Sarah walked to the entrance to the CAPERS unit and saw a young woman standing next to Gladys. Wide, dark eyes dominated a face that paled in the overhead neon. Sarah looked closely at the girl and recognized her as one of the hookers she had met that night with Angel. When had it been? It seemed like months ago. Today the girl was dressed in a tight leather mini-skirt and a red halter top, a black cardigan her only protection from the weather outside. "You wanted to see me?" Sarah asked, drawing the girl away from Gladys, who went back to her desk near the gate.

"Yeah." The girl flicked a nervous glance around the busy squad room.

"What's your name?"

"Mariella, uh . . . or do you want my real name?"

"That'll do for now." Sarah nodded toward the steps leading to the homicide area. "Let's talk back here."

Sarah led the way and motioned for the girl to sit in the wooden chair in front of her desk.

The girl perched on the chair's edge like a bird poised for a quick escape. "I heard what happened to Rosie."

"Do you know something about it?"

"Not really." Mariella shifted her gaze and her posture, and Sarah caught a whiff of the sour odor of sweat. Nervous sweat.

"Are you afraid of something?"

"Well, Reba told me not to come here."

"Why not?"

"Jingo. He's not going to like it."

"He scare you?"

"Some."

The girl shifted again, beads of perspiration popping out on her forehead. Sarah reined in her impulse to push, and Mariella looked at her again. "You think he did Rosie?"

"You think he would?"

"I guess." Mariella shrugged. "If he had a reason."

"What might that reason be?"

Mariella worried a scrap of cuticle on a well-chewed fingernail. "He likes us to stay in line."

"In line?"

"Yeah. Do what we're told. Remember who takes care of us."

"He doesn't like girls to leave?"

She shook her head.

"Was Rosie going to leave?"

"She never said so." The thumbnail got more attention. "It could have been that other guy."

Sarah sat up. "What other guy?"

"Reba said it was probably nothing. Lots of johns act a little strange."

"Strange how?"

"Quiet." The girl shrugged. "Course, they usually don't come to talk."

"Can you describe this guy? His car?"

"Big dark thing. Looked like money."

"Make. Model? Plate number?"

Mariella smiled. "Honey. We don't bother with plate numbers."

Sarah couldn't help but return the smile. There was something endearing about this young woman in spite of her profession. She looked like a waif from Appalachia. "What about the man?"

"He only came by a couple of times, so I never did get a good look at him." She paused to think for a moment. "But he wore a hat. Not like a baseball cap, but a real hat."

Sarah's mind made a quantum leap. Could that john be the mystery man from The Club? It didn't matter that McGregor considered the mystery man the least likely suspect. There was just something about him that jangled alarms for her every time she considered him. Of course, her alarms had jangled for dead ends before, too.

"Did you ever go with him?"

The girl shook her head, a slight movement that barely disturbed her long dark hair. "I thought about it. Figured he had some serious money, but Chrystal warned me off."

"Why?"

"She said he was wacko. Took her one night, but didn't do anything. Just wanted her to undress, then dance. Freaked her out."

"You have a number for this Chrystal?"

"Na. And I ain't seen her around in a while."

"What about the guy?"

"Ain't seen him neither."

Sarah slid a card across the table. "Call me if he shows up again."

Mariella reached for the card, then pulled her hand back. "Maybe I shouldn't. Jingo wouldn't like it."

Sarah resisted the urge to give the girl a version of the advice she'd given Amber. Something about these young, defenseless women made her want to mother them, and she didn't know where that was coming from. She'd never felt the slightest urge to mother anything. Was she having issues with her biological clock that she wasn't even aware of?

She shook the thought aside and walked Mariella out. Then she went to the break room to get a cup of coffee. It was dark and poured like sludge, releasing an odor reminiscent of burnt rubber, but it was caffeine. She added some creamer to counter the acid and was just sitting down at a table when Burtweiler walked in. "Got a forensic report for you," he said. "The lab picked up prints from the pimp at the motel where that hooker was found. According to the crime scene tech, the prints were recent. They were laid over other prints."

"Great." Sarah glanced at the report while she finished her coffee. Then she tossed the Styrofoam cup in the trash, grabbed the folder and headed out. "Thanks for bringing it by."

"No problem," Burt said to the empty room.

The door to McGregor's office was open, and he was seated behind his desk, suit coat off revealing a wrinkled white shirt with prominent sweat stains. Maybe he needed a mother, too. She stepped in. "We might have caught a break in the hooker's death."

McGregor motioned her to come all the way in. "What is it?"

"The lab picked up prints from the pimp. That guy Jingo."

"What the hell kind of name is that for a pimp?"

Sarah dropped the folder on top of the mess on his desk and sat down in the chair facing him. "I don't know, Lieu. I'm not responsible."

McGregor opened the folder and scanned the contents. "Anything to tie him to the Clemment girl?"

"No."

"We really need to get something." He looked up at her. "My ass is burning on this one."

Sarah knew what he meant. They were all feeling the heat. Helen had called her every day since the investigation started, and that was almost unheard of.

"We can't make anything stick if it doesn't have glue," Sarah said.

"I know. I know." He brushed a hand across a stubble of beard. "I wouldn't want you to."

"As much as I'd like to wrap these two cases up with the pimp, it's just not working for me," Sarah said, leaning forward. "We don't know if the Clemment girl knew the pimp or was even hooking. According to what her friend said, she wasn't. So I think we're better off focusing on the Alvarez kid. Or find that guy who ran from The Club the other day."

"How the hell do you plan to do that?"

"I just talked to this hooker who told me about a john the girls were all leery of. He fit the description of the guy we saw at The Club. One girl went with him and she could give us a lead."

"You know where this girl is?"

"No. But we can find out. That's what cops do."

"Don't be a smartass. I'm not in the mood."

Something in his tone made Sarah take a closer look at him. Were the lines of tension in his face deeper, or was that just her imagination? "Everything okay, Lieu?"

"Dandy. Just dandy."

"You're looking a little rough around the edges."

McGregor raised cold eyes to hers. "You gonna smooth me out?"

"No, sir. Just saying."

McGregor motioned toward the door, then swiveled his chair so he was facing the grimy little window behind his desk.

Sarah took the hint and left. She wasn't about to prod him when he was doing his grizzly bear impersonation. She could imagine the heat he was feeling from a lot of directions. The brass was probably all over him about his drinking, but she was sure that the drinking had not impaired his judgment . . . yet.

That was the problem. Yet. If he didn't ease up, no telling what would happen to his career. Stopping entirely was probably not an option, but he definitely could not keep escalating.

She shook off the thoughts and went back to the squad room just as Angel returned from her morning in court, looking all dapper in a dark blue blazer and gray skirt. She'd been testifying in an old robbery case that dated back to her days in uniform. A snail could move faster than the wheels of justice.

"How'd it go?" Sarah asked.

"Short and sweet," Angel said. "I spent more time waiting to be called than I did on the stand."

Sarah chuckled and reached for the phone. "I'm going to call O'Donnell in Vice to see if he can give us a lead on a girl we should talk to."

Angel shrugged off her blazer and sat down at her desk. "New case?"

"No. Just new information. That young hooker we saw on the streets came in today. Talked about a john who was a little hinky. Gave the name of a girl who might know more."

"And I suppose you're going to want to talk to this girl."

"If we can find her." Sarah held up one finger and spoke into the receiver. "Hey, it's Kingsly. You know a girl on the streets goes by the name Chrystal?"

"Yeah. I think so," Ryan said, "hold on a sec." Sarah could hear the sounds of paper shuffling, then Ryan came back on the line. "We hauled her in with a bunch of girls just last week. Her work name is Chrystal Strand. AKA Sandra White."

"Is she locked up?"

"Nope. Made bail the next day."

"You know where we can find her?"

"I know where she likes to set up. We can probably locate her."

"Okay. Let me know when you're free to go streetwalking."

"Is she connected to your case?"

"Maybe. Just exploring possibilities."

Sarah hung up and swiveled her chair to face Angel.

"Please don't ask me to go with you again," Angel said.

Sarah laughed. "I won't. Ryan and I can cover it."

Angel was filling out her daily report when Helen came striding into the squad room. She motioned to Angel and Sarah. "Conference room. Now."

From the look on the chief's face, Angel knew better than to ask why. She got up and followed the two women, Helen leading the way with long, purposeful strides that made Angel have to hustle to keep up. Chad and McGregor were already seated at the long wooden table, watching a news broadcast on the TV in the corner.

On screen, Burke Clemment addressed a group of reporters. He was flanked by his wife on one side and Mayor Talbert with Commissioner Hanson on the other. "It is unconscionable that the police can't seem to find this monster who stole our little girl from us."

At that, the wife dabbed her eyes and Clemment seemed to get a firmer set to his jaw. "We are offering a fifty thousand-dollar reward to anyone who can lead us to the killer."

Angel groaned, and Helen motioned her to be quiet. "Commissioner Hanson has promised me that a tip line will be set up by this evening. So we ask for the public's help. Please. If you know anything. Anything at all. Don't hesitate to call."

This time Helen did not try to silence the groans as the news show cut away to another story.

McGregor muted the TV as the three women took seats at

the long table. He nodded to Helen. "Couldn't you stop this bullshit?"

"I tried. But Clemment's got more juice upstairs than I do."

"So now we have to spend hours responding to every crackpot in town that's going to call?" Sarah asked. "We're stretched about as thin as we can get, and we have other leads to follow up on."

"What leads?" Helen asked.

"We've got this hooker I was going to try to find tonight," Sarah said, quickly briefing the chief on the mystery man they were looking for. "This john could be the same guy who bolted from us at the club."

"And you think he might have done the girl and the hooker?"

"Maybe," Angel said. "He seems more likely for both than the other two suspects we're looking at."

Helen looked to McGregor. "The boyfriend and the pimp you told me about?"

McGregor nodded. "The boyfriend could be good for the girl, but not for the hooker. And so far there is nothing showing a connection between the pimp and the girl."

"That's right," Chad said. "At first I thought the pimp could have done both. The two crime scenes did have some similarities. But we haven't found a single scrap of evidence to tie him to Tracy."

"He's still a lot stronger suspect than some mystery man," Helen said. "Find that hooker and see what she has to say. But don't overlook the boyfriend. Keep working all the angles and see what pops." She sighed. "We've got to get something soon or Clemment will have all our asses."

"How are we going to do that and man the tip line?" Angel said, barely concealing her irritation.

Helen shot her a sharp look, and Angel knew she had crossed the line. But she didn't care. The brass was always pissing on them from on high.

"I'm sure you can get the job done," Helen said.

As the detectives walked back to the squad room, Angel paused and held up a hand. "Do you hear that?"

"What?" Sarah asked.

"The ringing of a million telephones."

Sarah laughed and sat down at her desk. "I'll call Grotelli and see if he can spare a couple of Uniforms to help deal with the callers."

CHAPTER TWENTY-ONE

Sarah put a Lean Cuisine into the microwave, moving carefully from the freezer to the counter so she didn't trip over Cat, who was twining around her legs, his purr sounding like a diesel truck. "If you'd sit over there like a nice kitty, I could do this faster and get to your dinner."

Cat regarded her with his large, amber eyes, an expression in them that seemed to say, "What, you don't like the attention?"

At least that's the message Sarah pretended the cat was conveying instead of, "Get my dinner, bitch."

She managed to get his food dish filled, then gave him fresh water before going to her bedroom to change. Ryan had suggested they try not to look too much like cops when they went looking for Chrystal, but Sarah didn't want to look like a hooker either, especially since another cold front had blasted through, and the wind-chill was hovering in the teens. *Maybe I could be a hooker in a mink.* That thought made her laugh out loud. A hooker wouldn't be any more able to afford a mink than she would, at least not the ones who worked for a pimp like Jingo.

McGregor's right. What kind of name is that for a pimp?

The ding of the microwave ended her speculation. She ate from the container, disregarding the little voice in her head that sounded like her grandmother, "Sarah, civilized people sit down at the table to eat their dinner."

When she was finished, she put the container down for Cat to lick, ignoring another voice trying to remind her that cats should only eat cat food.

Cleanup was quick and easy, then she went into her bedroom to get ready. She pulled on some classy leather boots that rode high on her calf and grabbed a bold red sweater. With her trench coat as a buffer to the frigid weather, she would look more like a journalist than a cop.

When she pulled into the station parking lot, Ryan was already there. He was sitting in what could have been the same plain vanilla unmarked Buick that she and Angel used so often. She slid into the passenger seat and noted the deep gouge on the door panel.

It was the same car.

"All set?" Sarah asked.

"Yeah. As soon as you fasten your seat belt."

After pulling out into traffic, Ryan asked, "You really think this girl knows something pertinent to the murder of the Clemment girl?"

Sarah gave a slight shake of her head. "I don't know. Just pursuing all angles."

"From what Angel told me about the case, I wouldn't put any money on this little venture." Ryan paused to ease over to the right to take an exit ramp off I-75. "I don't think the girl was hooking, and I don't think she was connected to Jingo."

"You're probably right," Sarah said. "Pursuing that angle is probably a huge waste of time. But I also want to talk to her about a john Mariella told me about."

"Oh?"

"She mentioned some guy that came around now and then. Drove a big, dark luxury car, and always acted a bit strange. She said that Chrystal went with him once and all he wanted her to do was dance."

"You're shittin' me."

"Nope."

"I've heard a lot of strange practices, but that one beats them all. Nothing sexual at all?"

"Nope. Unless she did a strip-tease and the guy got off that way."

Ryan laughed, then pulled into the parking lot of a little dive called Loupe's and parked at the far end. Part of one wall was covered in old tin that reminded Sarah of the outbuildings where she grew up. Some people called them barns, but they weren't much more than the shacks the people lived in. This was definitely not a place she would come back to visit.

"Chrystal usually hangs on that next street." Ryan killed the engine and opened his door. "Figured we could walk around real casual like and maybe not spook her."

Sarah pulled her coat closed and jammed a knitted hat on her head. It made the cold barely tolerable as she followed Ryan down the street and around the corner. At first she didn't see any activity. The street was dark. Most of the street lamps were out, and the only light came from a bar that had a blinking Open sign with half the bulbs missing or broken. The window in the door of the joint was so grimy it might have been non-existent. "Geez," she said. "If a john wanted to pick up a girl here, how the hell would he see her?"

Ryan laughed. "The regulars know where to look. And these girls are cheap enough they have lots of regulars."

They approached the building, and Ryan pointed. "There she is."

Sarah saw a thin young woman with a tumble of blonde curls hanging well below her shoulders. She wore what Sarah was starting to think of as the "hooker's costume"—tight leather skirt, low-cut blouse, lots of makeup and sparkling jewelry.

As the detectives approached, Chrystal started to sidle away.

"Hold on there," Ryan said. "We just want to talk."

"Last time I talked to you, I ended up busted."

"Not this time." He held up two fingers. "Scout's honor."

"That don't mean shit to me."

Sarah took a half step closer. "Please. Just give us a minute."

"What's in it for me?"

"Maybe I can get you a free pass for the next time you're picked up by Vice."

Chrystal hesitated as if considering, then nodded. "Five minutes. Then get out of here. I have a quota to meet."

A quota? She's got a fuckin' quota? Sarah resisted the urge to slap the girl until her brain woke up. She took a deep breath to quell the flash of anger. "Ryan here tells me you work for Jingo," she said. "Is that right?"

The girl nodded.

"Has he ever been rough with you? Rough enough that you were scared of him?"

"Yeah." She glanced away, then back again. "He says he has to do it. Keep us in line."

Sarah shook her head. *Like I haven't heard that before.* "Did it ever get beyond 'keeping us in line'?"

"Not with me. But Rachel got hurt pretty bad once. Had broken ribs." She hugged herself as if protecting her own. "And a couple of girls haven't been around in a while. But I always figured they just left town."

"Did you hear about the girl who was found dead at the Cameo Motel the other day?" Ryan asked.

Chrystal nodded.

"She was one of Jingo's girls, wasn't she?"

"Maybe. I don't know. She was never down around here, but we all knew Jingo has other girls."

"Do you think he could have killed her?" Ryan asked.

The girl sucked in a breath and held it so long, Sarah wondered if she was ever going to let it out. "He could have," she finally said, the breath coming out in a soft whoosh and riding the cold air. "I saw him cut a dog's throat once for pee-ing on the tire of his car."

"Chrystal, I talked to Mariella today," Sarah said. "She told me about this john you went with once who acted kind of hinky."

"What do you mean? Hinky?"

"The one who only wanted you to dance."

"Is that how he . . . um . . . satisfied himself?" Ryan asked.

Chrystal laughed, a light pleasant sound that could have come from a child. "Look at you, all embarrassed," she said. "Big bad cop."

Sarah smiled. "Well, did he?"

"No. I don't think so." Chrystal paused to think a moment. "No. I'm positive. There was no hand-humping going on. He just watched, then gave me a hundred-dollar bill and left."

"Wait a minute," Sarah said. "He gave you a hundred-dollar bill? Not an assortment of bills?"

Chrystal nodded.

"Do many johns pay like that? With a single bill?"

Chrystal shook her head. "It's not common. That's one of the reasons I remembered him."

"What else do you remember about him?" Ryan asked.

"He was dressed formal-like. Dark suit and dark hat. And he never took the hat off. He gave me the creeps when he first stopped. That big black car sliding up alongside the curb made me think of a panther sidling up to a deer. And he was so soft-spoken . . ." She paused, as if going back to that night in her memory. "I almost didn't go with him, but it had been a slow night. I needed something to give to Jingo or he would have had my ass in more ways than one."

"So you went with the john," Sarah prompted.

"Yeah. He waved the money at me, and I was like a little dog responding to the offer of a treat."

"What can you tell me about the car?" Sarah asked. "Did you

get a plate number?"

"No. But I remember what kind of car it was. I don't often get a chance to ride in a Cadillac Seville."

The next morning, Sarah had barely settled at her desk to write up her report from the night before when Grotelli sauntered up to her desk. His uniform was so crisp, he could have been turning out for a parade or a visiting dignitary. "My guys finished running that partial plate from The Club," he said. "There are two hundred and twenty-five that go with some kind of large luxury car like Angel said she saw. Black ones, that is."

"Thanks." Sarah took the list from Grotelli and scanned it, stopping abruptly when she came to the fifth name. Rebecca Modine. She looked back at Grotelli. "Your guys check any of these out?"

"And deprive you of the pleasure? No way, ma'am." Grotelli gave her a mock salute, then marched away as if he really was in a parade.

Angel was in court again this morning, another long-ago crime finally getting prosecuted, so Sarah was on her own to start checking to see if any of the car owners frequented The Club. Based on what Chrystal had said, Sarah decided to start calling the people who owned a Cadillac. Over the next couple of hours, she got a variety of responses, ranging from threats to report her for harassing innocent people, to righteous indignation that she would even suggest such a thing. The loudest of that lot was a Mrs. Sandell, wife of a Baptist minister, who told Sarah she could rot in hell for even thinking such terrible things about a man of the cloth.

Sarah rolled her shoulders to ease the tension in her neck and considered Modine's name again. She'd skipped over it in making her calls, thinking it wouldn't pay to call a woman, especially not a woman who was so prim and proper, she would have more indignation than the minister's wife. On the other hand, she owned a Cadillac, and she could have a brother or a boyfriend who used her car. It wouldn't do to not check that out.

Reaching for the phone, Sarah was going to call the school, then paused and made a rash decision. She would go talk to Modine in person. Rattling her cage a little would be a lot more fun than sitting at her desk making calls. Angel was due back soon; they could both go.

"I didn't much care for this school the first time we came," Angel said. "And I like it even less the second time around."

Sarah laughed. "It's so quiet, it's eerie."

"If I didn't know better I'd swear the staff doped the kids."

"Maybe they do." Sarah opened a door and the detectives stepped into the outer office of the headmistress. Again, Sarah was struck by how much the room looked like a small alcove in a high-end hotel. Not that she had much personal experience in places like that, but she'd seen pictures.

The petite woman at the desk looked up, a flicker of surprise crossing her face before she offered a polite smile. "Detectives. I wasn't aware you had another appointment."

"We don't," Angel said. "But if Ms. Modine is free, we will only take a moment of her time."

"She's a busy—"

"We are aware that she is very busy," Sarah said. "But so are we. Trying to solve the murder of one of your former students."

The secretary had the good grace to blush as she picked up a phone to let Modine know they were there. She spoke in a hushed tone that Sarah could barely hear, then hung up. "She asked if you could please wait. She has a student with her."

Ten minutes later a girl bolted out of the back office, leaving the door open. She didn't look at the secretary or the detectives as she hustled past. Angel watched the girl and shook her head. "Wonder what she did to incur the wrath of the headmistress."

"We probably don't want to know."

Rebecca Modine came to the doorway of her office and motioned to the detectives. "You may come in now."

She turned abruptly and walked back toward her desk.

"Now I feel like *I'm* being called to the principal's office," Sarah said.

"Probably happened to you a lot, I'll bet."

Sarah shot her partner a sharp look, then took note of the smile and relaxed. It was just a joke. She wondered if there would come a time when they wouldn't be so touchy with each other, second-guessing every comment and gesture. She dismissed the thought with a sigh and followed Angel into the office. It looked much the same as it had last time, except today there was a paper on the desk. Modine had already taken a seat and had her hands on the paper, fingers laced together as if offering a supplication.

"What can I do for you today, Detectives?"

The tone took Sarah back to sixth grade when she had been caught trying to walk out of science class and out of the school forever. That young girl wanted to ask Modine if they could sit down, but the grown-up Sarah sat without asking.

"Would you mind telling us where you were two nights ago? Or, more specifically, where your car was?" Angel asked.

Modine unlaced her fingers and tapped them lightly on the paper. "Was there some kind of accident?"

Sarah shook her head. "We're tracking down cars that could have been at a gentleman's club Tuesday night. You wouldn't happen to be a fan of that kind of dancing, would you?"

"I resent the—"

"Please just answer the question, Ms. Modine."

"I was home Tuesday night." Modine spoke through lips

drawn so tight, the words barely made it out.

"Did anyone use your car that night?" Angel asked. "A brother? Boyfriend?"

Sarah noticed a slight twitch in the woman's face at the mention of a boyfriend. "Do you have a boyfriend, Ms. Modine?"

"No. Not really."

"Not really? What kind of answer is that? Either you do or you don't."

Modine puffed up with indignation. "I do not like your tone, young lady. Nor do I appreciate these personal questions. So, unless you have reason to take up my valuable time, I must ask you to leave."

Sarah leaned across the desk. "Can anyone confirm you were home Tuesday night?"

"I live alone. You could ask my dog."

"Nobody borrowed your car?"

"I'm not in the habit of lending my possessions."

"And you absolutely did not go to The Club that night?"

Modine's face turned a dangerous shade of red. "You will leave. Now."

"I'll leave when—"

"We're ready now." Angel stood and grabbed Sarah's arm, pulling her toward the door. "Thank you, Ms. Modine."

Out in the hall, Angel turned to Sarah. "What were you doing pushing so hard? Are you seriously taking a look at her, or do you just mistrust all rich people?"

"What the hell are you talking about?"

"First the father. Now the headmistress? You're treating them with more disdain than you do the scum on the streets."

"What makes you think she's rich?"

"I just . . ." Angel shook her head and started walking away.

Sarah hurried to catch up. "Let's just follow this and see where it leads."

"Follow what?" Angel stopped.

"The lady. Do a background check. Find out what was making her sweat while we were talking to her."

"You were making her sweat," Angel said. "It's like you enjoy pissing people off."

Sarah laughed. "She talks like a Yankee. I don't trust Yankees."

Angel shook her head again and this time she did walk away. Sarah followed slowly, stopping in the parking lot by a black Cadillac Seville parked in the spot reserved for the headmistress. Careful not to get too close and set off the alarm, Sarah walked around the car. Angel walked over. "What are you doing?"

"Could this be the car you saw that night?"

"Oh, for Pete's sake. You're relentless."

"Relentless solves cases."

Angel sighed. "What is with you? Modine's a woman. It was a man who went tearing out of The Club that night."

"You're right. But she never did answer our question about loaning out her car." Sarah's cell phone chirped and she pulled it out of her jacket pocket and flipped it open. "Kingsly."

She listened for just a moment, then closed the phone and appeared to forget all about Modine and the car. "Let's book," she said to Angel. "Chad caught a break. Got the pimp to confess to killing the prostitute."

CHAPTER TWENTY-TWO

Sarah looked through the one-way glass at the pimp, Jingo, slumped in a chair. He didn't look so full of himself now.

"He swears it was an accident," Chad said. "Didn't mean to kill Rosie. They fought and he pushed her. She fell and hit her head on the table. He didn't even realize she was dead until he couldn't find a pulse."

"How'd he explain cutting her throat?" Angel asked. "Another accident?"

"He said he did that to make it look the same as the other murder. Figured the perp from that would get blamed for both."

"But why go to all that trouble?" Sarah asked. "Why not just walk away? He's got to know that dead prostitutes get about as much attention as a girl with braces and pimples at a dance."

"McGregor's thinking maybe they look the same because they are the same," Chad said. "He wants us to sweat him."

"Did he forget we already took a run at him?" Angel asked.

"I reminded him. He said try again."

"The order came from higher up, didn't it." Sarah gave him a knowing look, her inflection making it clear that was not a question.

"Yup." Chad grinned. "So go in there and raise the humidity."

Angel waved and headed down the hall. "He's all yours, sister. Paperwork looks kind of appealing to me right about now."

Sarah walked into the interrogation room and pushed hard

against Jingo's chair as she crossed behind him. He whirled to look at her. "Hey, watch it, bitch."

"Don't."

The single word hung there for a moment, and Sarah noted that Jingo's arrogance slipped just a notch.

"Don't what?"

"Don't be calling me names. No telling what I might do if I get mad."

"I'm sposed to be scared of some honky?" The words were tough, but a nerve twitched in his cheek.

"See now, Jingo. That ain't right." Sarah kicked his chair again. "You calling me names like that. I might be the only thing standing between you and the death penalty."

"What you talkin' about? I tole that other cop I didn't mean to kill Rosie. Can't give me no death penalty for an accident."

"This isn't about Rosie. It's about that other girl, Tracy Clemment."

"Oh, man." Jingo wiped a hand across his face. "You can't hang that one on me."

"Actually, we can." Sarah took the other chair and straddled it. "We found your print where her body was found."

"Can't be. I was never there."

"You were never where, Jingo?"

"At that place the girl was killed."

"And what place was that?"

"I don't know."

"Then how do you know you weren't there?"

" 'Cause I never killed that girl."

"Maybe you didn't mean to. Maybe it was an accident like it was with Rosie."

"I tole you I never killed her." Jingo came flying out his chair so fast, Sarah barely had time to react. She jumped up and pushed him back down as Chad burst into the room. "Need some help?"

"No." Sarah didn't take her eyes from Jingo. "I got this."

Chad hesitated a moment, then backed out of the room. Sarah sat back down. "Why'd you kill Rosie?"

"Huh?"

"You heard me."

"I already said I didn't mean to."

"I know. And I think that's bullshit. Word is, you don't like your girls to give you any trouble. Not above using a little force if you have to."

"That don't mean nothin'."

"That's not what I heard. I heard you can get pretty rough if one of the girls steps out of line."

Jingo shrugged.

"Is that what happened with Tracy?"

"How many times I got to tell you?" Jingo leaned forward and punctuated each word with a loud thump on the table. "She was not one of my girls. And I did not kill her."

"Then how come your prints were found at the motel where she was killed?"

"I dunno. I don't remember every motel I was ever in. Maybe it was some place I did some business."

"You did some business all right." Sarah slapped the picture of Tracy on the table.

Jingo shook his head and crossed his arms across his chest.

"Look at her. She was just a kid. Why'd you have to go and do that?"

Jingo just kept shaking his head.

"You're going down for Rosie. You might as well come clean for this one, too." Sarah pushed the picture of Tracy closer to him. "You cooperate, maybe the DA won't ask for the death penalty."

"I want a lawyer." He said that with a smirk, but Sarah noted the little flicker of fear in his eyes. She waited a beat to see if he would say anything else, then sighed. She stood, slipped the picture back into the folder and walked out, joining Angel, Chad and McGregor in the viewing room.

"Nice try," Chad said.

"Thanks, but I don't think he did the girl."

"Send the paperwork to ADA Franklin anyway," McGregor said.

"What?"

"You heard me."

"But we don't have enough evidence."

"The print is enough for now. We'll get more."

"I'd like to know from where."

He gave her a glacial look. "Do it. That's an order."

McGregor left so quickly, he created a slight breeze as he passed Sarah.

Angel shook her head. "He can't be serious."

"Sounded pretty damn serious to me," Chad said. "I guess we turn it over to Jessica and see what happens."

Sarah was about to wrap it up for the day when she looked up to see ADA Jessica Franklin stride purposefully into the room, creating quite a stir. She had a way of commanding a room by virtue of her striking beauty—she could double for Halle Berry—but also by virtue of her ability. She was one tough prosecutor, and she took quarter from nobody. Sarah was always glad the woman was on their side of the table.

Jessica stopped by Sarah's desk, and Sarah recognized the signs of a pending storm in the firm set of the woman's jaw and flashes of anger in her brown eyes. "Just what in the hell were you thinking?"

Sarah waited. She knew an answer wasn't needed, or even wanted, until Jessica had a chance to finish venting.

"One stupid fingerprint. That's all you've got? You want me to add another murder charge on this pimp with barely a scrap of evidence?" She paused to take a short breath. "A judge just might order my arrest for stupidity."

Jessica sat down in the chair in front of Sarah's desk and shook her head. "I am not believing this. You guys keep throwing suspects at us like darts."

"It wasn't my idea to charge the pimp with the Clemment murder. That came from McGregor, and I think he got heat all the way from the top." Sarah closed the file she'd been looking at. "What did your boss have to say?"

"I haven't even told him yet. He likes to yell, and I'm not in the mood."

Sarah laughed.

"I'd join you if I could see a scrap of humor in this," Jessica said. "I'm going to keep the paperwork you sent over, but I'm not going to file the second murder charge. I can always add new charges later. If I go in with this at arraignment, I might not get anything to stick."

"You going to break that news to McGregor yourself?"

"Hell, no." Jessica pushed the chair away from the desk. "He likes to yell, too. I told you I wasn't in the mood."

For a moment that was funny, but after Jessica left, Sarah realized there was no way she wanted to face McGregor with this latest development. She considered her options: Call him. Send him an e-mail. Or just wait until tomorrow.

Waiting seemed like the wisest choice, so she put her files away and got ready to go home. Maybe she'd shop on the way home and fix herself a real dinner.

Sarah had just punched the elevator button for the lobby when her cell phone chirped. She answered it to hear a frantic voice that she didn't recognize, "Detective Kingsly, can you please help me? I'm so scared. He's . . . that man . . ."

"Whoa. Wait a minute. Who is this?"

"It's Amber."

"Okay, Amber, here's what I want you to do." Sarah stepped out of the elevator as the doors whooshed open. "Take a breath and calm down."

She waited a beat, listening as the girl worked to settle her panic. "Good," she finally said. "Now tell me what you're talking about."

"A man has been hanging around my apartment house for several nights. I didn't see him every time, but my neighbor just told me she has seen him almost every night. Then just now I saw him when I came home from the store. He was across the street and seemed to be watching me." She paused and took a ragged breath, then continued. "When I went to unlock the lobby door, he started across the street like he was going to follow me inside, but then Cherie came up and the man walked off."

"Who's Cherie?"

"My neighbor. She's the one who's seen the guy hanging around."

"Is he there now?"

"No."

"Can you describe him?"

"Not really. It was getting dark, and he was wearing dark clothes."

"Okay. We'll follow up on this. Meanwhile, you need to go somewhere else."

"I don't have anywhere to go. My folks are still mad at me. I can't go there."

Sarah bit back a sharp retort. Would this girl never learn? But now was not the time for giving her what-for. Amber was on the verge of panic.

Protocol dictated that Sarah call this in and have a patrol car go do a preliminary report, but she made a hasty decision to go talk to the girl herself. Maybe she could calm her down enough to get her to think of a friend she could stay with. She called dispatch to report what she was doing, then drove to Amber's apartment complex on Mockingbird. It was an older building, but decently maintained. Sarah did a quick check around the outside and didn't see anyone lurking about. She went to the entry and pushed the buzzer for Amber's apartment. When the lock released, she pushed the door open and hurried down the hall.

Amber stood in an open doorway and motioned frantically to Sarah. "Is he gone?"

"I didn't see anybody." Sarah hustled the girl into the small apartment and closed the door. "But you shouldn't have been standing in the hall like that. Geesh, did you even think?"

When the girl's eyes brimmed with tears, Sarah regretted her harsh tone. It was obvious Amber was terrified, and panic often trumped reason. She patted Amber awkwardly on the shoulder as a mute apology. Sarah never was good at this sort of thing and wished she wasn't always tempted to mother this poor child. She put on her business face. "Tell me again what you saw when you came home tonight."

"I had just parked my car down the street. There weren't any places close up." Amber walked over and sat on the faded brocade loveseat, motioning for Sarah to sit in the canvas director's chair across from her. "I looked across the street and saw this man kind of keeping pace with me. At first I didn't think anything of it. Could be just a coincidence, you know."

She paused as if expecting affirmation, so Sarah nodded. "When did you become alarmed?"

"He paused when I stopped at the door. I don't know what made me look over at him. Just some funny feeling. And he seemed to be looking at me. Then like I told you, he started to cross the street."

At this point Amber took a sharp breath and dropped her gaze. "I don't know what would have happened if Cherie hadn't showed up."

"There's no way to know for sure he was crossing to you," Sarah said. "Maybe he had a car parked down the street and he was headed there."

Amber's head came up quickly. "You don't believe me?"

"It's not a matter of believing. It's what we know and what we don't know. What about this man rang alarms for you?"

"At first it was just that he was this shadowy figure in the darkness. But I started to get nervous when I realized he was matching his steps to mine. And when he stepped out into the street, I swear he was looking right at me."

Sarah made a few notes then closed her notebook. "I can try to get some extra patrols out here for a few days. But that's real iffy with no description or anything concrete to go on. My gut is telling me that you might be right about a stalker, but I can't get my boss to act on a gut feeling. I still think your best course of action is to leave for a while."

"What if it's the guy who killed Tracy?"

"All the more reason for you to get out of here."

"I don't have anywhere to go." Amber lifted her chin. "Besides, I don't want to. I want him caught. You can watch or something, can't you? What do they call it? Surveillance?"

Sarah sighed and leaned back in the chair. "That would be harder to authorize than patrols. We can't take definitive action since there hasn't been a threat."

"But what about the note I got?"

"We have no way of knowing if the note came from this guy. We're not even sure this guy is stalking you."

"Still. I'm staying. You can't make me go, can you?"

Sarah recognized a determination that was uncomfortably close to home. Like it or not, there was a little bit of herself in this feisty young girl. "That isn't a smart idea."

"Probably not. But I owe this much to Tracy." She faltered over a break in her voice. "It's my fault she's dead."

Tears burst from the girl's eyes like water through a break in a dam, and Sarah patted Amber's arm, resisting the impulse to wrap her arms around the grief-stricken girl. If she loosened the cinch on her own grief, she might never get it under control again.

After what seemed like an eternity, Amber snuffled and reached for a tissue from the box on the coffee table. "Sorry about that."

"It's okay." Sarah swallowed hard. "Listen, I can't promise anything, but if you're determined to stay here, I'll see what I can do about some kind of protection."

"Just don't be too obvious." Amber offered a little smile. "We don't want to scare him away."

Chapter Twenty-Three

A light drizzle speckled the windshield, and Angel resisted the impulse to turn on the wipers. "If the rain picks up, we won't be able to see a thing."

"It won't," Sarah said. "Rain rain, go away. Come again another day."

"You trying to be funny?"

"Guess you never heard that little ditty before."

"Guess not." Angel shifted in the passenger seat of Sarah's car. "I can't believe I let you talk me into this. How long have we been sitting here, anyway? My butt is getting sore."

"It's only been two hours."

This was the third night of sitting outside Amber's apartment building, watching until she got home and safely inside. Sarah had done it by herself the first night, but then Angel joined her, leaving her own car parked around the corner out of sight. She'd told Sarah she was there because she didn't have anything better to do, but the truth was she worried about this silly girl who was so willing to use herself as bait.

They were off the clock, and hopefully off anyone's radar. Angel didn't know what McGregor would do if he knew they had staked out Amber's apartment on their own. He had been pretty adamant the other day when Sarah broached the subject of surveillance at the girl's apartment. In fact, Angel had worried about his blood pressure. Sarah had pleaded her case until he finally agreed to let her arrange for increased patrols in that area if Grotelli authorized it. But that was it. No time spent by them. Angel had sensed even then that Sarah was probably going to find some way around his orders. She'd done some pretty unorthodox things before and not gotten fired. Would they both squeak by this one?

"Did you see that?"

"What?" Angel leaned closer to the spattered windshield.

"There. That man. He just walked past the entrance to the apartment building and now he stopped in front of the alley."

"Yeah. Yeah. I see him. But it's so dark, he almost blends into the opening of the alley. Can you tell what he's doing?"

Sarah pulled a tissue out of her jacket pocket and swiped at the condensation their breath was creating on the glass. "He pulled something out of his pocket. Maybe he stopped to make a call."

"In the rain?"

"It's not rain. It's a light drizzle. Besides, he's got a hat and coat on. I saw the hat when he passed in front of the light at the apartment entrance."

A flicker of movement caught Angel's attention out the side window, and she tapped Sarah on the arm. "Here's our girl."

"How can you tell it's her buried in that parka?"

"The walk. Watch how she moves." Angel noticed that the man had turned toward Amber, and her internal alarm system went on overdrive. She fought the impulse to dash out of the car, hearing a faint "wait, wait, wait," from her partner.

Amber gave no indication that she saw the guy as she turned to walk up to the entrance to the apartment building. Pretty cool customer, Angel thought. Unless she really didn't see him.

Angel quietly eased her door open, while Sarah did the same. She had turned off the dome light so it wouldn't flash when they opened doors.

The man had turned and was walking in Amber's direction.

Again Angel stifled her urge to run across the street. They had to wait until he made a move. He could just be a neighbor out for a walk, although every instinct told Angel otherwise.

Amber appeared to be putting her key in the outer door when the man suddenly rushed her. Angel was there in two seconds, weapon drawn. "Police. Put your hands up."

Weapon drawn, Sarah ran up and took a position to Angel's left.

The man whirled, pulling Amber in front of him, and that's when Angel saw the knife. He had it braced across Amber's throat.

"Shoot the fucker," Amber shouted. "Kill him."

"Settle down," Sarah said, using that same tone she'd used to talk the jumper off the bridge. "Nobody has to get hurt here."

She moved farther to the left, away from Angel, forcing the man to turn his head from side to side to keep both her and Angel in sight. She focused on his eyes, trying to gauge how far over the edge he might be. She did not want to be responsible for another death. "Take it easy, mister. You don't want to do something you'll regret."

No response. Just the nervous flick of eyes moving from her to Angel and then back.

"Drop the knife and let the girl go," Sarah said, keeping her tone level. "There's no way out of this."

Sarah watched the man's eyes, hoping to see a sign of fear, of weakness. Something that would make him give it up.

Nothing. He tightened his grip on Amber and the knife touched the soft skin of her throat. *Oh, my God. He's going to do it.*

Sarah risked a glance at her partner, who had moved even farther away. *Did she have a shot?*

As if hearing the question, Angel gave a slight shake of her head.

Sarah looked back at the man, trying to ignore the frightened eyes of the girl and the drops of blood on her neck. "Drop the knife, or I take you out right now."

Time seemed to stand still for a moment, and Sarah could hear the pounding of her heart as she watched him watching her. Was he trying to see if it was a bluff?

Then suddenly he pushed Amber toward Angel. Sarah watched for one horrifying moment as the girl went down. She couldn't tell if the man had sliced her or not, but Amber's head hit the concrete with a sickening thud.

The man darted out of the doorway directly at her partner. Sarah tried to get a shot off, but Angel and the girl were in her line of fire. By the time Sarah ran into the clear, he had rounded the corner. She looked back at Angel, who was kneeling beside Amber and opening her cell phone. "Go," Angel said. "I've got this."

Sarah hesitated just a beat, then took off in the direction the man had gone. She could see him partway down the block, running fast, but she could run fast, too. All she had to do was wear him down. *You're gonna pay, you bastard.* Sarah made that her mantra as she concentrated on the pursuit.

For several blocks it looked like her plan would work. Her running shoes gave her traction on the wet pavement, and his footing didn't seem to be so steady. She thought the advantage was helping her to gain on him, but he didn't seem to be showing any signs of tiring. They appeared to be matched stride for stride, although hers were a bit shorter, and she willed her legs to pump faster to compensate. She was driven by the sight of the blood that had been pooling around Amber's head.

A sudden screech of a siren almost deafened her, and Sarah saw an ambulance barreling down the street, headed in the opposite direction. She only hoped they would get there in time as she kept on running. Her muscles were screaming, and she was started to lose the rhythm of her breathing. This had to end soon.

She repeated her mantra over and over, willing herself to get past the pain in her legs, in her side, in her chest, and slowly, the gap started to close. When the man turned to go through a park, she cut the angle and gained more precious yards on him. Closer . . . closer . . . closer, until she could launch herself in a sprawling tackle. The man went down, face first, sliding across the wet ground. His hat, which had somehow managed to stay on through the whole race, flew off and landed in a puddle.

The man twisted under her, trying to buck her off. "You bastard. Don't make me hurt you," Sarah said. "I don't need much of an excuse."

She wasn't sure if it was because of the threat or just that he was as winded as she was, but he suddenly went limp. She quickly cuffed him and turned him over.

Holy mother of God. Sarah blinked and looked again. It couldn't be.

But it was.

She was looking into the eyes of Rebecca Modine.

Still struggling to get her mind around what she saw, Sarah sat back on her haunches and wiped mud and dead leaves off her jacket. Her lungs were screaming for oxygen, and she took a few deep breaths. *Modine?*

The woman didn't move, and she didn't speak. She just stared at Sarah with eyes that revealed nothing.

Sarah heard someone running toward then and turned to see Angel with two uniformed officers. "How's Amber?" Sarah called out.

"Head trauma, but the paramedics got her stable to transport." Angel paused and looked down. "What the hell . . . ?"

"Yeah, that's what I said." Sarah stood and pulled Modine to her feet, then propelled her toward the officers in blue. "Take her down to the station and book her for assault and attempted murder."

The detectives watched the black and white pull away. Sarah shook her head. "Can you believe this?"

"I am not going to diss your instincts anymore, girlfriend."

"The only instinct I had about her was that she was too prissy," Sarah said. "And I thought maybe she was protecting some guy. But not this. No way was I thinking this."

"Are you going to call McGregor, or should I?"

"The stakeout was my idea. I'll make the call."

Sarah held the cell away from her ear, but she could still hear McGregor. "You did *what?*"

She waited a beat, then put the phone to her ear again. "Calm down, Lieu. I was right about this."

"Calm down? Calm down? You went against a direct order."

"Let me get to the good part before you fire my ass."

He didn't respond, and Sarah could hear him taking a couple of deep breaths. She quickly told him about Modine.

"You're shittin' me?"

"No. A couple of officers are taking her to booking as we speak."

"Why didn't you bring her in?"

"We're off the clock, remember?"

Sarah wasn't sure, but she thought she heard a little chuckle. "You want us to come in and question her tonight, Lieu?"

His response was negative. "Let her stew overnight."

Closing her phone, Sarah turned to Angel. "I'm going to check on the girl. Want to come?"

"I'll pass." Angel started out of the park. "Come on, I'll take you back to your car."

A half hour later, Sarah walked into the chaos of Parkland Hospital's ER. She knew it was organized chaos; the ER was noted as a top trauma center, but the noise was still deafening.

Babies and children screamed. Gurneys rattled down halls. Phones rang. The overhead blared.

Sarah wished she didn't have to keep coming here. First John, then Angel's mother, and now this. She walked up to the nurse's station and got the attention of a young male nurse who was writing in a patient chart. She showed her ID, then asked about Amber.

"They're getting ready to take her to ICU," he said.

"Is she going to be okay?"

"I'm afraid I can't give you that information."

"Because you don't know, or you don't want to say?"

The man put the chart in a slot and looked at Sarah. "Don't blame me for the privacy laws."

Sarah took a breath to steady herself before she pissed off this guy big time. "Is her family here?"

"Not yet," he said, then quickly added. "And, yes, they have been called."

"Can I see her?"

"Are you related?"

They stared at each other while seconds clicked off the clock, then Sarah finally broke the impasse. "It's my fault the girl is in here. I need to see that she's breathing."

The nurse gave a barely perceptible nod to his right. "Number eighteen."

Sarah hurried down the hall. Behind the curtain for cubicle eighteen, Amber lay on a narrow bed. An IV line dripped into her left arm, and the right was encased in a blood pressure cuff. Nurses stood on either side of the bed, making adjustments to equipment. One of the nurses looked over at Sarah. "We're getting ready to transport. Are you family?"

"No," Sarah said, taking a step closer and showing them her badge. "I was at the scene."

Sarah focused on the shallow, yet steady, respirations of the pale young woman in the bed. "Is she going to make it?"

"I'm sorry, I can't—"

"I know. Privacy issues."

"There is that. But I also just can't say. Her condition is grave. We'll have a better prognosis in twenty-four hours."

Sarah left the ER and stood just outside the doors for several minutes. The awning protected her from the rain, which had started up in earnest, and she mentally kicked herself for not grabbing her umbrella when she first arrived. The rain had increased even then, but she had been so intent on seeing Amber, she had ignored it. Now, she knew she would get drenched before she ever made it to her car.

She paced, wishing she had a cigarette, although a lot of good that would do, since she was in a smoke-free zone. Even though Sarah had seen the amount of blood from the injury to Amber, she had not really thought the girl would be critical. Critical came from gunshot wounds and knife wounds, not just a bang on the head. Yet she could still hear the hard thwack as Amber's head had hit the concrete.

"If she dies, your ass is mine, Modine."

Modine was so still, she could have been a rag doll slumped in the chair in the interrogation room. Sarah looked at her from the other side of the one-way mirror. "She didn't say a word, Lieu. Not until she asked for a lawyer."

McGregor stood to her right, Angel on the other side. Sarah had spent an hour trying to get the woman to talk, only to be met with a stony silence.

"I'm still having a hard time getting my head around this," McGregor said. "Is she the one you chased out of The Club?"

"Don't know for sure, Lieu. But we think so. And her car matches the one Angel saw tear out of the parking lot that night."

"But why is she dressing up like a man?"

"I don't know, Lieu. Maybe we should ask Sanchez or Peeples. Nothing about her fits the profile they gave us."

McGregor wiped a hand across his face. "Do you have anything to tie her to the other girl?"

Sarah shook her head. "Nothing besides the school connection. No hard evidence that puts her at The Club, or anywhere near the girls until tonight. Roberts is having some handwriting experts work on the note. See if the writing matches Modine's."

"Okay. So we move ahead. We've got her cold on the assault last night," McGregor said. "And the ADA might go for attempted murder, too."

"She did the other girl, Lieu. I just know it," Angel said.

"You got an instinct about it?" Sarah asked with a smile.

"Something like that."

McGregor looked from one woman to the other, a frown furrowing his brow. When neither of them chose to enlighten him on the private joke, he shrugged. "Instinct or fact, let's see what we can do about proving it."

With that, he left the viewing room and Angel turned to Sarah. "I'll get the knife to Roberts. Maybe we'll get lucky and he can prove it's the murder weapon."

"I'm having a hard time getting my mind around all this," Sarah said. "I just can't see a woman like that—so prim and proper—going to The Club."

"She's not very prim and proper now." Angel paused and looked back at Modine. "But the bigger question is what she had against Amber to stalk her like that."

Angel headed off to the lab, and Sarah went to her desk to make arrangements for a line-up. If they could place Modine at The Club, they would be one step closer to connecting her to Tracy's murder.

A couple of hours later, Sarah stood in another viewing room with McGregor, ADA Jessica and Modine's lawyer, Quentin

Macabee, a high-priced litigator from the same firm Clemment used. Sarah wondered if Clemment had arranged representation. If so, why would he do that for a prime suspect in his daughter's death?

On the other side of the glass, seven people stood in a row, all wearing a dark suit and black fedora. The first witness was the hostess from The Club. She was not able to identify the man she saw at The Club. That same scenario played out with the young hooker and Chrystal. Neither could say for sure that one of the five people they were looking at was the person known on the street as The Dark John. Sarah would never voice it aloud, but even she had trouble picking Modine out of the group.

"I guess that's it," Macabee said, turning to Jessica. "I'll see you at the arraignment."

He walked out and Jessica turned to Sarah. "I need some ammunition. I checked. She has no priors. So this slick lawyer of hers will do his damndest to get the charge reduced. She could even walk on probation."

"But she tried to kill Amber."

"That's what you say." Jessica folded her arms across her chest. "Don't underestimate the spin her lawyer will put on the scenario. 'My client was scared for her life, your Honor. These officers came running out of the dark, threatening her. She panicked and grabbed the girl. But she didn't intend to hurt her. It was all an unfortunate accident.' "

"Accident, my ass," Sarah said. "Modine deliberately pushed the girl to get away. If nothing else, she should be charged with reckless endangerment."

"Hey, I'm on your side. I'm just warning you that a judge might not be."

After Jessica left, Sarah took a minute to call the hospital. Earlier, she had jumped through all kinds of hoops to be able to get information on Amber's condition. Nothing had changed since last night, and again, nothing new to report now.

But at least the girl was still alive.

Sarah wasn't sure why she had all these mixed feelings about Amber. Partly, she felt responsible for her having been injured and wished now that she had not let the girl set herself up that way. Another part of her was starting to connect on a level that was not professional. She couldn't help but see some of the parallels between her life and Amber's. Not that Sarah had ever done anything as foolish as dance in a strip club. But she might have resorted to something equally unsavory had her grandmother not stepped in to salvage a very messed-up teen.

Back in the squad room, Sarah settled at her desk and booted up her computer. She found a website for the Pinewood School and saw a bio listed for Modine. She clicked on the link, and a PDF file opened to a detailed resume. Modine was from Maryland. Went to a small liberal arts college there, and started her teaching career at a private school in Baltimore. Sarah noted there was a gap in the employment history between her years in Baltimore and starting at Hockley ten years ago.

That didn't necessarily mean anything, but . . .

Sarah decided to do a search of Baltimore news for the last year Modine was there, and after following several links, she came upon a story: *Area Teacher Under Investigation.* The picture accompanying the story was of Rebecca Modine, younger, but with that same expression of stern disapproval on her face. According to the news report, a student at St. Mary's School for Girls accused Modine of threatening physical harm if she did not stop an illicit relationship she was having with another girl at the school.

"This is interesting."

Angel looked up from her desk. "What?"

Sarah kept her eyes on her computer screen. "Modine threatened a student in Baltimore."

"Threatened her how?"

"The exact threat was not reported. The story just said 'physical harm.' " Sarah paused to read more of the story. "And apparently the accusation never went anywhere after Modine hired a lawyer. She denied the charge and the whole thing came down to her word against the girl's. The school did ask her to leave because of the negative publicity but gave her a positive recommendation."

"Oh, sure, send the bad apples somewhere else."

Sarah looked over at her partner. "Feeling a bit cynical, are we?"

"I'm just tired of people sloughing their problems off on others. It happens too often in too many places."

At first Sarah thought Angel was speaking in general terms, but then a question popped into her head. *Does she mean us?* She tried to find the answer in Angel's expression, but Angel just resumed the paperwork she'd been filling out. *Okay. You're just being paranoid.*

Sarah turned back to the story and jotted down the name of the girl who'd filed the complaint, Stacy McBride. It was a real long shot, but maybe she could track her down and get more details about the threat.

CHAPTER TWENTY-FOUR

McGregor stepped into the stuffy room in the basement of Lord of Divine Light Church. Worn and dented metal chairs were lined up in uneven rows and about ten were occupied. He sat in a chair in the last row, and faced the man who was speaking at a small portable dais set up on a folding table. He had introduced himself with the standard AA opening, "Hi, I'm Larry, and I'm an alcoholic."

How many times McGregor had heard that, he couldn't count, and Larry's story was familiar. Most alcoholics had the same story. At least that had been his experience when he'd tried AA ten years ago. The stories, the meetings, the people were so depressing, he'd gone to a bar after each one.

So far, his current efforts to control his drinking were working. He had not had a drink while on the job since that day he'd met with Helen. But he knew she expected more of him, so here he was on his lunch hour in this dingy room with these losers.

"I see we have a visitor," Larry said. "Would you like to introduce yourself?"

McGregor looked around, then realized the guy was talking to him. He waved a dismissive hand.

"That's okay," Larry said. "Everyone's scared their first time. Just wait until you're comfortable."

As if that will ever happen. I don't need to be here spilling my guts. I need to be finding scumbags.

But McGregor stayed, listening to one sad story after another. At least they were supposed to be sad. Stories about being bullied in school and raised by tyrannical parents. Stories about abuse and strings of bad luck. Stories about loves lost. Stories about getting fired from one job after another.

Those weren't sad. They were pathetic. If they really wanted sad, McGregor could tell them about the nine-year-old girl who had been repeatedly raped, then sliced to ribbons and tossed into a Dumpster like last week's rotten meat. He could tell them about the young woman who had been abused for years, then had her head bashed in by an ex-husband because the law wouldn't let McGregor kill the bastard when he'd first collared him on the abuse. The woman was so battered, there wasn't an inch of her skin that was still pink. He could tell them about the three little children drowned by a mother who thought God wanted her to give them to Him.

Those stories made the others pale in comparison, but McGregor would not get up there and tell them. If he ever unlocked the box those memories were stored in, he was sure he would go nuts.

He waited out the hour, declined Larry's invitation to stay for coffee, and left. He had just enough time to get to the station for the briefing at one.

McGregor walked into the conference room and saw that the detectives working the Clemment murder were all there, and so was Burtweiler. McGregor had forgotten he'd asked Burt to follow up on the suspicions about Clemment. Of course, with Modine looming large in the suspect department, whatever Burt had might be moot.

"Hey, Burt, got something for us?" McGregor asked, sloughing off his jacket and putting it on the back of a chair.

"What I've got is nothing," Burt said. "Which is probably

fine. Sarah told me about the woman. Never figured a woman for this."

McGregor gestured for him to get on with it.

"I turned Clemment's alibi inside out and upside down. It's rock solid. Course he doesn't need it now, does he?"

"It's still good to know," Sarah said. "He may not be a suspect anymore, but we still have reports to file. It might even bring a smile to the commissioner's face to know his detectives are so diligent."

The comment elicited a chuckle from her fellow detectives, but a glare from McGregor. Burt swallowed his laugh and continued. "While you are being so diligent, you can also note that Simms and I went over Clemment's financials with the proverbial fine-toothed comb. Looking to see if maybe he hired some thug to take her out. All payments were accounted for. No large deposits in some unknown account."

"Too bad we can't indict him for being a crappy father and an officious son of a bitch," Sarah said.

"I wouldn't say that outside this room," Burt said. "People like that sue at the drop of an unkind word."

"I think we should drop the pimp as a suspect for the girl, as well," Angel said. "This case has gotten so snarled with possible suspects we could use a guest list to keep them all straight."

Chad laughed. "I agree about dropping the pimp," he said. "I've done some more checking, and there's nothing to connect him to the Clemment girl. Her friend swears Tracy had not been hooking before the night she decided to see what it was like. Didn't know this pimp. I talked to some more of his girls, too. None of them heard of Tracy being in the stable."

"Okay," McGregor said. "That leaves the kid and this Modine woman. What do we have on the kid?"

Sarah opened her notebook. "We've got motive. A shaky alibi for the TOD. And a possible murder weapon."

"When's the DNA test due back?"

"Hopefully pretty soon," Sarah answered. "Of course, if this were TV, we'd already have the results."

"Don't remind me," McGregor said. "Where do we stand with the woman?"

"Nothing concrete yet," Sarah said. "But I did some checking and found out she left Baltimore after being accused of harassing a student. Some kind of threat, but no luck so far in finding out what the threat was. I'm trying to trace the girl who filed the complaint."

"So, let's see what we get if we push more on the kid," McGregor said. "Chad, go back to the motel and lean on the clerk again. See if he can put the kid on the scene."

"And Modine?" Angel asked.

"For now, we just have her for the assault last night. Her lawyer is pushing for arraignment later today, and she'll probably make bail." McGregor slipped out of his suit coat and turned to Sarah. "What about that knife she had?"

"Roberts couldn't find any traces of blood. And the blade was too large to be the murder weapon."

"God, is anything in this case not going to lead us in circles?"

There was so much frustration in McGregor's voice, Sarah was sure it was not all coming from the case, but she pretended not to notice. Later she could worry about him. Right now they needed to focus on the job. "We'll all keep digging, Lieu," she said. "We're bound to come up with something to help our cause."

"Okay." McGregor swept the papers from the table and put them in a bulging file folder. "That's it, folks."

Sarah took the elevator downstairs and grabbed a soda and candy bar from the vending machines, then headed back to the squad room. She was just sitting down at her desk when Angel came in and nodded to the junk food. "That'll kill you, you know."

"Yeah, yeah. Forgot my carrot sticks."

Angel shook her head and went to her desk. Sarah finished off the candy bar, wiped chocolate from her fingers on a tissue, then booted up her computer.

"Still searching for that girl?" Angel asked.

Sarah nodded. She typed "Stacy McBride" into the Google search engine. Then she narrowed the search by adding "Baltimore." She got millions of hits, so she closed that search and went back to the article about Modine. She made a note of the reporter who had written the story for the *Baltimore Sun*— Luden Chancellor. The name conjured an image of some crusty old British reporter, but that image didn't fit with the *Baltimore Sun*. Dialing the number for the paper, Sarah wondered what the chances were that he was still on staff.

Not surprisingly, the editor she reached at the news desk said that Chancellor had retired five years ago. She managed to get his home number and dialed that. He answered on the fifth ring in a voice that did sound a bit British. Sarah told him who she was and what she was calling about.

"I'm not sure I recall the story," he said, and then chuckled. "The gray cells are dying out. They don't last forever, you know."

Sarah swallowed her own laughter and reminded him of the date and more details in the story. "I'd really like to contact the girl you wrote about and was hoping you might have kept a number for her."

"You may be in luck, young miss. I have saved all my interview notebooks. They are in storage, but I could have my son take me to the storage building to get the one for the month that story ran."

If his storage system was anything like hers, Sarah could picture boxes stacked in haphazard mountains against some wall, and probably not clearly marked. That didn't bode well for a prompt response to her request. "How long before you could get back to me?"

"Not long. I can see if my son is free tonight. And it won't take but a few minutes to find the notebook. I know exactly where they all are, and they're filed according to year. So it won't be any trouble at all."

Sarah left her number with him and hung up. What an odd, dear old man. He'd called her young miss. Made her feel like a teenager. Not a teenager in love, just a young, innocent teenager with no worries beyond Saturday's date. Not that she had ever lived that life. It was just one she'd always fantasized about.

An hour later she was about ready to quit for a while and stretch cramped muscles—maybe go downstairs for another snack—when she came across an article in the newspaper for a small town called Ellicott City that was near Baltimore. The story was about a tragic death of a Christina Modine, daughter of Bertrand and Francesca Modine and sister of Rebecca Modine.

"Hey, listen to this," Sarah called out. "Modine had a younger sister who died."

"How? Cancer? Car accident?"

"No. Horse accident. This article says she was an Olympic contender in dressage, whatever that means."

"Dancing."

Sarah looked over at her partner. "Did you say dancing?"

"Yeah. It's a type of horsemanship."

"And you know this how?"

"From LaVon."

"He does that?"

Angel sighed. "No. But he used to get horse magazines and I read them. He was only interested in what applied to Western riding or rodeo, but I liked the stories and pictures of the

English events, especially dressage. Have you ever seen the Lipp . . ." Angel paused. "No, I'm guessing not."

Sarah stood and stretched. "I don't even know what you are talking about."

"So, what's the deal about this girl?"

"The news article said she was thrown by her performance horse. It was labeled a freak accident."

"And you're finding this all so interesting because . . . ?"

"The groom was quoted as saying he was shocked that the horse threw the girl. He said it was 'bomb-proof.' Whatever that means."

"It means the horse didn't spook easily," Angel said. "But I don't see how this has any relevance to our case."

"Probably doesn't. I'm just being diligent here."

The phone on Angel's desk rang, and Sarah half listened to her partner's side of the conversation as she skimmed the rest of the story. What she heard consisted of one-word responses, and Sarah was ready to tune it out, when Angel hung up and said, "That was Modine's mother. She said it was 'convenient' for us to come over now."

Angel had called first thing this morning to talk to the woman and had reached an answering machine. Subsequent calls had met the same results. Angel had left several messages, and her frustration level had increased throughout the day when there had been no response.

"Oh, good. More fun with the upper crust." Sarah closed down her computer. "I can't wait."

Francesca Modine lived in a luxury condo in Turtle Creek. Sarah pulled the car to a stop at the curb, noting that the grounds were impeccable. Even in the dead of winter, it looked like the shrubs and hedges had daily attention. Not a scrap of litter blemished the small lawns or walkways. She followed Angel to the door, expecting their ring to be answered by a maid or butler, but was surprised when a woman who had to be Francesca opened the door. No maid would be wearing the latest fashions and have diamonds at her neck. Not that Sarah recognized the designer of the stylish cardigan or the tailored slacks, but she did know a diamond when she saw one.

"Please come in, Detectives."

Francesca was everything her daughter was not. Petite, beautiful, with porcelain skin and thick auburn hair that hung in waves to her shoulders. She also had a graciousness one normally associated with women of means who live in the Deep South, but Sarah had always been wary of those types of women. They might seem kind on the surface, but most of them never let kindness sink below the surface.

"Have a seat," Francesca said, gesturing to a plush, white leather couch. "I've made tea."

An ornate silver tea service was set up on a large square of dark granite that served as a table between the sofa and an antique rocking chair.

Sarah sat down, wondering about the facade of graciousness. Under the circumstances, she would have thought entertaining the detectives who had arrested her daughter would be the last thing this woman would want to do. She took the delicate cup Francesca handed over, not sure how to hold it, and finally wrapped her hands around it as if warming them. She knew she wouldn't drop it that way.

Angel, on the other hand, seemed to know exactly how to hold the thin China teacup and seemed quite comfortable sipping and smiling, looking every inch the young debutante at a social. Except for the badge.

Once the ritual of serving the tea concluded, Francesca sat in the rocking chair across from the detectives. The silence stretched into long minutes as she took a few sips of her tea, and Sarah waited it out. Finally, the woman set the cup down on the coffee table and smiled at the detectives. "Just what is it that you think my daughter has done?"

I guess we are not at a social function after all. Sarah returned the smile, giving it as much meaning as she was sure the woman had put into hers. "Rebecca assaulted a young woman the other day."

A sharp intake of breath was the only indication that she had rattled Francesca. "I'm sure there has been some mistake," she said. "Rebecca would never harm anyone."

"That's not exactly true, is it?" Sarah put her cup down. "What about that girl in Baltimore?"

"What girl is that?"

"The one who charged her with harassment and had her fired from that nice school she taught at."

"Oh." A lace-trimmed handkerchief was plucked from the pocket of her cardigan and touched to an upper lip. "That was nothing."

"It hardly seems like nothing to me."

Francesca straightened her spine. "Dredging up the past is hardly making good use of our time, now is it?" She pushed up her sleeve to check the time on a Cartier watch. "I have an appointment downtown in an hour, so I suggest we conclude this as soon as possible."

"How long have you lived here?" Angel asked.

If the sudden shift bothered Francesca, she gave no indication. "I've been here four years," she said. "I came here after my husband died. There was nothing to keep me in Baltimore anymore."

"Does Rebecca live here with you?"

"Oh, good heavens, no."

Sarah wondered at the vehement response, but decided not to interrupt her partner to ask about it.

"I'm surprised," Angel said. "It seems a perfect arrangement. Single daughter, widowed mother, sharing space."

"It's . . . we're not like that." Again the handkerchief appeared. "Rebecca's a grown woman. She needs her own . . . space. When we want to spend time together, we go to our cabin. She likes to get away from the city."

Angel pulled a small notebook out of her purse. "Where is that cabin?"

"Is this necessary?"

"Yes, it is. Please bear with us."

Francesca let out a deep sigh. "The cabin is on Cedar Creek Lake. Do you need the exact location?"

"That would be most helpful."

"I'll be right back."

Francesca stood and walked out of the room, returning in a few moments with a piece of paper she handed to Angel. Angel made a notation in her notebook and slipped the paper into the pocket of her jacket.

Waiting for the woman to get settled in the rocking chair again, Sarah picked up a small carving of a cat that sat in the middle of the table. She'd noticed it when they first sat down, but just now realized she had seen a similar sculpture in Modine's office at the school. "You and your daughter have the same tastes in artists, I see."

Francesca gave a very ladylike chuckle. "The artist is my daughter."

"Oh."

"Her grandfather taught her how to carve when she was a child. It was good therapy for her. Especially after . . ."

"Especially after what?" Sarah prompted.

"Her sister died when both girls were young."

"I saw a news story about that," Sarah said. "An accident, right?"

"It was terrible. Her horse threw her and she . . ."

The woman let the sentence hang, as if she couldn't bring herself to say any more.

"Was there ever any question that it was an accident?"

Francesca looked at Sarah, eyes wide in shock. "Of course not."

"Were the sisters close?"

"I would say so. They had their problems, of course. All sisters do."

"What kinds of problems?"

Francesca reached for her tea and took a sip before responding, and Sarah wondered if it was a stalling tactic. "Rebecca was always a little jealous of Christina. I think all first children resent the second child to a degree."

"Did that resentment ever get physical?" Sarah asked.

"What do you mean, 'physical'?"

This time Sarah recognized the stalling tactic and decided not to respond. The woman knew exactly what she was asking.

After fidgeting for a few moments, Francesca sighed. "All right. Yes, at times Rebecca would find a reason to hit her sister. But I read about that kind of behavior, and it is considered fairly normal for an older sibling."

"So you ignored it?"

"Of course not. My husband was a strict disciplinarian. He did not tolerate misbehavior."

"Did he utilize corporal punishment?"

"At times. When he deemed it necessary. He was a fundamentalist Christian and believed what the Bible said about raising children."

Ah, that whole "spare the rod" crap. Sarah glanced quickly at her partner, hoping she caught the implication in that. Nothing like a good case of Bible-thumping to turn a good girl bad. Sarah gave a nod to Angel to let her know she could take over the interview for a while.

"How did Rebecca react to the death of her sister?" Angel asked.

"How would you expect? She was inconsolable." Francesca paused to dab at her lips again, then took a breath and continued. "That was when we put her in boarding school. We thought it would be good for her to be around young people her age. Not as a substitute for her sister, of course. Nothing, or nobody, could replace Christina. We just thought it would be easier for Rebecca to recover from the loss if she was not at the farm with the constant reminders."

On the surface, that sounded like logical reasoning, but something in the practiced, almost rehearsed way it was delivered made Sarah start wondering. Did the woman repeat this to herself every time she questioned the wisdom of sending a grieving child away from home? And was it so logical for a couple who had lost a child to send their only other child away? Wouldn't it make more sense for a family in mourning to cling together?

That train of thought led to more questions. Was Mrs. Modine covering up something about this accident? Were the groom's concerns legitimate?

Before Sarah could decide whether she wanted to ask those questions out loud, Francesca said, "I would prefer that we not talk about Christina's accident anymore. You must understand how painful it is."

"Of course. That wasn't why we wanted to talk to you today, anyway." Angel set her cup on the coffee table, then continued. "Do you have any idea why Rebecca would assault that young woman?"

Francesca shook her head.

"What about The Club? Did you know your daughter went there?"

"That is a horrible lie. I read what they said in the newspaper about that place and that she was there." Francesca worried the handkerchief with thin, delicate fingers. "It's simply not true."

"I'm afraid it probably is," Angel said. "And we will know for sure when we get the DNA test results."

Noticing how agitated the woman was about The Club, Sarah decided to push a little. "I can see why your daughter changes her appearance to go to The Club. I'm sure the board of trustees at the school would frown on its headmistress attending such entertainment."

"Why do you refuse to believe me? She would not go there." Francesca glared at Sarah. "She was raised to be a good girl. We had very strict standards for both of our daughters."

"And they both lived up to those standards?"

Francesca checked her watch again, then looked at Sarah. "I'm sorry. I really need to get ready for my appointment." She stood. "Thank you both for coming."

Thank you for coming? As the woman escorted them to the door and then out, Sarah wondered about that abrupt shutdown. She had not expected much from this interview, but maybe it had been worth their time after all. If Modine was still into carving, she could have smaller knives than the one she was carrying the other night. Making her way to the car, Sarah glanced at her partner, who seemed as stunned as she was. "Did Roberts's team find any knives used for wood carving when they did their search at Modine's crib?"

"No. But they didn't know to look for them, either. Maybe we should get a warrant to search again. And one for that lake house."

Sarah opened her car door and got in behind the wheel, talking loudly so Angel could hear. "You know, my gut is telling me there's more to this family history than Mrs. Modine was willing to talk about. It would pay to do some digging into Modine's childhood, especially her sister's accident."

"Good idea," Angel said, slipping into the passenger seat of the car. "But there's a lot of digging we could do. Where do you want to start?"

"I don't know. I can't help thinking about her sister's death. What if the groom was right and it wasn't an accident?"

"What? You thinking Modine killed her sister?"

"It's within the realm of possibility. You heard what the mother said about the resentment."

"Yeah, but sibling rivalry usually just leads to a few bruises. This is a pretty long stretch, even for you."

Sarah laughed. "You may be right, but I'd still like to see if there is anything to the groom's concerns."

Angel pulled and buckled her seat belt. "We should probably ask my brother about it. He knows a lot more about horses than either of us do."

Sarah turned the key and brought the engine to life. "You think he'd tell us?"

"Sure. He's been fooling with horses since he was a kid."

"That's not what I meant," Sarah said. "I'm not sure he'd consider it a good idea to solicit information from the attorney of our primary suspect."

"But the question isn't related to his client. Who, in my book, is no longer the primary suspect."

"That's true." Sarah checked for traffic, then pulled away from the curb. "Can you talk to him this evening?"

"Nope. We're testing in Tae Kwan Do tonight. Trying for my high red belt."

"I thought you were already a black belt."

"Nope. Still one more level to go." Angel wrote something in her notebook and tore off the paper and handed it to Sarah. "This is the address of the stable. LaVon will be there tonight. He texted me earlier to see if I wanted to ride."

Sarah took the paper. "Why don't you text him or call him and tell him I'll stop by."

"Call him yourself. I wrote his personal cell number on that paper."

"Oh." Sarah looked. Sure enough. Cell number prominently written there.

Sarah's cell phone rang. She answered, listened for a minute, then flipped it closed. "That was McGregor. Wanted to let us know Modine made bail and is out."

"That'll make it more interesting for the forensic techs."

"And maybe it will rattle Modine a bit. Never can tell what will happen when you rattle a suspect."

"Does he want us to shadow her?"

"No. He's got Chad doing that."

CHAPTER TWENTY-FIVE

Sarah clocked out and managed to get to her car without a phone call interrupting her. She had hesitated about going to her desk after dropping Angel off, but she wanted to print out the news story about the accident that killed Christina Modine. And it would also help to find the location of the stable where LaVon kept his horse. She had left a voice-mail message on LaVon's phone, letting him know she was coming out, but she needed to know where she was coming out to.

After leaving the congestion of downtown traffic, she joined the stream of commuters heading north on I-75. Once past Richardson and Plano the traffic dropped by about half, and she was actually able to pick up some speed as she followed the directions she'd gotten from GoogleMaps. She took the last Allen exit and headed east. The countryside changed from concrete and housing developments to open land dotted with trees and sectioned with barbed-wire fences. Flyaway Stables was clearly marked on the county road, and Sarah turned onto a gravel drive that led to a large white barn. It was much like the stately horse barns she remembered seeing in Kentucky, so whoever owned this had deep pockets.

On one side of the large structure were an outdoor arena and several smaller round pens. The center door of the stable was open, revealing a large indoor arena. Four cars and a battered white pickup were parked just to the left of that opening, so Sarah assumed it was okay to park there and pulled into a space next to the truck. She got out of the car and immediately caught the strong scent of horse, leather, and manure. She wasn't sure she liked any of them.

She did like the relative quiet, compared to the buzz and hum of the city. There were a few birds flitting about the eaves of the barn, and she could hear the flutter of their wings and a few bird calls. She could also hear a rhythmic *thump, thump, thump* coming from inside. Curious, she stepped into the barn, losing her sight for a moment as her eyes adjusted to the dimness. Then she saw a rider on a dark horse going in large circles along the fence. When he passed in front of her, she recognized LaVon under the cowboy hat. *Hmmmm. He sure looks good.*

She shook that thought aside and waved when he nodded to her.

LaVon brought the horse to a halt so quickly, it looked like the animal might actually sit down in the dirt. Sarah took a step back, and LaVon chuckled as he dismounted and came to the other side of the fence. "Horse has got to stop like that when I rope a calf."

"Oh."

Now he laughed. "You ever been to a rodeo?"

"Nope."

"Well, maybe we'll have to remedy that."

"Oh." Sarah's cheeks burned. *Oh, great, the one-word wonder.*

LaVon chuckled. "Rodeo season doesn't start 'til spring. Plenty of time to get used to the idea."

Without giving her a chance to respond, LaVon led his horse to the gate, opened it, and came through. "I have to put him up. Want to come?"

Sarah nodded and followed him until he stopped in front of a stall. He tied the horse, then loosened the cinch and pulled the saddle off. "Your message said you had some questions about horses?"

The quick segue into business caught her a bit off guard. "Uh, right. Angel said you know a lot about horses and might know what it means to have one that is bomb-proof."

"And why would you need this information?"

Sarah hesitated for just a beat, hoping he didn't catch it. She had to be careful. "We're investigating a woman on an assault charge, and there was an incident in her past involving a horse. Her sister was killed in a freak accident, and the groom raised some questions that were never addressed. He stated that he considered the horse bomb-proof and had his suspicions the girl's fall was not an accident. I just want to know if there really is a horse like that."

"Here, let me show you." LaVon untied his horse and led him to one of the small round pens beside the barn. On the way out of the barn, he grabbed a stick with a thin rope on the end of it. The horse, his coat glistening in the late afternoon sun, pranced and danced when LaVon led him into the center of the round pen. LaVon led the horse in a few tight circles. He appeared to be talking to the horse, but Sarah couldn't make out what he was saying. She did notice that the horse visibly relaxed and slowly dropped his head until he was placidly walking next to LaVon. Then he stopped the horse and released the lead rope. The horse didn't move. LaVon took the stick and slowly rubbed it across the horse's back, under his belly, down his legs, and still the horse did not move. LaVon turned to Sarah. "That is a bomb-proof horse."

Sarah considered the animal for a moment. It could have been a dark bronze statue. "Then what would make a horse like this spook? Something jumping out of the brush?"

"Not unless the rider got spooked first. An inexperienced rider would probably get scared and react, and that would make the horse react."

"This girl was an Olympic-caliber rider."

"Then she would handle a sudden alarm with no problem," LaVon paused for a moment. "Was there any sign the horse had been injured?"

"Nothing noted in the report."

"Did anyone actually see the horse throw the girl?"

"No." Sarah dug the copy of the accident report out of the pocket of her jeans. "She was found just off a trail she rode on frequently. The coroner's report indicated that she had probably been thrown, hit her head on a large boulder, and the impact broke her neck. There were numerous contusions consistent with a fall like that."

"Who found the body?"

"The groom, who rode out after the horse came back to the barn without the rider."

LaVon attached the rope to his horse and led him out of the pen, motioning for Sarah to follow again. She was impressed with how the horse continued to move along without any pressure on the lead rope. It was as if the man and animal were communicating on some other level. LaVon brushed the horse and gave him treats, then put him in the stall. Sarah was content to sit on a nearby bale of hay and watch. This was a side of LaVon she had not expected, and it was endearing as well as a bit frightening. It was one thing to flirt, but she had a feeling they both could take it a step past flirting in a heartbeat.

He turned and faced her, and her whole body warmed. She remembered having that reaction the first time she saw Paul. *There is definitely something about a cowboy.*

"Is this at all related to the Clemment case?"

His question broke the mood as effectively as if he'd hit her with a bucket of cold water, yet she was relieved to get back to business. "You know I can't say."

"Interesting." LaVon poured some oats into a bucket and hung it on a nail for the horse, then stepped out and closed the stall door. "Does this mean you have another suspect?"

"Counselor!"

"Just checking." LaVon flashed a smile, and it was all Sarah could do to keep from smiling back.

The smile faded, but LaVon did not move away. "I'd like to kiss you."

For an agonizing moment Sarah teetered between stepping into his request and stepping back. He solved the dilemma by lowering his head and touching her lips with his, a soft kiss that was so light, the only way she knew for sure it happened was the bolt of electricity that shot through her body. She resisted the urge to wrap her arms around his neck and pulled away. "Professional boundaries, Counselor."

"Nobody knows but us." He glanced over his shoulder. "And Rebel."

Sarah considered him carefully. "And it won't happen again?" *God, what am I saying? I want it to happen again.*

"No, Miz Kingsly." He did such a perfect impression of a plantation houseboy, she burst out laughing.

"What happened to that lawyer who was just standing here?" Sarah made a big production out of looking around.

LaVon touched her arm to get her attention. Now his expression was serious. "It won't happen again. Not until the right time."

Sarah gave a quick nod. Matter settled. Subject closed. Thank you very much. Because if they stayed here bantering one more second, she would throw this man down on the hay and . . .

"Shall we?" LaVon gestured toward the doorway of the barn.

He walked her to her car and opened the door for her. Another gesture that was incredibly endearing. This man was full of all kinds of surprises.

Sarah walked into her apartment, threw her purse and jacket on the sofa and headed to her bedroom to change into clothes she could relax in, preferably sweats if she had any that were clean. Laundry was way overdue.

Cat met her in the hall with loud meows and twined his body around her feet. She picked him up, an action he normally barely tolerated, but today he seemed content to be carried into the bedroom. She dumped him on the bed and went in search of sweatpants. "What would you say if I told you I have the hots for this big black guy?" She addressed the question to Cat, who just stared at her. "But it's even more complicated than that— you know, white girl, black boy—my family in Tennessee would have a lot to say about that. Hell, folks here would have a lot to say about that."

She found her last pair of clean sweats and pulled them on, glancing back at Cat. "So why the hell am I telling you all this, anyway?"

He responded with a cat chirp that she was free to interpret any way she wanted to.

Sarah laughed, then headed to the kitchen. After fixing herself a bowl of soup and putting food down for Cat, she settled at the kitchen table and considered this latest romantic develop-ment. If that's really what it was.

Number one consideration, because she didn't give a rat's ass about what people thought of the color issue, was the profes-sional issue. Second to that was her partner. Things were get-ting better between them, but what would Angel think? Would she object if a relationship developed? *Should I ask her?*

That thought made Sarah spit out a mouthful of soup with her laugh. She couldn't even imagine how she would broach the subject. "Um, do you mind if I date your brother?"

She laughed again and shook her head. Better to just forget about it.

But the memory of that kiss made forgetting increasingly hard to do.

CHAPTER TWENTY-SIX

Sarah had just stepped into McGregor's office with Angel when the door opened and Roberts burst in. The Cheshire cat would have envied his grin. McGregor looked up from the paper he was scanning, "You have something good, I take it?"

"Yes, I do." Roberts dropped a plastic evidence bag on top of the pile of papers on McGregor's desk. "We found this in the trash under the sink in Modine's bathroom. She must be a closet smoker. I thought she would faint when she saw my tech pick this up."

Sarah stepped forward to look at the bag. It contained a cigarette butt. "I thought you went back to look for a possible murder weapon?"

"We did. And I'm sorry to say we didn't find anything. But this is still significant. It's the same brand as the one you found at The Club. And that matched one we found in that can at the crime scene."

"So . . . If we can tie all three to Modine . . ." Sarah let the rest of the sentence fade.

"Right," Roberts said. "We have some ammunition to give to the lovely Jessica."

"Do we have DNA back on any of them?" McGregor handed the bag back to Roberts.

"Nothing yet." Roberts slipped the bag into the pocket of his lab coat. "I didn't do any tests on the ones we found at the motel. There were about fifty, and there was no way the budget would allow that many tests, especially since it was a real long shot that any of them belonged to the perp. But we did get them sorted. Then we got lucky with finding the same brand at The Club, and now again at Modine's. Gitanes. I'm probably massacring the pronunciation, but it is a cigarette that comes from France."

"Have you checked tobacco shops to see how popular these are?" Angel asked.

"Working on it now. One of my guys called a few shops right away. Found out quite a few people buy imported smokes. A lot of local celebs are really into them."

McGregor drummed a pencil on his desk for a minute then looked back at Roberts, "We need that DNA to determine that the cigarette outside the motel was hers."

"I'll put a rush on it, but it's still going to take several days."

"Even if we get a match, that won't definitively put her at the murder scene," Angel pointed out. "How far was that can from the room?"

"I don't remember exactly," Roberts said. "I'd have to check my notes for verification, but I'm thinking it was about thirty-five feet." He looked to Sarah, who nodded.

"A good defense attorney can turn that distance into significant reasonable doubt," Angel said.

"Anything back from the search at the lake house?" McGregor asked.

"The crew isn't finished yet. But I'm expecting them to wrap it up by early afternoon."

"Okay," McGregor said, then looked at Sarah and Angel. "Anything to report?"

"I'm still waiting to hear back from that reporter," Sarah said. "Was hoping to talk to that girl who filed the complaint against Modine in Baltimore."

Sarah paused, wondering if she should also tell him about

her interview with LaVon, then decided not to. She really hadn't learned anything that led to concrete evidence to help put Modine away, so there was no need to bring up what could be a sensitive subject.

McGregor ran a hand through his hair, making it stick up like some punk hairdo. "That's it, then. We wait to see what turns up this afternoon."

Walking out into the hall, Angel put a hand on Sarah's arm to detain her. "Didn't you want to tell him about the sister and the accident?"

"What's to tell? McGregor's made it clear on more than one occasion that he doesn't care to hear about my gut feelings."

Angel laughed. "How did it go with LaVon last night?"

Sarah immediately thought about the kiss and felt the heat of a blush creep into her cheeks. She averted her face before Angel could see it. *Should I tell her? Will he? Aw, crap. What a mess this could turn out to be.*

"Sarah?"

"Huh?"

"I asked if LaVon had anything to help with our case."

"Not directly." Sarah went on to give her a condensed version of what she had learned from LaVon, leaving out the part about the kiss.

"Maybe we should try to contact that groom. See if he has any more to offer."

"Good idea. You want to do that? I'm going to follow up with the reporter to see if he found contact information for that girl."

Two hours later, Sarah finally got a call back from Chancellor. He was very apologetic about taking so long to find the information for her, and Sarah listened to a rather convoluted story about all the things that had to be taken care of before his son could take him to the storage area. It was way too much information, but Sarah bit back her impatience and listened until he got around to giving her a phone number. "This was at her parents'," he explained. "So if they are still at the same residence, they should have a current number for the girl."

"Did you do any more stories about the incident?"

"There was nothing to follow up on. The case, if there ever was one officially, went away. I suspect because the teacher's parents had money and clout, and the girl had nothing."

"I hear you," Sarah said. "Thanks for the help."

She hung up, then dialed the number he'd given her. After a few rings, Sarah heard a timid response. She identified herself and established that she was talking to Stacy McBride's mother.

"Has something happened, Officer?"

"No. I'm calling about that incident of harassment at that private school your daughter attended in two thousand." Sarah paused, waiting for a response of some kind, but there was none. "I was hoping to talk to her about that."

"Why, after all this time?"

"It might relate to another case we're investigating."

"I don't understand. The charges were dropped. There was no case."

"I realize that. But there must have been something that initiated a call to the police."

The woman was quiet for so long, Sarah started to wonder if she had hung up. Finally, she heard a deep sigh, then, "I don't think it would be good for Stacy to talk about the incident. It's best left in the past."

"Mrs. McBride, it might be extremely helpful to our current case."

Nothing.

"The teacher might have escalated from threats."

A sharp intake of breath, then, "Is Stacy in danger?"

"No. Not at all. The danger is here in Texas. To another young girl."

Again Sarah waited while the woman apparently thought this through. When the silence stretched too long, Sarah said, "Perhaps you could tell me the circumstances surrounding the threat Modine made to your daughter."

"Please, Detective. I don't see how—"

"This is very important, Mrs. McBride. I wouldn't be calling otherwise."

"You have to understand. The girls were young. Experimenting."

"I read the news reports, Mrs. McBride. I know the teacher caught Stacy and another girl in a rather compromising situation."

"Not like they were the only girls there doing that."

"I'm sure they weren't." Sarah paused to let the woman compose herself, then continued. "So what did the teacher do?"

"It was awful. It took Stacy two weeks to even tell me." A hesitation, then Mrs. McBride plunged on. "The teacher screamed at both girls. Told them they were whores, filth, destined to go to hell. She pushed Stacy against a desk and her cheek split open."

"Didn't you wonder about the injury?"

"Stacy said she fell. That it was an accident. I had no reason to doubt her at the time."

"But eventually she told you the truth?"

"Yes. Apparently she told the teacher she was going to tell the headmistress about the assault. And the teacher threatened to do more than give her a little push. That's when Stacy told me. She didn't want me to, but I went to the school. The headmistress did nothing."

"So why did you go to the police?"

"Because my daughter was terrified. She said the teacher

intimidated her every chance she got over the next week."

"Maybe the headmistress did talk to Modine after your visit?"

"I really couldn't say."

Sarah shifted to a more comfortable position in the chair. "Did the police take your case seriously?"

"At first. They took pictures of Stacy's injury and did a full report. Turned it all over to the district attorney."

"But the charges were eventually dropped?"

"It came down to my daughter's word against the teacher's. The teacher said it was an accident. She won."

Sarah was about to conclude the interview when she thought of one more thing. "Was Modine asked to leave the school because of the incident with your daughter?"

"I suspect so, but don't know for sure. We pulled Stacy out after that *accident,* and the school didn't seem inclined to keep us informed thereafter."

There didn't seem to be anything else to ask, so Sarah started to thank Mrs. McBride, who interrupted. "Are you going to nail the bitch?"

Sarah was taken aback by the question as well as the vehemence behind the words, but that's what comes of ten years of no vindication. "Yes," she answered. "We're nailing the bitch."

"Good."

The next thing Sarah heard was the dial tone.

CHAPTER TWENTY-SEVEN

Sarah took advantage of an evening at home to do some much-needed laundry. When she brought a load of warm clothes from the dryer and dumped them on the bed, Cat plopped in the middle of the pile and gave her a look that seemed to say, "Gonna do something about this, lady?"

"I've got a gun, you know."

Cat yawned and proceeded to lick his crotch.

"Aw, yuck!" Sarah pulled clothes out from under him, careful to avoid his claws as he periodically swatted at her efforts. She carried the basket into the kitchen and set it on the table just as her cell phone rang. She grabbed it off the counter and took note of the number. McGregor.

"Yeah, boss."

"Just got a call from Chad. He lost Modine."

"What do you mean he lost her?"

"He was tailing her. Staying a few cars behind, so she wouldn't spot him. They came to a railroad crossing where the bars were already down for an oncoming train. Woman drove around the barriers just ahead of the train."

"Think she jumped bail?"

"Dodging a train doesn't seem like something she'd do just driving to the grocery store and back."

"Okay. Okay. I get it. Stupid question." Sarah grabbed the cup of coffee she'd left on the counter earlier and took a sip. "Am I back on the clock?"

"Everyone is until we find her. Chad is going to stay near her place just in case she comes back. A couple of Uniforms are going to The Club. It's a long shot she'd go there, but we're not taking any chances."

"What about the hospital? What if she goes there to finish what she started with Amber?"

"That's another long shot, but we'll alert hospital security. Burt and Simms are going to the mother's place, so that leaves the cabin for you and Angel."

Sarah hung up and called her partner, making arrangements to pick her up at her place. It was a good thing she'd eaten as soon as she came home. No time for food now. She glanced over at the laundry basket, wondering if she should take a few minutes to fold some things and put them away. Cat was nestled in the basket, sound asleep. Well, at least he wasn't doing anything disgusting.

Angel called her mother and cancelled out of the family dinner, surprised that her mother didn't raise too many objections.

"Are you okay, Mom?"

"I'm fine. You need to stop with the alarms every time I'm a little tired. People get tired all the time."

Angel bit back a laugh. Her mother was right. Ever since that awful scare last year, Angel was quick to jump to the wrong conclusion. "Okay. You guys have fun without me."

That elicited a chuckle from her mother before she hung up. Then Angel went in search of her old running shoes. She hadn't done much running since starting Tae Kwan Do a couple of years ago, but had kept the shoes. That was a good thing, since she didn't want to go tromping around in the wilderness in her good shoes. She didn't care much for the great outdoors, and wished she had been put on surveillance instead of sent out to the boonies.

Since it would be dark out there in those boonies, Angel also dug out her big Mag-Lite.

A car horn sounded out on the street, and Angel looked out her front window to see Sarah's car. She grabbed her parka, gloves, scarf and flashlight and went out.

"Heading to Alaska?" Sarah asked as Angel got in.

Angel just gave her a look. "Drive."

Cedar Creek Lake was about sixty miles south of Dallas, and once they cleared the city, traffic was light enough that Sarah was comfortable to set the car to cruise at eighty-five. To be safe, she ran with lights, but no siren. They made it to the lake in just under forty-five minutes. Once they turned off the main entrance to the lakefront development, Hidden Bay, they rolled down a bumpy dirt road and darkness settled in with a vengeance. Clouds blanketed the stars, and the twin tunnels of illumination from the headlights created a ghostly glow that bounced off trees and brush.

Angel checked the GPS on her phone. "We're at the turnoff. The cabin should be about a hundred yards to our right."

"I'm going to pull up a ways. If she's not here already, don't want her to see the car."

Sarah eased the car to a stop about twenty-five yards down the road, and they stepped out into a strong wind off the lake. It had to be a good ten to fifteen degrees colder here than it had been in town. Angel zipped up her parka and just smiled at Sarah, who shivered in a light jacket.

"I know. You were probably a Girl Scout," Sarah said.

"No. But my mama taught me well."

The silence was eerie as they made their way back to the turnoff for the cabin, reminding Angel of one more reason she did not like the wilderness. Give her the hum of traffic any old day. And the darkness. God, it was like a blanket had been thrown over the area. Even with the slight illumination from the flashlight, she stumbled over rocks and downed tree limbs. The whole area was thick with trees and brush, and when they finally located the path to the cabin, it was just two deep ruts in the dirt, with high grass growing between them.

"Doesn't even look wide enough for a car," Sarah said.

Angel muted the illumination from the flashlight, so only a small beam of light lit the path through the trees. If Modine was at the cabin, it wouldn't do to announce their arrival. "How do you want to do this?"

"Carefully."

It was hard going as they tried to walk abreast, using the ruts as individual paths.

"Wonder if this is any easier in daylight," Angel said.

Sarah chuckled. "Probably. Might even be prettier."

They walked another twenty feet or so, then Sarah touched Angel's arm and pointed. Ahead they could see flickers of light. "That must be the cabin," Sarah said in a soft whisper.

Angel doused the flashlight. "Think that's her in there?"

"I'd put money on it."

Now that they were trying to approach the cabin without alerting whoever was in there, it seemed like every noise was amplified. Every twig that broke sounded like a gunshot.

Sarah pointed to her eyes and then to the window to let Angel know what she was going to do. Angel nodded and signaled that she was going to the right of the front door.

Sarah pushed her way through the brush below the window. In another life it had probably been a hedge of some sort. Now it was an overgrown mess of small limbs that seemed bent on denying her access. She used the barrel of her gun to push branches aside and plowed on, trying to ignore the scratches on her hands. Finally, she broke through and sidled up to a window and peeked in. The interior was dim, lit only by a kerosene lamp on a table made of rough timber, but Sarah could see

Modine silhouetted in the dim light. She could also see what looked like an assortment of small knives on the table. Beside the knives was a small stack of money, and it appeared that Modine was stuffing the money into a leather satchel. What Sarah wasn't sure about was whether the woman had a gun.

Only one way to find out.

"Modine. This is the police. We're coming in."

Sarah watched as the woman whirled and looked toward the door. Her hands were empty. "No gun," Sarah called out, already moving toward the porch. "Go, go, go!"

Angel breached the door with one good kick and rolled to the right. Sarah followed, moving quickly to the left. She looked at Modine and saw the woman had picked up one of the knives.

Oh, shit. Not another suicide by cop.

"Put the knife down, Modine," Sarah said. "It's over."

Modine looked from Sarah to Angel, then back, but didn't move.

"Hey, Sarah. Didn't we do this once before?" Angel called out, moving to put Modine between her and Sarah.

"Yeah. And I didn't like the way that one ended. Not at all."

Modine licked her lips, glancing quickly from one detective to another, then back again. Sarah recognized the signs of pressure. They had to contain this, and quickly, if they were going to bring her in alive. "Either you walk out of here, or you're carried out," Sarah said. "Your call."

Modine didn't respond. It was almost as if she hadn't heard. Sarah watched Angel move a few steps closer to the woman, and sent her a silent message to stop. She did. Then Sarah faced Modine again. "It's over, Modine. Drop the knife and put your hands on your head.

Nothing. Not even the bizarre dance with her eyes anymore, and a long, thin silence that seemed to go on forever.

Then Modine lunged.

Sarah saw the hand with the knife go down, ready to come back up after making contact, and the muscles in her stomach contracted. She took a half step back and jigged to the left.

"Take her down, Sarah. I don't have a clean shot."

"No. She deserves to fry."

At that, Modine hesitated for just a beat, and Angel dove into her with a roundhouse kick to the center of her back. Modine staggered, but didn't go down. She charged at Sarah again, this time swinging the knife back and forth in a blind rage. Shooting the woman would have been the prudent thing to do, but Sarah wanted to bring her in alive—needed to bring her in alive.

Sarah took a step to the side and the blade grazed her right arm, slicing a long line in her jacket sleeve. If the blade touched skin, Sarah couldn't feel it. Visually, she followed the arc of the swing and when it was at its peak, she reached up and grabbed Modine's arm, wrenching it back hard.

Modine went down, with Sarah on top of her. Sarah tried to maintain her grip on the hand holding the knife but felt it slipping as Modine bucked and twisted like some crazed bull. She was strong and desperate, driven by adrenaline. But so was Sarah. She hung on even when the muscles in her left arm screamed for release and a thin trail of blood started to soak her jacket sleeve on the right. *The bitch cut me.*

Maybe the thought distracted Sarah, or maybe the woman was just stronger, but all of a sudden Modine gave a mighty lurch and Sarah was down, her grasp on the woman's arm broken.

Sarah saw the point of the blade as Modine thrust the knife at her throat. She reached up, caught the arm in midair, and held it . . . held it . . . in some macabre arm-wrestling match. For a moment, Sarah thought she had the advantage and could push the woman off, but then the muscles in her arm started to twitch and the knife slowly started to descend. "Any time there, partner."

Angel landed another kick, this one to Modine's side, and the woman fell over. Sarah maintained her grip on the hand holding the knife, slamming it against the floor over and over until Modine let go.

Angel grabbed the other arm, and they hauled Modine to her feet, cuffed her and dragged her to a chair. The woman sat, mute and motionless. She could have been an oversized doll. Sarah leaned against the edge of the table, taking a few deep breaths to stop the erratic beat of her heart. Then she glanced over to see Angel was already putting the knife in an evidence bag. "Think this is enough for Jessica?" Angel asked.

"Oh, yeah." Then to Modine. "They're gonna fry your ass down in Huntsville."

"God is my judge. Not man."

"You'd better be rethinking that."

Angel was barely through the doorway when her phone chirped. She kicked the door shut and grabbed her phone. What now? The woman was in lock-up. What could McGregor want now?

But it wasn't McGregor. "What do you want, LaVon?"

"We missed you tonight. No need to get all snippy on me."

Angel kicked off her shoes and buried her toes in the pile of the carpeting. "Sorry. It's been a rough night."

"Can you talk about it?"

"We caught the killer. On the Clemment case."

"That's good news. Let's my client off the hook and . . ."

Angel waited for him to finish, and when he didn't she prompted him. "And what?"

"Nothing."

"Didn't sound like nothing to me."

LaVon didn't respond, so she continued. "I know when nothing is really nothing. And this isn't it."

"Okay. I'm going to ask Sarah out."

"What? Like on a date? Are you nuts? Has she been putting moves on you?"

Angel could hear her brother laugh.

"This is just so wrong on so many levels, I don't even know where to start."

"Simmer down, little sis. It's just a date. And the woman might even say no."

CHAPTER TWENTY-EIGHT

Sarah noted the lines of fatigue in her face as she faced the mirror while washing her hands. She always hated the florescent lighting in the station washroom. It was never flattering, even in the best of times, and this was definitely not the best of times. Her arm still throbbed, even though the wound had not been as long or deep as she'd first thought. A quick trip to the ER and ten stitches had fixed her right up. At least that's what the ER doc had said. It didn't feel so fixed up this morning.

While she'd been at the hospital, the other detectives had been here until close to eleven last night, getting Modine through booking. Then Chad had called her cell to tell her that everyone wanted to go celebrate. Angel had left after one drink. Probably was the smart thing to do, but Sarah had stayed and closed the bar with McGregor. Definitely not a smart thing. And Sarah knew she was going to have to stop supporting him in his drinking. What was the term the shrinks used? Enabling? Yeah. That was it. But she preferred to think of it as aiding and abetting. She was definitely going to have to stop pretending that it didn't hurt to stop after work for a few drinks with a friend.

The door suddenly burst open and Angel stormed in. "Is there any line you will not cross?"

Shaking the water off her hands, Sarah reached for a paper towel. "What's got you so riled up?"

"LaVon called me last night. Wanted to know what I'd think

if he asked you out."

"Oh." Sarah flashed on the scene at the barn and remembered his kiss.

"Were you hitting on my brother?"

The question was so absurd, Sarah almost laughed, but she feared Angel's reaction if she did. The woman had a nasty kick. "Is that what he said?"

"No." Angel's voice was closer to normal now. "He just wanted to know how I would feel about the two of you dating."

Sarah tossed the towel in the trash can. It still had the dents from the last time the two of them had been in here talking about black and white, and the great divide between the two. "What did you tell him?"

"That I don't know. There is a bit of a shock factor here, you know. Hard to think when you're in shock." The volume of Angel's voice rose a notch. "He said there was an attraction. Just when did you have time to establish an attraction? When you were supposed to be talking to him about the case? Or maybe when you were supposed to be *not* talking to him about the case?"

"Hold on there." Sarah stopped and took a breath to stifle her anger. "Aside from the fact that you have no call to question my professional ethics—"

"I wasn't aware that you had any."

Before Sarah had a chance to respond, the door opened again and Jessica walked in. She looked from Sarah to Angel, then back to Sarah. "Do I need to come back?"

"No," Angel said. "I'm leaving."

She opened the door, then looked back at Sarah. "I've decided. Stay away from my brother."

After the door closed, Jessica looked at Sarah, one eyebrow raised in question. Sarah shook her head. "Don't even ask."

"Okay." Jessica headed to a stall. "You coming to the arraignment?"

"Wouldn't miss it."

Sarah walked out, wishing she could be as definitive about what she was going to do about LaVon. He had called her last night, too. Before or after he talked to Angel? He hadn't mentioned the call to his sister, so Sarah guessed he had called her first. After some hesitation—actually, considerable hesitation—Sarah had agreed to meet him for dinner on Friday. Should she call and cancel?

No. I will not let Angel dictate who I can date and who I can't.

An hour later, Sarah sat in the back of the courtroom and watched as Rebecca Modine was brought in and the arraignment proceeded. She noted that Angel was on the other side of the aisle, keeping her face averted. Sarah was sure she could see an aura of hostility hovering over the woman. *Great. This bodes real well for our next case.*

The arraignment didn't take long. Fifteen minutes from the time the bailiff formally opened the proceedings to the final bang of the judge's gavel. Modine was charged with one count of first-degree murder, one count of attempted murder, one count of assault, and one count of threatening a law enforcement officer. Her bail was revoked, and the woman would never see the outside of a prison before she died, which could be sooner rather than later, if the DA went for the death penalty.

Sarah sat in the back row of the gallery and watched the woman being taken by the guards. Modine turned and shot Sarah a look of pure hatred.

"I don't think she likes you," McGregor said, sliding into the seat beside her.

"Ask me if I care."

McGregor let out a great burst of laughter, and after a moment Sarah joined him. *God, it's good to have this case wrapped up.*

"How's your arm?"

Sarah touched the bandage covering the cut. "Not bad. Just a flesh wound, as they say in the old westerns."

McGregor shook his head. "Who would have guessed a woman?"

"Yeah. Peeples missed this one big time."

"We always knew the fibbies weren't perfect."

Sarah stood up. "I'm out of here."

"Go home. Get some rest. You look like shit."

"Yeah, yeah, yeah."

Sarah didn't go home. She went to the hospital and found that Amber had been moved out of ICU. The nurse on duty didn't seem concerned about privacy when Sarah showed her badge. She told Sarah what room Amber was in.

The girl was asleep when Sarah stepped in, and she was about to leave when a soft voice called out, "Detective?"

Sarah went back to the bed. "How are you doing?"

"I'm good. The doctor said there is no permanent brain damage."

"That was quite a nasty fall."

"Yeah. Tell me about it."

Sarah pulled a chair up to the side of the bed. "Has anyone told you what happened after you fell?"

"My mother did. She said it was that headmistress from school who attacked me and killed Tracy."

"Yes."

"But why?"

"We don't know. She hasn't said why. But piecing some things together, I think it was because you girls were dancing at The Club."

Amber turned her face away.

"Hey," Sarah coaxed her to look back. "This isn't about judgments. These are the facts. Modine assaulted a girl before. One who was in a homosexual relationship. And I suspect she might have killed her sister years ago."

"Why?"

"I don't know that either."

"Are you going to find out?"

Sarah shook her head. "That case belongs to the authorities in Maryland. Where it happened. I sent them a report, and they will either reopen the case or not. It's their call."

"What makes a person do these horrible things?"

"All kinds of reasons. I think Modine saw herself as some kind of avenger of evil."

Amber glanced away again. "This was all my fault. It was my idea to go dance at that stupid place."

"So what are you going to do about it?"

"What?" Amber shot her a sharp glance.

"You have a choice here. Learn from this mistake and do something good with your life . . . Or not."

Tears leaked out of the girl's eyes and trickled down her cheeks. "I don't know what to do."

"Let your parents help you."

"They won't"

"Even after all this?" Sarah gestured vaguely at the hospital room.

"Mom said she was done trying to straighten me out."

Sarah looked at the girl, bandages covering the top of her head, an IV tube stuck in her left arm, appearing even smaller and more vulnerable in the hospital bed.

It wasn't the prudent thing to do, but she said, "Then let me help you."

ABOUT THE AUTHOR

Maryann Miller is an award-winning author of numerous books, screenplays and stage plays. This is her third book with Five Star Cengage/Gale, and the second in the Seasons Mystery Series. In addition to the mystery, Miller has a suspense novel, *One Small Victory*, published as an e-book and in paperback. It was originally published in hardback in 2008. Her young adult novel, *Friends Forever*, is also available as an e-book and paperback. *Play it Again, Sam*, a contemporary romance, is available as an e-book, and a short story collection, *The Wisdom of Ages*, is also available as an e-book.

Among the awards she has received for her writing are the Page Edwards Short Story Award, the New York Library Best Books for Teens Award, first place in the screenwriting competition at the Houston Writer's Conference, placing as a semifinalist at Sundance, and placing as a semi-finalist in the Chesterfield Screenwriting Competition with the screenplay for *Open Season*.

Miller lives in east Texas with her husband, where she is the theatre director for the Winnsboro Center for the Arts.